Home Fire

Home Fire

Kamila Shamsie

THORNDIKE PRESS
A part of Gale, a Cengage Company

Farmington Hills, Mich • San Francisco • New York • Waterville, Maine
Meriden, Conn • Mason, Ohio • Chicago

Copyright © 2018 by Kamila Shamsie.
Thorndike Press, a part of Gale, a Cengage Company.

Thorndike Press® Large Print Core.
The text of this Large Print edition is unabridged.
Other aspects of the book may vary from the original edition.
Set in 16 pt. Plantin.

LIBRARY OF CONGRESS CIP DATA ON FILE.
CATALOGUING IN PUBLICATION FOR THIS BOOK
IS AVAILABLE FROM THE LIBRARY OF CONGRESS

ISBN-13: 978-1-4328-6099-8 (hardcover)

Published in 2018 by arrangement with Riverhead Books, an imprint of Penguin Publishing Group, a division of Penguin Random House LLC

Printed in Mexico
1 2 3 4 5 6 7 22 21 20 19 18

For Gillian Slovo

The ones we love . . .
are enemies of the state.

— Sophocles, *Antigone*
(translated by Seamus Heaney)

ISMA

1

Isma was going to miss her flight. The ticket wouldn't be refunded, because the airline took no responsibility for passengers who arrived at the airport three hours ahead of the departure time and were escorted to an interrogation room. She had expected the interrogation, but not the hours of waiting that would precede it, nor that it would feel so humiliating to have the contents of her suitcase inspected. She'd made sure not to pack anything that would invite comment or questions — no Quran, no family pictures, no books on her area of academic interest — but even so, the officer took hold of every item of Isma's clothing and ran it between her thumb and fingers, not so much searching for hidden pockets as judging the quality of the material. Finally she reached for the designer-label down jacket Isma had folded over a chair back when she entered, and held it up, one hand pinching each shoulder.

"This isn't yours," she said, and Isma was sure she didn't mean *because it's at least a size too large* but rather *it's too nice for someone like you.*

"I used to work at a dry-cleaning shop. The woman who brought this in said she didn't want it when we couldn't get rid of the stain." She pointed to the grease mark on the pocket.

"Does the manager know you took it?"

"I was the manager."

"You were the manager of a dry-cleaning shop and now you're on your way to a PhD program in sociology?"

"Yes."

"And how did that happen?"

"My siblings and I were orphaned just after I finished uni. They were twelve years old — twins. I took the first job I could find. Now they've grown up; I can go back to my life."

"You're going back to your life . . . in Amherst, Massachusetts."

"I meant the academic life. My former tutor from LSE teaches in Amherst now, at the university there. Her name is Hira Shah. You can call her. I'll be staying with her when I arrive, until I find a place of my own."

12

"In Amherst."

"No. I don't know. Sorry, do you mean her place or the place of my own? She lives in Northampton — that's close to Amherst. I'll look all around the area for whatever suits me best. So it might be Amherst, but it might not. There are some real estate listings on my phone. Which you have." She stopped herself. The official was doing that thing that she'd encountered before in security personnel — staying quiet when you answered their question in a straightforward manner, which made you think you had to say more. And the more you said, the more guilty you sounded.

The woman dropped the jacket into the jumble of clothes and shoes and told Isma to wait.

That had been a while ago. The plane would be boarding now. Isma looked over at the suitcase. She'd repacked when the woman left the room and spent the time since worrying if doing that without permission constituted an offense. Should she empty the clothes out into a haphazard pile, or would that make things even worse? She stood up, unzipped the suitcase, and flipped it open so its contents were visible.

A man entered the office, carrying Isma's passport, laptop, and phone. She allowed herself to hope, but he sat down, gestured for her to do the same, and placed a voice recorder between them.

"Do you consider yourself British?" the man said.

"I am British."

"But do you consider yourself British?"

"I've lived here all my life." She meant there was no other country of which she could feel herself a part, but the words came out sounding evasive.

The interrogation continued for nearly two hours. He wanted to know her thoughts on Shias, homosexuals, the Queen, democracy, *The Great British Bake Off,* the invasion of Iraq, Israel, suicide bombers, dating websites. After that early slip regarding her Britishness, she settled into the manner that she'd practiced with Aneeka playing the role of the interrogating officer, Isma responding to her sister as though she were a customer of dubious political opinions whose business Isma didn't want to lose by voicing strenuously opposing views, but to whom she didn't see the need to lie either. ("When people talk about the enmity between Shias and Sunnis, it usually centers on some political imbalance of power, such as in Iraq or Syria — as a Brit, I don't distinguish between one Muslim and another." "Occupying other people's territory generally causes more problems than it solves" — this served for both Iraq and Israel. "Killing civilians is sinful — that's equally true whether the manner of killing is a suicide bombing or aerial bombardments or drone strikes.") There were long intervals of silence between each answer and the next question as the man clicked keys on her laptop, examining her browser history. He knew that she was interested in the marital status of an actor from a popular TV series; that wearing a hijab didn't stop her from buying expensive products to tame her frizzy hair; that she had searched for "how to make small talk with Americans."

You know, you don't have to be so compliant about everything, Aneeka had said during the role-playing. Isma's sister, not quite nineteen, with her law student brain, who knew everything about her rights and nothing about the fragility of her place in the world. *For instance, if they ask you about the Queen, just say, "As an Asian I have to admire her color palette." It's important to show at least a tiny bit of contempt for the whole process.* Instead, Isma had responded, *I greatly admire Her Majesty's commitment to her role.* But there had been comfort in hearing her sister's alternative answers in

15

her head, her *Ha!* of triumph when the official asked a question that she'd anticipated and Isma had dismissed, such as the *Great British Bake Off* one. Well, if they didn't let her board this plane — or any one after this — she would go home to Aneeka, which is what half Isma's heart knew it should do in any case. How much of Aneeka's heart wanted that was a hard question to answer — she'd been so adamant that Isma not change her plans for America, and whether this was selflessness or a wish to be left alone was something even Aneeka herself didn't seem to know. A tiny flicker in Isma's brain signaled a thought about Parvaiz that was trying to surface, before it was submerged by the strength of her refusal ever to think about him again.

Eventually, the door opened and the woman official walked in. Perhaps she would be the one to ask the family questions — the ones most difficult to answer, the most fraught when she'd prepared with her sister.

"Sorry about that," the woman said, unconvincingly. "Just had to wait for America to wake up and confirm some details about your student visa. All checked out. Here." She handed a stiff rectangle of paper to Isma with an air of magnanimity. It was the boarding pass for the plane she'd already missed.

Isma stood up, unsteady because of the pins and needles in her feet, which she'd been afraid to shake off in case she accidentally kicked the man across the desk from her. As she wheeled out her luggage she thanked the woman whose thumbprints were on her underwear, not allowing even a shade of sarcasm to enter her voice.

The cold bit down on every exposed piece of skin before cutting through the layers of clothing. Isma opened her mouth and tilted her head back, breathing in the lip-numbing, teeth-aching air. Crusted snow lay all about, glinting in the lights of the terminal. Leaving her suitcase with Dr. Hira Shah, who had driven two hours across Massachusetts to meet her at Logan Airport, she walked over to a mound of snow at the edge of the parking lot, took off her gloves, and pressed her fingertips down on it. At first it resisted, but then it gave way, and her fingers burrowed into the softer layers beneath. She licked snow out of her palm, relieving the dryness of her mouth. The woman in customer services at Heathrow — a Muslim — had found her a place on the next flight out, without charge; she

17

had spent the whole journey worrying about the interrogation awaiting her in Boston, certain they would detain her or put her on a plane back to London. But the immigration official had asked only where she was going to study, said something she didn't follow but tried to look interested in regarding the university basketball team, and waved her through. And then, as she walked out of the arrivals area, there was Dr. Shah, mentor and savior, unchanged since Isma's undergraduate days except for a few silver strands threaded through her cropped dark hair. Seeing her raise a hand in welcome, Isma understood how it might have felt, in another age, to step out on deck and see the upstretched arm of the Statue of Liberty and know you had made it, you were going to be all right.

While there was still some feeling in her gloveless hands she typed a message into her phone: Arrived safely. Through security — no problems. Dr. Shah here. How things with you?

Her sister wrote back: Fine, now I know they've let you through.

Really fine?

Stop worrying about me. Go live your life

18

— I really want you to.

The parking lot with large, confident vehicles; the broad avenues beyond; the lights gleaming everywhere, their brightness multiplied by reflecting surfaces of glass and snow. Here, there was swagger and certainty and — on this New Year's Day of 2015 — a promise of new beginnings.

Isma awoke into light to see two figures leaving the sky and falling toward her, bright colors billowing above their heads.

When Hira Shah had brought her to see this studio apartment, the morning after her arrival in America, the landlord had drawn attention to the skylight as a selling point to offset the dank built-in cupboard, and promised her comets and lunar eclipses. With the memory of the Heathrow inter-rogation still jangling her nerves, she had been able to think only of surveillance satel-lites wheeling through the sky, and had rejected the studio. But by the end of the day's viewings it had become clear that she wouldn't be able to afford anything nicer without the encumbrance of a roommate. Now, some ten weeks later, she could stretch out in the bed, knowing herself to be seeing but unseen. How slowly the parachutists seemed to move, trailing golds and reds. In almost all human history, figures descending from the sky would have been angels or gods or demons — or Icarus hurtling down, his father, Daedalus, following too slowly to catch the vainglorious boy. What must it have felt like to inhabit a commonality of human experience — all eyes to the sky, watching for something mythic to land? She took a picture of the parachutists and sent it to Aneeka with the caption Try this someday? and then stepped out of bed, wondering if spring had arrived early or if this was merely a lull.

Overnight the temperature had climbed vertiginously, melting the snow into a river. She had heard it at her first waking, for the dawn prayer, as it rushed down the gentle slope of the street. It had been a winter of snowstorms, more than usual, she'd been told, and as she dressed she imagined people exiting their homes and, on patches of ground glimpsed for the first time in months, finding lost items — a glove, keys, pens, and pennies. The weight of snow pressing familiarity out of the objects, so that the glove placed beside its former pair looked no more than a distant relative. And what then do you do? Throw away both gloves, or wear them mismatched to acknowledge the miracle of their reunion?

She folded her pajamas and put them under her pillow, smoothed out the duvet. Looked around the clean, spare lines of her apartment — single bed, desk and desk chair, chest of drawers. She felt, as she did most mornings, the deep pleasure of daily life distilled to the essentials: books, walks, spaces in which to think and work.

When she pushed open the heavy door of the two-story stone-veneer house, the morning air was free of its hundred-blade knife for the first time. The thaw had widened the streets and sidewalks, and she felt — what was the word? — "boundless"! as she set off walking at a pace that didn't worry about slipping on ice. Past double-storied colonial houses, past cars announcing all their political beliefs on bumper stickers, past vintage clothing, past antiques and yoga. She turned onto Main Street, where City Hall with its inexplicable Norman towers inset with arrow slits gave the vista an edge of hilarity.

She made her way into her favorite café and walked down the stairs with a mug in hand to the book-lined basement — a haven of warm lamplight, worn armchairs, and strong coffee. Punched keys on the keyboard to wake her laptop, barely registered from overfamiliarity the desktop picture of her mother as a young woman of the 1980s, big hair and chunky earrings, dropping a kiss on Isma's infant scalp. As a matter of morning routine, she opened the Skype window to check if her sister was online. She wasn't, and Isma was about to click out when a new name appeared on the online contacts list: *Parvaiz Pasha.*

Isma lifted her hands off the keyboard, set them down on either side of the laptop, and looked at her brother's name. She hadn't seen it here since that day in December when he'd called to tell them the decision he'd made for his life without any consideration of what it would mean for his sisters. Now he would be looking at her name, the green check mark next to it telling him she was available to chat. The Skype window was positioned so that her mother's lips were touching it. Zainab Pasha's slim, fine-boned features had skipped Isma and passed on to the twins, who laughed with their mother's mouth, smiled with their mother's eyes. Isma maximized the Skype window so it filled the entire screen, encircled her throat with the palms of her hands, and felt her heart's reaction to the sight of his name in the high-speed propulsion of blood through her arteries. The seconds passed, and there was nothing from him. She kept watching the screen, just as she knew he was watching his, both for the same reason: waiting for Aneeka.

A few weeks earlier, at Hira Shah's condo, a strange music had cut through the sound of Hira slicing potatoes — a whistling, high-pitched twang. Isma and Hira checked phones and speakers, placed ears against walls and floorboards, stepped out into the corridor, opened closets, entered empty rooms, and still it kept on, eerie loveliness, impossible to pinpoint as any known instrument, voice, or birdcall. A neighbor stopped by, looking for the source. "Ghosts," he said with a wink before leaving.

Isma laughed, but Hira drew her shoulders in tighter, reached out to touch the evil eye that hung on her wall, which Isma had always assumed to be merely decorative.

The music kept on, coming from everywhere and nowhere, following them as they moved through the apartment. Hira, gripping her knife, whispered something that turned out to be the Lord's Prayer — she'd been educated at a convent school in Kashmir. Finally, the supremely rational, razor-minded Dr. Shah said they should go out for dinner despite the unpleasant hail. Perhaps the sound would have stopped by

23

the time they returned. Isma went upstairs to the bathroom to wash the grime of concealed corners off her hands. While standing at the sink, looking out of the window beside it, she saw the source of the music.

Running down, she caught Hira's arm and pulled her out of the backdoor entrance, ducking her head against the hail. All along the redbrick building, end to end, icicles hung from the eaves, a foot or more in length. Against these broadswords, pellets rained down and made music. The acoustics of ice on ice, a thing unimaginable until experienced.

Pain swerved at her then, physical, bringing her to her knees. Hira moved toward her but Isma held up a hand, lay back in the snow, and allowed the pain to roil through her while the hail and icicles continued their synthetic-edged symphony. Parvaiz, a boy never seen without his headphones and a mic, would have lain out here for as long as the song continued, the wet of snow seeping through his clothes, the thud of hail beating down on him, uncaring of anything except capturing something previously unheard, eyes hazy with pleasure.

That had been the only time she had truly, purely missed her brother without adjectives such as "ungrateful" and "selfish" slicing through the feeling of loss. Now she looked at his name on the screen, her mouth forming prayers to keep Aneeka from logging on, the adjectives thick in her mind. Aneeka must learn to think of him as lost forever. It was possible to do this with someone you loved, Isma had learned that early on. But you could learn it only if there was a complete vacuum where the other person had been.

His name vanished from the screen. She touched her shoulder, muscles knotted beneath the skin. Pressed down, and knew what it was to be without family; no one's hands but your own to minister to your suffering. *We'll be in touch all the time,* she and Aneeka had said to each other in the weeks before she had left. But "touch" was the one thing modern technology didn't allow, and without it she and her sister had lost something vital to their way of being together. Touch was where it had started with them — as an infant, Aneeka was bathed and changed and fed and rocked to sleep by her grandmother and nine-year-old sister while Parvaiz, the weaker, sicklier twin, was the one who suckled at their mother's breast (she produced only enough milk for one) and cried unless she was the one to tend to him. When the twins grew older and formed their own self-enclosed universe, there was less and less Aneeka needed from Isma, but even so, there remained a physical closeness — Parvaiz was the person Aneeka talked to about all her griefs and worries, but it was Isma she came to for an embrace, or a hand to rub her back, or a body to curl up against on the sofa. And when the burden of the universe seemed too great for Isma to bear — particularly in those early days after their grandmother and mother had died within the space of a year, leaving Isma to parent and provide for two grief-struck twelve-year-olds — it was Aneeka who would place her hands on her sister's shoulders and massage away the ache.

Clicking her tongue against her teeth in remonstration of her self-pity, Isma pulled up the essay she was writing and returned to the refuge of work.

By midafternoon the temperature had passed the 50 degree Fahrenheit mark, which sounded, and felt, far warmer than 11 degrees Celsius, and a bout of spring madness had largely emptied the café basement. Isma tilted her post-lunch mug of coffee toward herself, touched the tip of her finger to the liquid, considered how much of a faux pas it might be to ask to have it microwaved. She had just decided she would risk the opprobrium when the door opened and the scent of cigarettes curled in from the smoking area outside, followed by a young man of startling looks.

His looks weren't startling because they were exceptional — thick dark hair, milky-tea skin, well-proportioned features, good height, nice shoulders. Stand on any street corner in Wembley long enough and you'd see a version of this, though rarely attached to such an air of privilege. No, what was startling was the stomach-turning familiarity of the man's features.

In her uncle's house — not an uncle by blood or even affection, merely by the habitual nature of his presence in her family's life — there was a photograph from the 1970s of a neighborhood cricket team posing with a trophy; it was a photograph Isma had sometimes stopped to look at as a child, wondering at the contrast between the glorious, swaggering boys and the unprepossessing middle-aged men they'd grown into. It was really only the ones she knew as middle-aged men she paid much attention to, and so she'd never given particular thought to the unsmiling one in the badly fitting clothes until the day her grandmother stood in front of the picture and said, "Shameless!" poking her finger at the young man.

"Oh yes, the new MP," the uncle said, coming to see what had drawn out a pronouncement of such uncharacteristic venom. "On the day of the final we were a player short and this one, Mr. Serious, was visiting his cousin, our wicketkeeper, so we said, *Okay, you play for us,* and gave him our injured batsman's uniform. Did nothing all match except drop a catch, and then ended up holding the trophy in this official photograph, which went into the local newspaper. We were just being polite to offer it to him, since he was an outsider, and only because we were sure he'd have enough manners to say thanks but the captain — that was me — should be the one to hold it. We should have known then he would grow up to be a politician. Twenty pounds says he has it framed on his wall and tells everyone he was man-of-the-match."

Later that day, Isma overheard her grandmother talking to her best friend and neighbor, Aunty Naseem, and learned the real reason for that "Shameless!" It was not the unsmiling one's choice of career but a cruelty he'd recently shown to their family when it would have been easy for him to act otherwise. In the years after that, she'd paid close attention to him — the only one in the picture to grow up slim and sharp, bigger and brighter trophies forever in his sights. And now here he was, walking across the café floor — not the hated-admired figure he'd grown into but a slightly older version of the boy posing with the team, except his hair floppier and his expression more open. This must be, had to be, the son. She'd seen a photo that included him as well, but he'd ducked his head so that the floppy hair obscured his features — she'd wondered then whether that was by design. Eamonn, that was his name. How they'd laughed in Wembley when the newspaper article accompanying the family picture revealed this detail. An Irish spelling to disguise a Muslim name — "Ayman" become "Eamonn" so that people would know the father had integrated. (His Irish-American wife was seen as another indicator of this integrationist posing rather than an explanation for the son's name.)

The son was standing at the counter, in blue jeans and a quilted olive-green jacket, waiting.

She stood up, mug in hand, and walked over to him. "They only open up this counter when it's busy."

"Thanks. Kind of you to say. Where is — ?" His vowels unashamedly posh where she had expected the more class-obscuring London accent of his father.

"Upstairs. I'll show you. I mean, I'm sure you understand 'upstairs.' I should have said, I'm going there myself. Coffee's cold." Why so many words?

He took the mug from her hand with unexpected familiarity. "Allow me. As thanks for rescuing me from being the Englishman Who Stood at the Counter for All Eternity. Who you could be forgiven for confusing with the Englishman Who Gets Lost Going Upstairs."

"I just want it heated up."

"Right you are." He sniffed the contents of the mug, another over-familiar gesture. "Smells amazing. What is it? I wouldn't know an Ethiopian from a Colombian if . . ." He stopped. "That sentence doesn't know where to go from there."

"Probably just as well. It's the house brew."

She stood where she was a moment, watching him walk up the stairs, which were bracketed on one side by potted ferns and on the other by a wall with ferns painted on it. When he glanced down toward her, mouthing "Not lost yet," she pretended she had simply been preoccupied by her thoughts and returned to the little table in the alcove, angling her body so that her own shadow kept the sunlight from her computer screen. Slid her fingers over the wooden tabletop, its knots, its burns. Guess who, she started to type into her phone, then stopped and deleted it. She could too easily imagine the tone of Aneeka's response: Ugh! she'd say, or Why did you even talk to him?

He didn't return. She imagined him seeing a short line at the counter and placing her mug down with a shrug before walking out the upstairs exit; it left her both vindicated and disappointed. She went up to buy herself another coffee and found that the machine had broken down, so had to settle for hot water and a tea bag that leaked color into it. Returning downstairs, she saw a mug of fresh coffee at her table and a man folded into the chair next to it, legs thrown over the arm, reading a book in the shape of the gap in the bookshelf above his head.

"What is it?" he said, looking at the cup of tea she set down on an empty table. He examined the tag at the end of the tea bag. "Ruby Red. Not even pretending it's a flavor."

She held up the mug in thanks. The coffee wasn't as hot as it could have been, but he

31

must have had to carry it down the street. "How much do I owe you?"

"Five minutes of conversation. That's what I spent standing in the queue. But after you're finished with whatever you're doing."

"That could be a while."

"Good. Gives me time to catch up on essential reading about . . ." He shut the book, looked at its cover. *"The Holy Book of Women's Mysteries. Complete in One Volume. Feminist Witchcraft, Goddess Rituals, Spellcasting, and Other Womanly Arts . . ."*

One of the undergraduates looked up, glared.

Isma slung the laptop into her backpack, downed her coffee. "You can walk to the supermarket with me."

During the short walk to the supermarket, she learned that he'd quit his job with a management consultancy and was taking some time to live life beyond office walls — which included visiting his maternal grandparents in Amherst, a town he loved for its association with childhood summer holidays.

While she tried to choose between one variety of unconvincing tomato and another for tonight's pasta sauce, Eamonn wandered off and brought back a can of plum tomatoes, as well as leaves for the salad she hadn't intended to make. "Arugula," he said, rolling the *r* extravagantly. "Halfway between a Latin American dance and an ointment for verrucas." She couldn't tell if he was trying to impress her or if he was the kind of man in love with his own charm. When she had finished placing the shopping in her backpack he picked it up from the checkout counter and looped it over one shoulder, saying he liked the schoolboy feeling of it, would she mind very much if he carried it for a while? She thought he was making a show of the polished manners that passed as virtue among people like him, but when she said there was no need for such chivalry he said it was the opposite of chivalry to burden a woman with his company just because he was feeling lonely and a London accent was the best possible antidote. So they continued on together, walking toward the nearby woods since the day was so lovely. On the way he asked for a detour via Main Street (he said the name with the slight deprecation of someone newly arrived from a metropolis) so they could stop at an outdoor-clothing store, and in little more than the time it took her to cross the street and withdraw twenty dollars from the ATM he was out again, wearing expensive walking shoes, the backpack more weighed down than previously.

The woods were slushy, but the light piercing through between scrabbling branches was a pleasure, and the river, swollen with snowmelt, roared. They turned up their collars against the dripping from the branches; he didn't seem to mind yelping when fat, cold drops fell on his head, merely commented on the stylish protection of her wool turban and called her "Greta Garbo." Every now and then they heard the *whump!* of a section of dislodged snow landing on the ground, but they felt safe enough to keep going. Their talk was insubstantial — the weather, the overfriendliness of strangers in America, favorite London bus routes (which revealed nothing so much as the distinct geography of their lives) — but even so, the Englishness of his humor, and his cultural references, were a greater treat than she would have expected. Small talk came more naturally to him than to her, but he was careful not to dominate the conversation — listening with interest to even her most banal observations, asking follow-up questions rather than using her lines as springboards to monologues of his own in the manner of most of the men she knew.

Someone raised him the way I tried to raise Parvaiz, she couldn't stop herself from thinking.

Along one of the calmer stretches of water, a fallen tree extended out twenty or more feet from the bank. Isma walked across it, arms out for balance, while he remained behind, making noises that were half anxious, half admiring, wholly pleasing to hear. The sky was a rich blue, the water surged like blood leaving a heart, a lean young man from a world very distant from hers was waiting for her to walk back to him. She breathed in the moment, tried to catch her reflection in the water, but it was too quick, nothing like the slow-moving waterways to which she was accustomed.

She came from a city veined with canals: that had been the revelation of her adolescence while her school friends were embarking on other kinds of discovery that discomforted more than appealed to her. In Alperton, two miles from her old home, she could descend into waterside avenues of calm, unpeopled in comparison to the streets, thick with noise, she'd traveled to arrive there. She knew her mother and grandmother would say it was dangerous, a lone girl walking past industrial estates and along silent stretches with no company other than the foliage, as in the countryside (to her family nowhere was more dangerous than the countryside, where you could scream for help without being heard), so she never said anything more specific than "I'm going for a walk," which they found both amusing and unthreatening.

Her foot slipped on the slick surface of the branch, and she had to drop to her knees to keep from falling in. The cold water a spray on her hands and sleeves. She walked back cautiously, registering the anxiety in Eamonn's expression.

After that, he asked more direct questions about her life, as though seeing her walk away from him across a fallen tree had brought her into focus. She gave him the easiest version: Grew up in North London, as he already knew because of the bus routes — the Preston Road neighborhood to be precise, which was obviously too precise for him. Two siblings — much younger. Raised by her mother and grandmother, now both dead; she'd never really known her father. She was here for a PhD program, fully funded, with a stipend from a position as a research assistant that would give her enough to live on. She'd applied too late for the autumn semester, but her former tutor Dr. Shah had arranged permission for her to start in January, and here she now was.

"And so you're doing what you want to be doing? You lucky thing!"

"Yes," she said. "Very lucky." She wondered if she should respond to his questions about her life with some about his. But then he might mention his father, of whom she couldn't pretend to be unaware, and that might lead them down a road she didn't want to travel.

The river was dark now, the first indication that the day was ending although there was still abundant light in the sky. She led the way back onto the road, bringing them out near the high school, where long-limbed teenagers were running on the outdoor track, piles of muddy snow pushed to the corners of the field.

"Can I ask you something?" he said. "The turban. Is that a style thing or a Muslim thing?"

"You know, the only two people in Massachusetts who have ever asked me about it both wanted to know if it's a style thing or a chemo thing."

Laughing, he said, "Cancer or Islam — which is the greater affliction?"

There were still moments when a statement like that could catch a person off-

37

guard. He held his hands up quickly in apology. "Jesus. I mean, sorry. That came out really badly. I meant, it must be difficult to be Muslim in the world these days."

"I'd find it more difficult to not be Muslim," she said, and after that they walked on in a silence that became more than a little uncomfortable by the time they were back on Main Street. She had assumed that in some way, however secular, however political rather than religious, he identified as Muslim. Though what a foolish thing to assume of his father's son.

"Well, good-bye," she said as they approached the café, holding out a hand for him to shake, aware that the gesture was strangely formal only after she'd made it.

"Thanks for the company. Perhaps we'll run into each other again," he said, extracting his shoes and delivering the backpack into her extended hand as though that's what it was there for. Assuming women who wore turbans as "a Muslim thing" couldn't possibly shake hands with men. As she walked home she thought how much more pleasant life was when you lived among foreigners whose subtexts you couldn't hear. That way you didn't need to know that "Perhaps we'll run into each other again" really meant "I have no particular wish to see you after this."

Aunty Naseem, the neighbor who had taken the place of their grandmother when she died and with whom Aneeka was now staying, called to say she didn't want to worry Isma but could she check on Aneeka? "She stays out so often now, and I thought she was with her friends, but I just saw Gita and she says the friends don't see her very much at all anymore."

Gita of Preston Road was a link between Aneeka's home and university lives — a year older than the twins and with a new stepmother who didn't want her around, she had a room in student halls to which Aneeka had a spare key; Gita herself never used the room because she was living with her boyfriend, though none of the older generation of Preston Road knew this.

When Aneeka had first started staying over at Gita's, because Aneeka was in the library or out socializing in one way or another until after the tube stopped running, Isma hadn't been happy about it. All those boys at university, whose families no one knew. And unlike Isma, Aneeka had always been someone boys looked at — and someone who looked back. More than looked, though Aneeka always guarded that part of her life from her sister, who was, perhaps, too inclined to lecture. It was Parvaiz who had talked Isma into accepting it — if there was anything worrying going on with Aneeka he'd know, and would tell Isma if he needed backup in talking sense to his twin. But there was no need to start having nightmares about Aneeka out alone in the cold, impersonal heart of London — she'd always been good at finding people who would look out for her. There was an instant appeal in her contradictory characteristics: sharp-tongued and considerate, serious-minded and capable of unbridled goofiness, as open to absorbing other people's pain as she was incapable of acknowledging the damage of having been abandoned and orphaned ("I have you and P. That's enough"). Whereas Parvaiz and Isma stayed at the margins of all groups so that no one would start to ask questions about their lives ("Where is your father? Are the rumors about him true?"), Aneeka simply knew how to place herself in the middle of a gathering, delineate her boundaries, and fashion intimacies around the no-go areas. Even as a young girl she'd known how to do this: someone would approach the subject of their father, and Aneeka would turn cold — an experience so disconcerting to those accustomed to her warmth that they'd quickly back away and be rewarded with the return of the Aneeka they knew. But now Parvaiz was a no-go area too, and not one that Aneeka could confine to a little corner of her life.

After the conversation with Aunty Naseem, Isma called her sister repeatedly, but it was late at night London time before she replied. The lamp at her bedside cast a small pool of light that illuminated the book resting on her chest — an *Asterix* comic, an old childhood favorite — but left her face in darkness.

"The Migrants have a new car. A BMW. A BMW in our driveway. What next? A pony? An AGA? An au pair?" When the tenants had moved into the house in which the siblings had grown up, and replaced the net curtains with obviously expensive blinds that were almost always lowered, Aneeka said she sympathized for the first time with residents of a neighborhood who felt aggrieved when migrants moved in. The nickname had stuck despite Isma's attempts to change it.

"I'm surprised you noticed — Aunty Naseem says she hardly sees you. And neither do your uni friends."

"I must really be behaving badly if Aunty

Naseem is driven to complaining," Aneeka said.

"She's concerned, that's all."

"I know. I'm sorry. I don't mean to worry her. Or you. It's just easier being on my own these days. I suppose I'm learning why solitude has always been so appealing to you."

"I'll come home. Spring break is starting soon. We can at least have a week together." The thought of London was oppressive, but Isma kept that out of her voice.

"You know you can't afford it, and anyway, you don't want to have to go through that airport interrogation again. What if they don't let you board this time? Or if they give you a hard time when you return to Boston? Also, I've got papers due. That's the main reason why no one's seen me. I'm working. The law makes you work. Not like sociology, where you get to watch TV and call it research."

"Since when do we lie to each other?"

"Since I was fourteen and said I was going to watch Parvaiz at cricket nets, but instead I went to meet Jimmy Singh at McDonald's."

"Jimmy-Singh-from-Poundland Jimmy Singh? Aneeka! Did Parvaiz know?"

"Course he knew. He always knew everything I did."

The night they discovered what Parvaiz had done, Aneeka had allowed Isma to brush out her long dark hair as their mother used to do when she had a daughter in need of comforting, and partway through Aneeka leaned back into her sister and said, "He never explained why he didn't tell me about the Ibsen tickets." Months after their mother died, Parvaiz, a boy suddenly arrived into adolescence in a house where bills and grief filled all crevices, had decided he needed a laptop of his own so that his sisters wouldn't disrupt his work on the sound projects that had recently become an obsession. One night he sneaked out of the house when everyone had gone to sleep, took the bus to Central London, and waited from midnight until mid-morning outside a theater in the West End for return tickets to the opening night of an Ibsen play that an actor recently elevated, via a superhero role, to the Hollywood A-list was using to reestablish his credentials as a serious thespian. Parvaiz bought two tickets with money he'd "borrowed" from the household account using Isma's debit card, and quickly sold them both for an astronomical sum. He announced all this, sauntering into the house like a conquering hero, only to be confronted with his sisters' rage. Isma's anger came from the thought of the overtime she worked to keep the debt collector from the door, and from the thought of every horror that could befall a young boy in a world of racists and pedophiles; but Aneeka's rage was far greater. "Why didn't you tell me? I tell you everything — how could you not tell me?" Both Parvaiz and Isma, accustomed to Aneeka's being the buffer between them, had been completely unprepared for this. Six years later, that story was all Aneeka could grasp to help her understand her brother's subterfuge. Isma had an easier answer: his father's son; a fecklessness in the gene pool.

"Boys are different from us," Isma said. "They see what they want through tunnel vision."

The screen became a place of confusion, all motion and shapes, for a few seconds, and then she saw her sister lying in bed, face turned toward the phone that had been settled in its dock.

"Maybe if we start looking now for cheap flights I could come to you for my Easter break," Aneeka said, but Isma shook her head firmly before the sentence was finished.

"Don't want me telling the security mon-

44

keys at Heathrow how much I admire the Queen's color palette?"

"I do not." Her muscles tightened at the thought of Aneeka in the interrogation room. "Are we really not going to talk about the fact that Parvaiz has reappeared on Skype?"

"If we talk about him we'll argue. I don't want to argue right now."

"Neither do I. But I want to know if you've spoken to him."

"He sent a chat message just to say he's okay. You get the same?"

"No, I got nothing."

"Oh, Isma. I was sure you had. I would have told you otherwise. Yes, just that. He's okay. He must have assumed I'd tell you as soon as I heard."

"That would imply he remembers how to think about anyone other than himself."

"Don't, please. I know anger is the way you express your concern but, just don't."

Anger is the way I express my anger, she would have said on another night, but tonight she said "I miss you."

"Stay with me until I fall asleep," Aneeka said, her hand reaching toward Isma, swerving to switch off the light.

"Once upon a time, there lived a girl and a boy called Aneeka and Parvaiz, who had the power to talk to animals."

Aneeka laughed. "Tell the one with the ostrich," she said, voice muffled by her pillow.

She was asleep before Isma was done telling the childhood story their mother had invented for her firstborn and Isma had modified for the twins, but Isma stayed on the line, listening to their breath rise and fall together as in all those times when Aneeka would crawl into Isma's bed, awakened from or into some night terror, and only the older sister's steady heartbeat could teach the younger one's frantic heart how to quiet, until there was no sound except their breath in unison, the universe still around them.

2

All morning she pretended not to notice him sitting across the café basement, working on a crossword. But when she ordered a sandwich for lunch and brought it to her table, he came over and said he was. about to have a bite himself, would it be all right if he sat with her.

"Preston Road," he said, returning a few minutes later with a plate of pasta. "It sounded familiar when you said that's where you grew up but I didn't know why until I looked it up on a map. That's in Wembley. My father's family lives some-where around there. I used to visit every Eid."

"Oh, really?" she said, choosing not to mention that she knew exactly where his father's family used to live, and that she also knew, as he seemed not to, that they'd moved away, to Canada.

"There was a song my cousins used to

sing to my little sister when the adults weren't around. I've had a line of it stuck in my head for years. Drives me crazy that I can't remember the rest, and my sister has no memory of it. Do you know it?" Unexpectedly he broke into a Pakistani pop song that predated his birth — he was four years her junior, she'd discovered. She recognized the song by the tune more than the words, which came out as gibberish tinged with Urdu. He sang two lines, softly, face turning red — a self-consciousness she wouldn't have expected, particularly given how pretty his voice was. She pulled up a song for him from the music library on her phone and watched as Eamonn plugged in his headphones — unconscionably expensive; Parvaiz had coveted such a pair. He listened, eyes closed, recognition rather than pleasure in his expression.

"Thank you," he said, when he was done. "What does it actually mean?"

"It's in praise of fair-skinned girls, who have nothing to fear in life because everyone will always love their fair skin and their blue eyes."

"Oh, yes," he said, laughing. "I knew that once. They sang it to tease my sister, but she just treated it as a compliment and made it one. That's my sister for you."

48

"And you? Are you like that too?"

He frowned a little, sliding the tines of his fork into the little tubes of pasta. "No, I don't think so," he said in the unconvinced manner of someone who isn't accustomed to being asked to account for his own character. He raised the fork to his face and with little sucking sounds drew the pasta into his mouth. "Oh, sorry. My table manners are usually better than this."

"I don't mind. Do you know any Urdu?" He shook his head, a response his singing had anticipated, and she said, "So you don't understand 'bay-takalufi.' "

He sat up straight and raised his hand like a schoolboy. "I do know that one. It's informality as an expression of intimacy."

She experienced a brief moment of wonder that a father who hadn't taught his son basic Urdu had still thought to teach him this word. "I wouldn't say intimacy. It's about feeling comfortable with someone. Comfortable enough to forget good table manners. If done right, it's a sort of honor you confer on the other person when you feel able to be that comfortable with them, particularly if you haven't known them long." The words rushing out to cover how her voice had caught at "intimacy."

"Okay," he said, as if accepting a proposition. "Let's be comfortable with each other beyond table manners." He pushed his plate toward her. Extravagantly, she dipped the crust of her sandwich into his pasta sauce and leaned forward over his plate to bite into it.

At the end of lunch — a lunch that was relaxed, swift-flowing — he stood up and said, "See you here again one of these days? I've discovered that when the coffee machine is working, this place has the best cappuccino in town."

"I only have afternoon classes, and this is my favorite place to spend my mornings," she said. In fact, she sometimes went to her second-favorite café when it seemed too crowded in here, but really, what was the need for such fussiness?

The siblings watched one another, and watched one another watching one another. At least it felt that way, though in all probability she was far more aware of the twins than they were of her. She raised her eyes briefly from the screen to see Eamonn at a table neither too close nor too far away from her, so intent on some story in the local paper that he didn't take his eyes off the page even as he lifted his mug of coffee and drank. Existing in another world entirely from the one she now inhabited for these few seconds each morning at eleven a.m. Her brother had always been a creature of habit, and that at least was something to be grateful for, else hours of every day might go like this: watching Aneeka waiting for Parvaiz to come online, then that moment when the green check mark appeared next to his name, Isma wondering, *What is he saying is he telling her something that will upset her is he asking her to become part of this madness he's joined oh no please he wouldn't do that but why can't he just leave her alone;* but every day it was only a few seconds before his name moved into the offline column again. Just after, Aneeka would text Isma to say: he checked in. *Check in,* one twin used to say to the other when there were school trips or sleepovers that kept them apart, and at some prearranged hour a text would arrive saying nothing more than *checking in.*

When Parvaiz logged off, followed shortly by Aneeka, Isma felt herself released of the day's burdens and texted a steaming-mug emoji across the room to Eamonn, who in response went upstairs to buy them both fresh cups of coffee. This too had become part of the morning routine over the last week or so — why pretend she wasn't keeping track? It was nine days since he decided they should be informal in intimacy together. "What's happening in the world today?" she asked when he returned and sat down across from her, and he presented her his highlights of the local news stories: a bear was reported clawing at a garage door, traffic in the adjoining town was briefly held up because of a three-car accident in which no one was injured, a statue of Ronald McDonald was reported missing from a family's garden. She said it was clear the Ronald won gold medal for "most local" of the local news stories, but he disagreed on the grounds that Ronald was a global icon.

Daily, after their elevenses, he'd set off to "wander" by wheel and on foot, a Christopher Columbus of modest ambitions, retracing childhood paths and discovering new ones. He would sometimes arrive at the café the next morning with an offering from his journey: a jug of maple syrup from a sugarhouse, a one-dollar bill he'd found nailed to an oak tree with an oak-leaf shape cut out of it, a rubbing from Emily Dickinson's gravestone, with its peculiar wording — "CALLED BACK" — which he said made Dickinson sound like a faulty product. She learned more about this part of the world from his retelling than from her own living, but when she asked him the point of it all — imagining a travel book — he said surely experience and observation were point enough. What would happen when his savings ran out, she asked, and he said, actually, those savings he'd mentioned were his mother's — she had recently semiretired and decided that people gave too much of their lives and relationships to work; while there was no talking her daughter out of her seventeen-hour days, she had quite easily convinced her son to try to find other ways of constructing meaning in life than via paychecks and promotions. Isma found this idea compelling and Eamonn's less-than-halfhearted pursuit of it disappointing. Surely he should be learning a new language, or piloting a ship through waters where refugees in search of safety were known to capsize in their pitiful dinghies.

In the first few days she had thought he might suggest they do something together past elevenses — a movie, a meal, another walk — but she now understood that she was just part of the way he divided up his days, which had structure in place of content. Between "morning newspaper" and "daily wander" there was "coffee with Isma." Even the fact that spring break had now started and she'd made it clear she had time on her hands hadn't changed that.

His father was often a topic of conversation during coffee, but always as "my father," never as a man in the public eye. The picture Eamonn conjured up, of a devoted, indulgent, practical-joking parent, was so at odds with Isma's image of the man that she sometimes wondered if the whole thing were an elaborate fiction to disguise the truth about his father. But then she'd observe Eamonn's unguarded manner and know this wasn't true.

One morning he was late to the café. She thought it was because of the weather — winter had returned. Snow slashed across the windowpanes, the sky was white, cars alerted cops that they'd overstayed their two-hour parking limit by the depth of snow on their roofs. Just as she'd got past the distraction of his absence and submerged herself in the problem of missing variables for her statistics course, a text arrived from Aneeka:

> Have you heard? Lone Wolf
> new home secretary.

She must have said something out loud because the woman sitting next to her asked, "Are you okay?" but she was already clicking on a bookmark in her browser, pulling up a news site with a BREAKING NEWS banner announcing a cabinet reshuffle, the most significant change of which was the appointment of a new home secretary. There he was — the man whom she had thought Eamonn looked just like before she'd spent enough mornings noticing the particulars of his face, his mannerisms. The accompanying article described the newly elevated minister as a man "from a Muslim background," which is what they always said about him, as though Muslim-ness was something he had boldly stridden away from. Inevitably, the sentence went on to use the phrase "strong on security."

She felt sick before she could form the thoughts to understand why. Her phone buzzed and she looked down to a series of messages.

It's all going to get worse.

He has to prove he's one of them, not one of us, doesn't he? As if he hasn't already.

I hate this country.

Don't call me, I'll say things I shouldn't.

Stop spying on our messages you arse-holes and find some bankers to arrest.

"Hey, Greta Garbo, why so serious?"

He sat down across from her, one arm slung over the back of the chair. Such a languid contrast to the coiled spring of his father. She slammed the lid of the laptop, flipped the phone screen over.

"You're late," she said.

"Big family news." He leaned forward, smiling, a proud son. The table was so small his knees knocked against hers. "My father's just been appointed the new home secretary. Karamat Lone. You know who he is, right?" She nodded, took a sip of coffee for something to do. "I guess you're one of the people who doesn't see my face, hear the surname, and put two and two together."

"It's not an uncommon Pakistani sur-name." An evasion rather than a lie, she told herself.

"I know. Anyway, I'm glad I can finally tell you. Also, this is why I haven't been able to answer your question of how long I'm staying. I hate all the old muck they scrape up about him every time he's in the head-lines, and this time it'll be worse. I came to avoid it. He's good at dealing with it; I'm not. So if you see me obsessing over stuff they're saying online, take my phone away from me, would you?" He tapped her fingers with his as he spoke to emphasize the final point.

All the old muck. He meant the picture of Karamat Lone entering a mosque that had been in the news for its "hate preacher." LONE WOLF'S PACK REVEALED, the headlines screamed when a tabloid got hold of it, near the end of his first term as an MP. The Lone Wolf's response had been to point out that the picture was several years old, he had been there only for his uncle's funeral prayers and would otherwise never enter a gender-segregated space. This was followed by pictures of him and his wife walking hand in hand into a church. His Muslim-majority constituency voted him out in the elections that took place just a few weeks later, but he was quickly back in Parliament via a by-election, in a safe seat with a largely white constituency, and the tabloids that had attacked him now championed him as a LONE CRUSADER taking on the backwardness of British Muslims. Isma doubted very much that "the old muck" would rise again — oh, unless he meant the opposing side of that story: all the accusations she'd heard, and that seemed entirely accurate, that Karamat Lone had precisely calculated the short-term losses and long-term gains of showing such contempt for the conventions of a mosque. Sellout, coconut, opportunist, traitor.

"You're close to him, aren't you?"

"You know what fathers and sons are like."

"Not really, no."

"They're our guides into manhood, for starters."

She'd never understood this, though she'd heard and seen enough anecdotally and academically to know there was something to it. For girls, becoming women was inevitability; for boys, becoming men was ambition. He must have seen her look of incomprehension, because he tried again.

"We want to be like them, we want to be better than them. We want to be the only people in the world who are allowed to be better than them." He gestured at himself and around the café with a shrug that encompassed the mediocrity of everything. "Obviously, I worked out long ago that such an attempt would be futile."

"That's not true. You're a much better person than he is."

"What do you know about it?"

She didn't answer, didn't know how to, and he said, "Why were you acting so furtive when I came in?"

She hesitated, turned her laptop around so it faced him, and opened the lid.

"You were reading about him. Isma, did you already know he was my father?"

"Yes."

"Why did you lie about it?"

She clasped her hands together, looked down at the interlacing of her fingers, which he'd touched so familiarly just a few moments ago.

"You're one of them? The Muslims who say those ugly things about him?"

"Yes."

He waited, but there was nothing more she could say.

"I see. Well, I'm very sorry to hear it." She heard the scraping of the chair and looked up as he stood. "I suppose one day I'll see the irony in running here to try and escape certain attitudes only to find myself having coffee with their embodiment." Gone was the friendly, considerate boy, and in his place a man carrying all the wounds his father was almost certainly too thick-skinned to feel as anything more than pinpricks. When he said good-bye there was no mistaking the finality of his tone.

The wind had dropped, and the snow drifted down in large flakes that retained their shape for a moment on her sleeve before melting into the fabric. Isma walked the short distance home, but as she approached her front door the thought of her studio with its clanging pipes was intolerable. She carried on down to the tree-lined graveyard at the end of the street, unexpectedly positioned beside a nursery school, across the road from a baseball diamond. In the summer it must be a place of shade, in autumn a feast of color; but she had known it only as the white of snow, the gray of stone.

She started on a cleared pathway before cutting across a snowdrift that came halfway up her knee-high boots, and pulled herself onto a nineteenth-century gravestone, feet dangling. Sometimes the dead were a friendly presence, but today they were only dead, and every chiseled slab was a marker of someone's sorrow. She kicked her heels against the gravestone. "Stupid," she said.

That was the only word for this sense of enormous loss where there had been so very little to lose.

"You don't have to decide that's the end of it," Hira Shah said that evening, when they sat down together for a typically elaborate meal. A single woman in her mid-fifties who had never had to cook on a regular basis for anyone, Hira retained the idea that company for dinner must be occasion for pyrotechnics in the kitchen, no matter how frequently company was over — or perhaps she did that only when her company hadn't had anyone to mother her in a long time. "You should at least try explaining why you feel the way you do. What is there to lose?"

"What is there to gain? He'll be going back to London soon in any case."

Hira looked at her over a forkful of rogan josh. "Do you know when you were at LSE I thought you found me offensive?"

"That's ridiculous. Oh, you mean that first term. When I rolled my eyes at you?"

It overturned seven hundred ninety years of precedent in British law, the Kashmiri lecturer had been saying during an impassioned presentation on control orders and their impact on civil liberties when Hira saw the quiet girl in the third row roll her eyes. *Would you like to say something, Ms. Pasha?* Yes, Dr. Shah, if you look at colonial laws you'll see plenty of precedent for depriving people of their rights; the only difference is this time it's applied to British citizens, and even that's not as much of a change as you might think, because they're rhetorically being made un-British. *Say more.* The 7/7 terrorists were never described by the media as "British terrorists." Even when the word "British" was used, it was always "British of Pakistani descent" or "British Muslim" or, my favorite, "British passport holders," always something interposed between their Britishness and terrorism. *Well, you have quite a voice when you decide to use it.*

Isma had gone home that evening and stood in front of the mirror, pressing down on her larynx, and felt the slight tremor of something on the cusp of waking. And wake it had — her suppressed anger distilled and abstracted into essays about the sociological impact of the War on Terror. Then Isma's mother died, and that voice was lost — until now. Dr. Shah was coaxing it back with the shared paper they were working on — "The Insecurity State: Britain and the Instrumentalization of Fear" — which took Isma's experience in the interrogation room and made it research.

"No, not then. All the way through until you graduated. I thought you disliked something in me personally, and that's why you acted so distant when I tried to talk about anything other than work. It was only after your mother died and you told me everything that you made sense."

How she'd wept that day in Hira Shah's

office. For her mother, for the grandmother who had predeceased her daughter-in-law by less than a year, for her father, for the orphaned twins who had never really known their mother before bitterness and stress ate away the laughing, affectionate woman she'd once been — and, most of all, for herself.

"I don't want Eamonn's pity, if that's what you're driving at here."

"I'm driving at the fact that habits of secrecy are damaging things," Hira said in her most professorial voice. "And they underestimate other people's willingness to accept the complicated truths of your life."

"So — what? I should just call him up —" She held the saltshaker to her ear, miming a phone. "Eamonn, here's a funny story about my father."

"Maybe without the word 'funny.'"

"And then? Do I follow up with the even funnier story of my brother? To the son of the new home secretary?"

"Mmm. Maybe start with your father, and see how it goes from there. And one other piece of advice. Reconsider the hijab." She pointed at the turban that Isma had left near the door along with her shoes, the latter out of consideration for Hira's hardwood floors and Persian carpets, the former out of consideration for her sensibility.

"Don't miss an opportunity with that one, do you, Dr. Shah?"

"It might be keeping your young man at a distance. He'll read things into what it means."

"He's not my young man and his reading won't be so wrong. And when did I say I wanted anything from him in that way?" It had been so long since anything approaching "that way" that she didn't know if she knew how to want it anymore. Mo at university had been the last and — barring some forgettable fumbling — the first man with whom she'd known any physical intimacy. Perhaps if they'd gone further than they had she'd have a sense of missing something, but Mo worried about their eternal damnation and Isma thought you should at least be able to imagine marrying someone before doing something so significant with them. In retrospect, it was a mystery they'd stayed together almost their entire second year of university.

"You know the Quran tells us to enjoy sex as one of God's blessings?" Hira said.

"Within marriage!"

"We all have our versions of selective reading when it comes to the Holy Book."

Isma laughed and stood to clear the plates.

From her greathearted vantage point Hira Shah saw Isma clearly — so careworn, so blemished by all the circumstances of her life that certain options had simply crossed their arms and turned away from her. But when a boy stepped into Isma's path, his laughter trailing a promise that life could be joyful if you stayed near enough to him, Hira turned her attention to a piece of fabric and said, *There, that and an untold story are the only obstacles between you and him.*

For a moment Isma stood in the kitchen, with its familiar scents and the warm glow of its lamps, and allowed herself to believe it. There was perfectly good cappuccino near his grandparents' house; he didn't have to drive twenty-five minutes every morning to the same café. She caught her reflection in the window. She had no idea where he went in the evenings, where he spent his nights. Where he was right now.

"Stupid," she said, and turned her attention to loading the dishwasher.

Eamonn opened his mouth and the sound that came out was that of a grasshopper. *Say something,* she said. *Chirp.* Isma opened her eyes from one darkness into another that was interrupted by a rectangle of light.

65

It was 2:17 a.m. Why was Aneeka calling at this hour? No, no, no, no, no. Her baby, her brother, the child she'd raised. She grabbed at the phone — images in her mind of his death, violent, unbearable — and pressed the answer button. Aneeka's face a death mask.

"It was you," her sister said.

"Parvaiz?" her own voice strange with sleep and fear.

"You were the one who told the police what he'd done."

One kind of panic ending, another beginning. "Who told you that?"

"Aunty Naseem is on the phone talking to Razia Apa about it. So you admit it?"

"They would have found out anyway."

"You don't know that." Her sister's voice all hurt and confusion. "They might not have. And then he could have come home. He could just have turned around the moment he knew he'd made a mistake and come home. You've made him not able to come home." She cried out, as if she'd only just then felt the wound that had been delivered to her. "Isma, you've made our brother not able to come home."

Isma touched her sister's face on the screen, felt the cold glass. "Shh, listen to me. People in the neighborhood knew. The

66

police would have found out. There was nothing I could do for him, so I did what I could for you, for us."

"For me?"

"We're in no position to let the state question our loyalties. Don't you understand that? If you cooperate, it makes a difference. I wasn't going to let him make you suffer for the choices he'd made."

"Is this me not suffering? Parvaiz is gone."

"He did that, not me. When they treat us this way the only thing we can do for our own sanity is let them go."

"Parvaiz is not our father. He's my twin. He's me. But you, you're not our sister anymore."

"Aneeka . . ."

"I mean it. You betrayed us, both of us. And then you tried to hide it from me. Don't call, don't text, don't send me pictures, don't fly across the ocean and expect me to ever agree to see your face again. We have no sister."

One moment her face was there, enraged, and then it was replaced by Isma's phone's wallpaper: yellow and green leaves floating on the surface of the Grand Union Canal. Isma tried FaceTime, Skype, WhatsApp, and even the expense of an international phone call, not with any hope of Aneeka answering but to let her sister know how desperately she wanted to communicate.

Finally, when the sound of ringing became more than she could bear, she lay back in bed, wrapping the duvet tightly around her. The stars were cold above her head. A verse from the Quran came to mind: *By the sky and the night visitor! / And what is the night visitor? / A piercingly bright star.* She got up, pulled the prayer rug out from under her bed, and knelt down on it. "Bismillah ir-Rahman ir-Rahim." The Arabic words her companions since childhood, passed on to her within her grandmother's embrace when no one thought she was old enough to learn them. *In the name of Allah the Beneficent, the Merciful.* This rocking motion that accompanied her prayers was her grandmother rocking her to sleep, whispering these verses to protect her. At first the words were just a language she didn't know, but as she continued, closing her eyes to shut out the world, they burrowed inside her, flared into light, dispelled the darkness. And then the light softened, diffused, enveloping her in the peace that comes from knowing your own powerlessness.

At least, that's how it usually worked. But today she couldn't make them anything other than words in a foreign language, spoken out loud in a room that didn't anticipate anyone's being out from under covers at this hour, and so was too cold. She returned to bed, hugged a pillow close to her chest, placed another against her back. She had only been fooling herself that night when she thought she still knew how to calm the frantic pacing of her sister's heart. Aneeka's had learned to beat in the company of her twin brother, in the world of their mother's womb. As children the twins would lie in the garden, fingers on each other's pulses, listening to the trains go by on the tracks behind their house. Waiting for those moments when their hearts were synchronized, first with each other and then with the sound of the train pulling out of Preston Road station.

Please call me please call me please call me she Skyped, WhatsApped, texted her sister.

Aunty Naseem called, horrified at her own role in what had happened. She and her daughter Razia had been discussing something in the news and she had said what a good thing it was, in this climate, that Isma had reported what Parvaiz had done. She hadn't heard Aneeka come in the night before and assumed she was miles away, at Gita's. "She was rude to me," Aunty Naseem said, the sentence conveying a whole universe and its behavior patterns upturned.

So then Isma had to convince her that it was a mistake easily made, and that there was nothing to forgive, and Aneeka would come around eventually, when really she wanted to shout into the phone *How could you have been so careless!* When the call finally ended she felt as tired as she'd ever been. She leaned into the pillow against her back, Eamonn holding her tight. "Oh," she said, surprised and not. This wasn't the first time she'd found him there, but she'd always banished him before. Now she pressed herself closer, taking the comfort it was suddenly obvious only he could give. At first, and for a long time, it was warmth that spread through her limbs, then, eventually, heat. She turned toward him in the darkness. By the time the first light appeared in the sky she felt herself transformed by the desire to be known, completely. Before the day and its realities could dispel this headiness, she reached for the phone and sent Eamonn a text: I'm sorry. I envy you your father. Mine died while being taken to Guantánamo. I want to explain it all to you.

He answered, earlier than she imagined

he would be awake: Tell me where to meet you.

From Aneeka, no word. FaceTime, Skype, WhatsApp, phone call. Nothing.

Isma looked at her reflection in the mirror, hair "texturized" into "beachy waves," as Mona of Persepolis Hair in Wembley had promised when she recommended a product that could counter frizzy, flyaway hair without attaining the miracle of straightening it. Her hair said "playful" and "surprising." Or it would if it didn't come attached to her face. She opened the drawer in which she kept her turbans and headscarves, closed it, looked in the mirror once more, opened it again.

A diffidence of knuckles on her door. She had expected him to call when downstairs, but one of her neighbors must have left the front door open, and now he was here, sooner than she'd anticipated, and she was still in her bathrobe. "Wait," she called out, and grabbed the nearest clothes at hand. Jeans, bra discolored in the wash — for heaven's sake, what difference did that make? — and fleece-lined sweatshirt.

She opened the door, a little breathless, as self-conscious as on the day she'd offered to walk him upstairs to the coffee counter.

There was a slight, spiced scent of aftershave coming off him. Specially for this meeting, or did she usually not see him until late enough in the day that it had worn off?

"Hello," he said, in a tone that wasn't unfriendly but more formal than his usual "hey." Was it because of their last conversation or because she was without a turban? His eyes slipped across her face and beyond it, as if he thought it might be impolite to look straight at her while she was uncovered. She saw him take in the glass and plate in the drying rack, the bare walls, the single bed with its white duvet and sheets.

"It's nice," he said. "Uncluttered." He unbuttoned his coat, the popping sound intimate in the silence of the studio. She wondered if "uncluttered" was a polite word for "austere," or if he really saw the studio as she had until that moment — a home that made almost no demands on you, allowed you simply to be. Now she wished she'd put a little more care into it, and that the single bed wasn't so determinedly single.

"Sorry about yesterday," he said.

"I'm the one who should be saying that. Tea?"

He kicked off his Wellies, and while she was filling the kettle she could hear him walking over to the desk, then a low whistle telling her he'd seen the photograph of Aneeka.

"That's my sister," she said.

He turned toward her, photo frame in his hands. The picture had been taken the previous year, soon after the twins graduated. Aneeka was dressed to go out in her favorite ensemble: black knee-high boots, black leggings, and long white tunic, a black bonnet cap accentuating the angles of her face, a scarf of black and white gauze wrapped loosely over it. One hand on hip, jutting her chin in a show of attitude to her twin behind the camera while Isma, elbow resting on her sister's shoulder, smiled indulgently. How broad her face looked next to her sister's, how washed-out her features compared to the lipstick-and-mascara enhancements at which Aneeka was so skillful.

"How old is she?"

"Nineteen." A woman-child, a mature-immature. Isma couldn't think of any words that would reach her.

He put the photograph down. "Attractive family," he said. He finally looked straight at her. "You have nice hair." The remark followed the one before it in going straight to her stomach, but he'd already turned his attention to the other frame on her desk, which contained an Arabic verse, handwritten on lined paper. "And this?"

"It's from the Quran. La yukallifullahu nafsan ilia wus-ahaa. Allah does not burden a soul with more than it can bear." When her grandmother died she had found this taped inside her bedside-table drawer.

He looked at her with more pity than she could endure, which he must have seen, because when he spoke his tone was lightly wry: "Here ends the small-talk part of the conversation, then."

She sat down on her bed, wondering if he'd sit next to her or choose the desk chair several feet away. He did neither, settling himself on the floor instead, knees drawn up to his chest.

"Tell me about your father," he said.

"I don't really know what to tell you about him, is the thing. I didn't know him. He tried his hand at many things in his life — guitarist, salesman, gambler, con man, jihadi, but he was most consistent in the role of absentee father."

She told him everything as she remembered it, without evasion. The first time her father had abandoned his family she was too young to remember either his departure or his presence before it. So she grew up in a house with her mother and grandparents, unaware that her heart was missing anything. When Isma was eight years old, he reappeared — Adil Pasha, known to his friends as "Pash, short for Passion," a laughing, broad-shouldered man who delighted in her resemblance to him. Like every woman in his life she quickly fell for his charm, which was so devastatingly effective it gained his readmittance to the marital bed, even though when he first walked through the door her mother overrode her in-laws and insisted he sleep on the couch. He stayed long enough to impregnate his wife with twins and to ensure his daughter found the thought of his ever leaving again unbearable, and then he was gone once more. This time his excuse for going wasn't a get-rich-quick scheme but an aid convoy to Bosnia, which was then in the final months of war, allowing him to cloak his departure in righteousness. The convoy returned a few weeks later, but he didn't, and Isma never saw him again.

Every so often a card in his scribbly handwriting would arrive to say how invaluable he was to some fight or other against oppression, or a bearded man would appear at the doorstep with some small amount of money and the name of wherever Pash was fighting — Kashmir, Chechnya, Kosovo. In

October 2001 he called. He was in Pakistan, en route to Afghanistan, and had heard of his father's death. He wanted to speak to his mother, and also to hear his son's voice. His wife hung up without waiting to find out if he might also want to hear Isma's voice — the voice of the only one of his children he'd ever known.

Eamonn shifted, rested his ankle against hers, an act of sympathy just small enough for her to bear.

"A few months later MI5 and Special Branch officers came around, asking about him, though they wouldn't say why. We knew something was wrong, and my grandmother said maybe we should try to contact someone — the Red Cross, the government, a lawyer — to find out where he was. If my grandfather had still been alive that might have happened, but he wasn't, and my mother said if we tried looking for him we'd be harassed by Special Branch, and by people in the neighborhood, who would start to suspect our sympathies. My grandmother went to the mosque looking for support, but the Imam sided with my mother — he'd heard too many stories of abuse suffered by the families of British men who'd been arrested in Afghanistan. One of my grandmother's friends had said the British government would withdraw all the benefits of the welfare state — including state school and the NHS — from any family it suspected of siding with the terrorists."

Eamonn made a face of distaste, clearly offended in a way that told her he saw the state as part of himself, something that had never been possible for anyone in her family. She raised a hand to hold off his objections. "My mother knew that wasn't true, but she allowed my grandmother to believe it. So that was that until 2004, when a Pakistani man released from Guantánamo contacted my father's family in Pakistan to say he had been imprisoned at Bagram with my father from early 2002. In June that year both he and my father were among the men put on a plane for transport to Guantánamo. My father died during takeoff, some sort of seizure. He said other things also, about what happened to my father in Bagram, but the family in Pakistan said no one needed those images in their head, and didn't tell us."

"No one told you he was dead for two years?"

"Who was going to tell us? The Americans? British intelligence? We weren't told anything. We still haven't been told anything. They haven't released records of

Bagram from that time period. We don't even know if anyone bothered to dig a grave."

"I'm sure they dug a grave," he said.

"Why? Because they're so civilized?" She had promised herself she wouldn't lie to him, and that included not curtailing her rage.

"I'm sorry. I was trying to . . . I'm sorry. I can't imagine what that must have been like for you, for your whole family."

She made a helpless, hopeless gesture. "We didn't talk about it. We were forbidden to talk about it. Only Aunty Naseem and her daughters who lived across the road knew because we were essentially one family divided into two households. Other than that there was only one other person who was told — a man who my grandparents had known since they first moved to Wembley and there were so few Asian families around that all of them knew each other. On my grandmother's behalf, this man went to visit his cousin's son, a first-term MP, and asked if the British government could find out any information about Adil Pasha, who died on his way to Guantánamo, and whose family deserved answers. 'They're better off without him,' the MP said, and left the room."

"That was my father?"

"Yes."

He slumped forward, his face in his hands.

She wanted to run her fingers through his thick hair, stroke his arm. There was a lightness inside her, entirely new, that made the whole world rearrange itself into a place of undreamt-of possibilities. In this lightness Aneeka's anger was short-lived, Parvaiz's choices reversible.

He looked up, held her gaze. "Can I?" he said, pointing to a spot on the bed next to her. She nodded, not trusting her voice enough to use it.

The mattress dipped slightly beneath his weight. He took her hand, looked at her with deep feeling in those brown eyes of his. "I'm so sorry for everything you've suffered," he said. "You're a remarkable woman." And then he patted her hand, once, twice, and let go of it. "You need to understand something about my father."

She didn't want to understand anything about his father. She wanted his hand back sending currents through her, including in the most intimate places. Almost as if he'd touched her there.

"It's harder for him," he said. "Because of his background. Early on, in particular, he had to be more careful than any other MP,

79

and at times that meant doing things he regretted. But everything he did, even the wrong choices, were because he had a sense of purpose. Public service, national good, British values. He deeply believes in these things. All the wrong choices he made, they were necessary to get him to the right place, the place he is now."

There he sat, his father's son. It didn't matter if they were on this or that side of the political spectrum, or whether the fathers were absent or present, or if someone else had loved them better, loved them more: in the end they were always their fathers' sons.

"I'm not saying that makes it okay," he said. He touched two fingers to his temple, rubbed. Perfect half-moons in his finger-nails. "I'm not very good at this. He should be the one explaining. I'll tell you what — next time you're in London, you two can meet. I'll set it up. Confront him with this — make him account for it. He'd be up for that. My guess is, you'll feel more favorably about him at the end."

"Me? Meet Karamat Lone?"

Mr. British Values. Mr. Strong on Security. Mr. Striding Away from Muslim-ness. He would say, *I know about your family. You're better off without your brother, too.* And

80

Eamonn, his devoted son, would sadly have to agree.

"Don't sound so worried about it. He'll be nice. For my sake." He took hold of a strand of her hair, pulled it lightly. "Now that I've seen your head uncovered, I'm practically your brother, aren't I?"

"Is that what you are?"

"Sorry, is that too presumptuous?"

She stood, turned, shrugged. "No, it's fine," she said, making her voice light, making him seem absurd for sounding so serious about it. "Oh, look, I never made you that cup of tea, and now I have to go out. Appointment."

"Will you come to the café after?"

"Probably not today. Actually, maybe not for a while. A friend has invited me to come and spend the rest of spring break at her place." Not strictly untrue. At the end of their meal the previous night Hira had said, *You're welcome to move into my spare room for a few days if you want company. Don't be heartbroken alone.*

"Oh, but then we won't see each other. I'll be leaving in the next day or two. News cycle already moving on from my father. And to tell you the truth, I think I'm cramping my grandparents' social life."

"Well, then. I'm glad we cleared the air,"

she said, holding herself straight-backed, upright.

"Me too. Well. Good-bye. Thanks for being such a fantastic coffee companion." He stepped forward and held his arms out slightly awkwardly. What followed was not an embrace so much as two bodies knocking into each other then moving away. He smiled, pushed his hair back from his face in a way that already felt as familiar to her as the tics of people she'd grown up with. She watched him put on his Wellies, button up his coat, smile again, turn to go. His hand reached for the doorknob, and then he paused.

"Isma?"

"Yes?" The trace of hope still working its way through her veins.

He picked up the padded envelope from the kitchen counter, which was filled with M&M's — there was a long-running joke between the neighboring households about Aunty Naseem's sweet tooth for American confectionery after a vacation there in the 1980s.

"This the same package you had in the café last week? Weren't you going to the post office with it?"

"Keep forgetting," she said.

He tucked it under his arm. "I'll post it

from London."

"There's no need."

"It's really no problem. Cheaper and quicker."

"Oh, okay. Thanks."

"Bye, sis," he said with a wink. Then he stepped through the door and closed it behind him.

She ran over to her balcony. Moments later, he stepped out onto the street, rolling back his shoulders as if released from the weight of her company. He walked away without looking up, his stride long.

Isma knelt down on the snow-dusted balcony floor and wept.

■ ■ ■ ■

EAMONN

■ ■ ■ ■

3

A kayak glided high above the stationary traffic of the North Circular Road, two ducks paddling in its wake. Eamonn stopped along the canal path, looked over the edge of the railing. Cars backed up as far as he could see. All the years he'd been down there he'd taken this aqueduct for just another bridge, nothing to tell you that canal boats and waterfowl were being carried along above your head. Always these other Londons in London. He typed "canal above north circular" into his phone, followed a link that led to another link, and was soon watching news footage of a bomb planted on this bridge by the IRA in 1939. When the newsreader came to details of what would have happened if the bridge had been destroyed, he clicked pause mid-sentence, and hurriedly strode on.

But today was not a day to worry about the precariousness of things. It was the start of April, and London was bursting into spring, magnolia flowers opening voluptuously on the trees in Little Venice where he'd entered the tow path. Now he was walking along a wilder terrain, weeds and bushes growing in all directions, sometimes tall enough to hide the industrial blight that lay beyond, sometimes not. And then it changed again, became beautiful, almost rural — swans on the bank, yellow buds studding the trees, a man and his dog both snoring on the roof of a canal boat, the sky an expanse of blue smeared with white. Isma the invisible presence walking alongside him, her expression intense except when he could make her smile. He wondered if she would get in touch next time she was in London. Probably not. Despite their attempt to clear the air, the history of their fathers had made things between them far too strange. He tried to imagine growing up knowing your father to be a fanatic, his death a mystery open to terrible speculation, but the attempt was defeated by his simple inability to know how such a man as Adil Pasha could have existed in Britain to begin with.

He left the canal path near high-rises embodying the word "regeneration" and was soon on Ealing Road, walking past

Gurkha Superstore, Gama Halal Meat, a Hindu temple intricately carved of limestone, cheerful stalls and restaurants. He couldn't point to anything in particular he recognized, yet he had complete certainty that he had looked out a car window onto this street many times in his childhood. "We're going," is all his father would say before the annual outings to Eamonn's great-uncle's house every Eid, a holiday that his mother explained as "marking the end of the month of not observing Ramzan for all of us." On that one day of the year, his father became someone else, and it was this that he knew his mother hated as much as he did. Surrounded by his extended family, Karamat Lone disappeared into another language, with its own gestures and intonations — even when he was speaking English. One year, when Eamonn was nine or ten, Eid fell just after Christmas. The American family was visiting, and there were plans every day for outings with cousins. "You don't have to come this year," his father agreed after some judiciously timed postprandial Christmas Day pleading, and went on his own. The next year it was "Do you want to come?" and he didn't seem to mind when his wife and children said no. Just when Eamonn was becoming old enough to want to know the part of his father's life that remained so mysterious, there was the whole business with the mosque photographs and a falling-out with the cousins over the necessary damage control.

He was nearing a mosque, crossed the street to avoid it, then crossed back so as not to be seen trying to avoid a mosque. Everyone always went on about the racism his father had had to face when a section of the press tried to brand him an extremist, but it was London's Muslim population who had turned their back on Karamat Lone and voted him out, despite all the good he'd done for his constituents. All because he'd expressed a completely enlightened preference for the conventions of a church over those of a mosque and spoke of the need for British Muslims to lift themselves out of the Dark Ages if they wanted the rest of the nation to treat them with respect.

On the High Road now, with its pound stores and pawnshops, glancing up every so often at the bone-white rainbow of Wembley Stadium for its reassuring familiarity — and then north toward Preston Road, where everything turned residential, suburban. Any one of these semidetached houses could be the home in which he'd spent all those Eid afternoons, sitting pressed against his mother in an alliance she tried to push him out of, knowing that he would rather be in the garden playing cricket with the boy cousins whose invitations to join them were located confusingly at the border between the merely polite and the genuine. His sister, habitually free of the burden of alliances, would be upstairs with the girl cousins, throwing herself into a rapture of family feeling that would disappear as soon as they were back in Holland Park. She was, everyone said, her father's daughter, a claim she was proving with her determined ascent, at twenty-two, through the world of investment banking in Manhattan.

On the rare occasions he remembered his father's family it was only to recall the feelings of estrangement that visits to them brought up, but spending time with Isma had reminded him that there were other, more familial feelings. She evoked in particular his father's youngest cousin, the one who once affixed a Band-Aid and a healing kiss on his elbow when he took a tumble in the garden, gashing open his skin. He wondered if, in turn, he reminded Isma of Parvaiz, the younger brother to whom she referred only in passing, twin to the beautiful woman in the photograph.

He was walking past curving side streets that he seemed to know had been laid directly over country roads more recently than a person might assume. The distance between his father's life and his own revealed itself here more acutely than in West London. This was the London of Karamat Lone's childhood, these were the homes of the affluent relatives whose lives his father had aspired to when he sat up all night in his cramped flat in Bradford, studying for exams. Late at night was the only time he could spread his books onto the surface that was kitchen counter, dining table, and workspace for his seamstress mother. On the wall across from him a large poster of the Ka'aba, the faithful prostrating themselves around it. Eamonn knew this from a photograph, one of the few his father had from his childhood, about which he had always been too embarrassed to ask.

Finally, he approached the street on which Isma had grown up, just off a commercial stretch of Preston Road. Now that he was here he felt awkward about not simply posting the package, and he walked up Preston Road for a while — past a Jewish bakery beside an Islamic bookshop beside a Romanian butcher — before turning back toward Isma's street again. He was unable to let go of the feeling that behind these doors existed a piece of his childhood — of his father — that he'd been too ready to forget. He knocked on the door of a pebble-dash house and an elderly woman made small by age answered, wearing a shalwar kameez with a thick cardigan that signaled her internal thermometer was still set to another country. This must be the old friend and neighbor, Aunty Naseem, in whose house Isma's sister was living while studying law at LSE. He said he had brought something for her from Isma, which made her open the door wide and reach up to place the palm of her hand against his cheek before turning to walk back inside with the words "Come, have some tea."

The Arabic calligraphy on the wall, the carpeted stairs, the plastic flowers in a vase, the scent of spices in the kitchen despite there being nothing on the stove: all brought back his great-uncle's home, and with it the shameful memory of his own embarrassment about it.

He took Isma's envelope out of his satchel and handed it to the old lady, who laughed in delight when she shook it, guessing the contents. "Such a thoughtful girl, that girl. Tea — with sugar?" At his response she said, "You British, never any sugar in your tea.

My grandchildren are all the same. My daughters, half-and-half — one yes, one no. How did you meet Isma? What do you do for a living?"

She was amused by the story of the man who needed rescuing from an unmanned coffee counter but made a disapproving face at "taking a year off," which made him say "probably return to consultancy but perhaps a more boutique firm." "One of those personal shoppers?" she asked, and it took him a moment of placing together "consultancy" and "boutique" to understand how she'd reached that conclusion. When he explained, she laughed, slapping his hand in a show of mirth, and he laughed too, wishing he'd known a paternal grandmother — a dadi. His had died the year before he was born, and her husband — a newspaper-kiosk vendor — had followed soon after, "dead of helplessness," as Eamonn's father explained.

Soon she was frying samosas for him, as though determined to inhabit a stereotype, while, as instructed, he licked the end of a thread and guided it through the eye of a needle. She had moved to London from Gujranwala in the fifties, she said; his grandparents had come then from Sialkot, he said. No, he didn't speak Punjabi. No, not

94

Urdu either. "Only English?" Some French. She said, "My father fought in the British Indian army during World War One. He was in France for a while, billeted with a family there — the sons and husband were soldiers, so it was just the women he lived with. *Je t'adore,* he used to say to his children years later. After he died, I wondered who had taught him those words. Here, hold out your arm."

The threaded needle was for him, it turned out. She had noticed the loose button on his sleeve, and he found himself looking at the parting of her dyed black hair as she bent down to set it right, still talking away. "Shukriya," he said, the Urdu word clumsy on his tongue, and after a moment's pause in which something else seemed necessary he added "Aunty," and was rewarded by another pat on his cheek. He assumed all this affection and the generosity of her welcome was just the famed Pakistani hospitality his father sometimes sighingly spoke of when regretting how "English" his children's lives had turned out (to which Eamonn's mother would reply, "It's wonderful in the abstract but when you actually encounter it you call it intrusive and overbearing"); but then she said, "So, Isma sent you to meet us."

He set down the samosa, which, it was suddenly clear, had been given to him under a false assumption. "Not exactly. In fact, no. I told her I would post the package, but it was such a nice day I thought I would take a long walk and drop it off."

"You walked here? All the way from Notting Hill, to see us."

"It's a nice walk. I like discovering new bits of London — in this case, the canal," he said, which seemed an effective way of dispelling her misconception without either of them actually mentioning it.

"Oh, she told you how much she loves walking along the canal." He picked up the samosa and bit into it. Isma could set her straight when they spoke — he didn't doubt Aunty Naseem would be on the phone to her as soon as he left. "You know, I've known her since the day she was born. Her grandmother was my first friend — we were living off the High Road, nothing like today. There were no other Asians at all. And then one day, across the street I saw a woman in a shalwar kameez. I ran across, in the middle of traffic, and caught her by the arm, and we stayed there talking for so long my husband came out looking for me. When we moved to this street, we said to them, 'Come on, we can't separate.' So they came. And here Isma was born, and grew up. So much sadness in her life, looking after the twins from such a young age. It's time someone looked after her."

He was spared the further embarrassment of this conversation by the sound of footsteps coming down the stairs.

"We have a guest. A very nice young man. Isma sent him." The footsteps retreated up the stairs and the old woman's voice dropped. "Aneeka. She'll come down again once she's fixed herself up. In my days either you were the kind of girl who covered your head or you were the kind who wore makeup. Now everyone is everything at the same time."

He had been about to leave, but instead he reached for another samosa. A few minutes later, the footsteps approached again. The woman who walked in was smaller than he'd expected from the picture — petite, really, and without any of the sense of mischief he'd seen in the photograph — but just as beautiful. Eamonn stood up, conscious of his greasy fingers and of the question of how he might use them to unpin the white hijab that framed her face. She greeted him with a puzzled look, which confirmed how unlikely it was for Isma to have sent someone like him to meet

97

her family. The old lady introduced him by his first name — which was all he had given her — and Aneeka's expression didn't so much change as ossify.

"That's spelled with an *e*, not an *a*, Aunty. Eamonn Lone, isn't it?"

"Isma told you about me?"

"What do you want here? Why do you know my sister?"

"He met Isma in Northampton. At a café," the old woman said, coming to stand next to Eamonn and place a hand on his arm, looking at him apologetically, not only for the girl's behavior but for her own "oh" of disappointment when the girl mentioned his surname. "He walked all the way from Notting Hill to bring me M&M's from Isma. Along the canal."

The beautiful girl looked at the envelope with Isma's handwriting on it and then at him, her face confused.

"It's a lovely walk. The canal flows above the North Circular, along an aqueduct. I never knew that. The IRA tried to bomb it in 1939. It would have flooded all of Wembley." He had no idea if this last detail was actually true, but he wanted to say something interesting so the girl would see that he might be the kind of person her sister would choose to have coffee with, not just the posh toff who seemed so out of place in this kitchen and in Isma's life. "You can see news footage about it. Just search for 'north circular canal bomb' or something like that and it'll come up."

"Right — because that's a good idea if you're GWM, isn't it?"

"I don't know what that is."

"Googling While Muslim. Aunty, did Isma tell you anything about this person?"

"Why don't we all call her now?" Aunty Naseem said brightly, and the girl — who made less sense with every second — said, "Please stop trying to make me speak to her. Anyway, I have to go out now. And Mr. Lone, since you've delivered the M&M's you can leave with me."

Despite Aunty's noises of protest, he followed the girl out. She didn't say anything until they were at the end of the street, and then she turned sharply on her heels to face him.

"What's going on here?"

"I really don't know what you mean," he said, holding up his hands. "I was just delivering a package for Isma. As your . . . aunty said, we met in a café. In Massachusetts. Became friends, sort of. Two-Brits-abroad kind of thing."

A man in a bright red suit that appeared

99

not to have been washed in several years stopped next to Aneeka and held out a filthy square of fur. "Have you met my cat?"

Before Eamonn could chivalrously interpose himself, Aneeka was reaching out to stroke the matted fur as if it were the smoothest mink. "Of course I've met Mog, Charlie. She and I are old friends." The man made happy noises, tucked the fur into his jacket against his heart, and carried on.

After that moment of gentleness, the harshness of her voice when she turned her attention back to him was particularly unsettling. "That doesn't explain why she asked you to come here."

"She didn't. I offered to post it." He couldn't imagine articulating to this woman his curiosity about a lost piece of his father, so instead he said, "Okay, this is embarrassing, but I saw a photograph of Isma's sister, and wanted to know if anyone could really look that beautiful in person."

She gave him precisely the look of disgust he deserved for such a statement, and strode away without another word.

The train pulled out of Preston Road station, and he turned in his seat to look out at the houses alongside the tracks. Beyond the back wall and garden sheds of one property a girl flew up, hovered for a moment, fell, flew up again. A trampoline. She made her body a starfish, and though he knew she couldn't see him, he raised his own hands to mirror hers. He continued to look through the window after the train picked up speed and left Preston Road behind.

When he finally turned to face forward, a woman standing farther along the mostly empty carriage came over and sat next to him.

"Do you live alone?" Aneeka said.

"Yes."

"Take me there."

After the boldness of that line, she barely spoke all the way from Preston Road to Notting Hill. At first he tried to fill the silence with conversation about Isma, but her response made it clear theirs was not the relationship of closeness Isma had portrayed. "Did she tell you —" he started to say, and she replied, "I'm discovering the list of things Isma hasn't told me is far longer than I would have believed," which made any further conversation along that line impossible.

On the walk from the tube station to his home she looked around like a tourist, and he was embarrassed by the affluence of the neighborhood he lived in while unemployed. It was an embarrassment not aided by entering his flat, which was paid for and decorated by his mother, with its central open-plan space that combined kitchen, living room, and dining area in an expanse that could double as a playing field and provoked Aneeka to say, "You really live here alone?"

He nodded, offered her tea or coffee. She asked for coffee, before turning to walk the length of his flat, looking at the framed photographs on his shelves — family picture, graduation picture, his friends Max and Alice's engagement-party picture.

"One of these your girlfriend?" she asked, looking up from the last photograph.

He was all the way at the other end of the flat, by the coffee machine, but his emphatic "No, I'm single" would have carried down a room twice as long. He waited for her to return to the kitchen end and slide onto a high stool at the counter before asking, "And you? Boyfriend?"

She shook her head, dipped a finger into the coffee foam, checking its depth, didn't meet his eye. *Why are you here?* didn't seem like a question he could ask, and might make her leave, which he didn't think he wanted, although it was hard to know what to want of a silent, beautiful woman in a hijab sipping coffee in your flat.

"Isma prefers turbans," he said, to say something, indicating her head covering.

She unpinned the hijab, folded it carefully, and placed it between the two of them on the counter, then pulled off the tight-fitting cap beneath it. She shook her head slightly and her hair, long and dark, fell about her shoulders like something out of a shampoo advertisement. She looked at him, expectant.

Eamonn knew what to do when a woman asked to come home with him and began to undress. It was not a situation he was unfamiliar with. But he didn't know if this was that situation. Though what was it, if not that?

He leaned forward, placed one elbow on the counter, and extended the rest of his arm across the glass-topped distance between them, palm up, resting it close enough to her hand to be an invitation, but distant enough to be ignored without too much awkwardness. She downed the rest of the coffee in a gulp, wiped the back of her hand across her mouth, which slightly smeared her lipstick, and placed the hand on his wrist. Coffee foam and lipstick on her skin.

He was conscious of the hammering of his heart, the pulse leaping out at her. She smiled then, finally. Taking his other hand, she placed it on her breast but over her shirt. That too was confusing until he realized, no, not her breast, she had placed his hand on her heart, which was beating frantically too.

"We match," she said, and the promise of her voice made the situation familiar, and thrillingly new.

The next morning, he is pressing his nose against the sofa, breathing in the smell of her. All these surfaces of his home — walls, bed, sofa — marked with her scent. He walks from one surface to the next, his senses still filled with her.

He glances around the room. How is it possible that it appears exactly the same as yesterday? It should look as though a storm has been through. There should be broken vases, torn blinds, upturned furniture. Something to mirror this feeling of turmoil, of everything having changed. He stands in front of the mirror, touches the scratch on his shoulder as though it's a holy relic. At least there's this. Cups his hands and lifts them to his face, breathing in. His personal act of prayer.

To start with she'd been hesitant, tentative. During their first kiss, she'd broken away and started to put her hijab back on, before his entreaties convinced her to stay. Then things swung the other way, and she seemed to think she had to prove to him that she really wanted to stay, in the way of a certain kind of adolescent girl who had always made him uncomfortable in his teenage years — the ones who thought they were required to give to the older boys without anything in return. So he stopped her, showed that wasn't how this would work, and she said, "You're nice," as if that was a surprise, and they set about discovering each other in that slow-quick way of new lovers — testing, exploring, building on what each was learning about the other.

At daybreak he woke to discover she'd risen from the bed, to which they'd finally made their way. Hearing the sound of the shower, so early, he thought she was planning to leave without saying good-bye. But when she left the bathroom her footsteps didn't move in the direction of the door. Eventually he swung himself out of bed and walked into the living room to find her praying, a towel as her prayer mat, the hijab nothing more alien than a scarf loosely covering her head without the elaborate pinning or the tightly fitted cap beneath. She made no sign of being aware of him except a slight adjustment of her shoulders, angling away from his naked form. He should have left immediately, but he couldn't help watching this woman, this stranger, prostrating herself to God in the room where she'd been down on her knees for a very different purpose just hours earlier. Finally, the depth of her immersion in a world other than that of bodies and senses made him go back to the bed, wondering if she'd return.

"What were you praying for?" he asked when she came back in and started to unbutton her long-sleeved shirt, starting at the base of her neck.

"Prayer isn't about transaction, Mr. Capitalist. It's about starting the day right."

"You had to put on a bra for God?" he said, as she unbuttoned further, needing her to laugh with him about it. "Did you think He might get distracted by your . . . distractions?"

"You do other things better than you do talk."

That burned in ways both good and bad. He held back from mentioning that he could say the same for her. When openings for conversation had arisen she preferred to pillow her head in her arms and look up at the ceiling, or doze with her back to him, the soles of her feet pressed against his legs, combining rejection and intimacy. He watched as she continued to undress until there was nothing left but the white scarf covering her head, one end of the soft fabric falling just below her breast, the other thrown over her shoulder.

"Leave this on?" she said. He had learned already that everything new she offered was posed as a question. It was not because she doubted his desire, as he'd thought the first time, but because it seemed important to her to hear the "yes," its tones of want and need. Now he hesitated, though his body's reactions were answer enough as she touched her nipple through the white cotton, colors contrasting. He reached a hand out to her, but she stepped back and repeated the question. "Yes," he said, "please."

Now he picks the white fabric off the sofa, wraps it around himself like a loincloth, beats his chest, and makes gorilla sounds. Just before leaving she had put on that tight-fitting object she referred to as a "bonnet cap," ignoring his comment that this was as superfluous a name as "chai tea" or "na'an bread," and taken a blue scarf from his hall closet, which she started to wrap around her head. "Why'd you have to do that?" he said, and she brushed the end of the scarf against his throat and said, "I get to choose which parts of me I want strangers to look at, and which are for you." He had liked that. Against his will, against his own self, he had liked it. Dumb ape.

After breakfast they lay together on the sofa in a square of sunlight, and either the dimensions of the cushions, or the thought that she soon had to leave, made her finally curl up against him, her head on his chest.

"So, Isma," he said tentatively. "She speaks about you as if you're close."

There was silence for a while, and he wondered if mentioning Isma had been a bad idea. He felt strangely guilty about her; straitlaced, pious Isma. She wouldn't approve of what they had done here. If he was thinking that, surely Aneeka was too. He threaded his fingers through her hair, wondered if her sister's disapproval would be a reason for her never to come to him again, held her tighter.

"We used to be close," she said. "But now I don't want her anywhere near my life. Are you in touch with her?"

"Not since I left. But I thought I'd drop her a line to say I'd been to Aunty Naseem's. Why, would you rather I wasn't in touch with her?"

"Would you do that for me if I asked?"

"I think I would do any number of outrageous things for you if you asked," he said, tracing a beauty mark on the back of her hand. "But don't give me too much credit for this one — it's not as if she's written to me. I think we both recognize it was just one of those holiday friendships, which there's no point trying to carry into the rest of your life." The complication of fathers was not an issue he felt any need to bring up while they were lying naked together.

There was another stretch of silence, then she said, "When I leave, will you want to see me again?"

"That can't possibly be a serious question."

"If this is something that's continuing, then I do want you to do something outrageous for me. Let me be your secret."

"How do you mean?"

She placed her open palm against his face and dragged it slowly down. "I won't tell anyone about you, you don't tell anyone about me. We'll be each other's secret."

"Why?"

"I don't ask 'why' about your fantasies, do I?" she said, sliding a bare thigh between his legs.

"Oh, this is a fantasy, is it?" Distracted by

the beginnings of a rocking motion she was making, the friction of her skin against his.

"I don't want my friends wanting to know when they can meet you. I don't want Aunty Naseem inviting you round for a meal. I don't want Isma thinking she can use you as a conduit to me. I don't want other people interpreting us. I don't want you wanting any of those things either. Just want me, here, with you. Say yes."

"Yes." Yes, yes, yes.

Over the next few days he discovered her version of secrecy meant he didn't have her phone number, couldn't contact her online (couldn't find her there, in fact), wasn't permitted to know when she was planning to come and go. She'd simply turn up at some point in the day, sometimes staying for so short a time they never even got completely undressed, other times remaining overnight. Secrecy was an aphrodisiac that gained potency the longer it continued, every moment filled with the possibility that she might appear, so there was no time when he was away from home that he didn't want to return there, and no moment at home when he didn't race to the front door at every imagined footstep, every pressed buzzer. Soon he found himself almost incapable of thinking about anything but her. And not just the sex, though he thought about that often enough. The other things also: the concentration with which she brushed her teeth, her fingers tapping on the sink, counting out the number of strokes up and down and to the side; her habit of spraying on his aftershave before showering, claiming the scent would linger under the shower gel, so subtle only she would know it; the way her face transformed into a cartoon — eyes narrowed, lips pressed together, nose wrinkled — when she ate slices of lemon with salt with her morning tea; the precision with which she followed recipes, one tooth biting her lip as she measured out ingredients, even while praising his skill at culinary improvisation. Aneeka drying her hair with a towel, Aneeka balanced cross-legged on a kitchen stool, Aneeka's face settling into contentment when he took hold of her feet and massaged them.

In the beginning, he was afraid she might choose simply to stop coming around one day. There was a skittishness to her manner, now passionate, now distant. Once she'd even broken off at a moment that left him crying out in dismay to say, "No, I can't," dressing quickly and leaving, refusing to explain. He suspected it was her God and His demands that made her want to deny what she clearly had no wish to be denied; he knew he couldn't win an argument on that score, so there was nothing to do but stay quiet and trust that her headstrong nature ensured that no abstract entity would set the rules for her life.

Sometimes he thought of calling Isma, just to speak to someone who knew Aneeka, just to hear her name. But Aneeka didn't want him to, and he wasn't going to get caught in the rupture between sisters that, it turned out, centered around some issue of inheritance. "There was something that belonged to me. She had some claim on it, but mostly it was mine. From our mother. And she took it away from me." Although he couldn't believe that Isma would steal something, he could imagine her deciding to sell some family heirloom for financial reasons and seeing no reason to discuss it with the sister whom she sometimes spoke of as though she were still a child in need of parenting.

"And what does your brother say about this?" he asked.

In Eamonn's mind this brother — Parvaiz — was a slippery ghost, sometimes an ally, sometimes a rival. The slipperiness came from the fractured nature of Aneeka's stories about him. In her tales of growing up he was her ever-present partner in crime, the shadow who sometimes strode ahead, sometimes followed behind, without ever becoming detached from their twinness, an introspective boy who disapproved of her relationships ("always with older boys, of course") but helped her keep them hidden from her sister and Aunty Naseem, while remaining perpetually in love with one or another of Aneeka's friends, who all insisted they loved him as a brother. (Eamonn knew well the pain of this, thanks to his sister's childhood friend Tilly, of the long legs and bee-stung lips — "I don't want to know about it," Aneeka said, which was a balm to her mention of the older boys.) But after school, their lives diverged. Unlike Aneeka, Parvaiz hadn't received any scholarships; unwilling to start his adult life by taking on crippling loans, he'd instead gone traveling, in the time-honored fashion of drifting British boys. Here he disappeared from her stories.

"I haven't told him what she did. When he comes back, I will."

"And when is he coming back?"

She shrugged, and continued clicking through the photographs on his computer, watching his life from childhood to the present day — all the family holidays, all the girlfriends, all the hairstyles and fashion choices and unguarded moments.

"I can't actually tell if you're on better terms with him than you are with your sister."

She zoomed in on a picture of Eamonn with his arm around his father's shoulder, both in matching T-shirts with the words "lone star" written on them, the resemblance between them everywhere, from smile to stance. Unlike her sister, Aneeka didn't seem to have much of an opinion of his father as a political figure, and he sometimes wondered if she'd been too young when her own father had died to have been told what Karamat Lone had said about him.

"He knew Isma was leaving and then he went and left too. It's nothing I won't forgive when he comes back. Until then, I'm holding it against him."

It struck him as unfair to take issue with a nineteen-year-old boy wanting to see the world instead of sitting at home keeping his sister company. But then Aneeka clicked to the next photograph — the Lone parents and children hamming it up for the camera in Addams Family Halloween costumes — and he reminded himself that growing up an orphan obviously created an interdependence between siblings that he, with his affectionate yet disengaged relationship to his sister, couldn't understand.

There was, in fact, a great deal about her he didn't understand. Most days that was part of her allure, but one morning, less than two weeks after they'd first met, he woke up resentful. The previous afternoon he had returned from the bakery around the corner to find a note she'd slipped through the communal letter slot in the front door saying "Was here. Left." He canceled his evening plans in case she came back, but she hadn't, and all that secrecy he'd been enjoying suddenly seemed a tiresome game in which she held all the power. Impulsively, he packed his bags for a week away and caught the train to an old school friend's home in Norfolk. To begin with, he enjoyed the thought of her returning repeatedly to his front door only to find him gone. Let her know what it felt like to be the one who did the waiting around. But on the second night, when his hosts were asleep, he called his father's personal assistant and asked him to find a cab company nearby that could get him back to London.

He arrived home at nearly three a.m., half asleep as he came up the stairs to his front door, and saw a figure curled up on the landing, his doormat rolled up as a pillow. He crouched down next to her, and when she opened her eyes her relief was both shaming and thrilling.

Once they were inside he walked straight to the living room, withdrew a set of keys from a ceramic bowl on a shelf, and handed it to her, saying it was hers to use anytime, day or night. She butted her head against his shoulder and said, "Don't be this nice." He asked her what she meant and she replied by kissing him, slow and intense.

Something shifted between them that night. When he woke up the next morning and walked toward the sound of Aneeka making breakfast in the kitchen, she left off blending a smoothie to show him the chart she'd made of all the blocks of time when he shouldn't expect to see her — times when she was on campus, or in study groups, or the Wednesday evenings when Aunty Naseem insisted on a family dinner, and any day between three and five p.m. "Why not then?" he said, and she nipped his shoulder and said, "Let a woman hold on to her mystique!"

"Okay, okay. Block out Sunday afternoons too," he said.

She kissed his shoulder where she had nipped at it. "The weekly Lone family lunch

116

in Holland Park. Is it very civilized? Do you say 'please' and 'thank you' and 'sorry' and talk about the weather?"

"Why don't you come some Sunday and see for yourself."

She stepped back. She was wearing nothing but his T-shirt, and the tightening of her shoulders transformed the look from sexy to vulnerable. So she did know about her father and his. He caught her hands in his, reassuring them both that they could survive the conversation he knew they had to have. "I know that'll be difficult for you. Isma told me. About your father. And about what my father said about him."

"You know about my father?"

"Yes."

"Why did she tell you? We don't talk about that to anyone."

"If you ever speak to her again you could ask."

She walked away, poured out a smoothie, left it next to the blender, and returned to him. Shoulders still held in, looking at him with some of the mistrust she'd shown at their first meeting.

"Who else did she tell you about?"

"What do you mean?"

"Not who else. I meant what else. What else did she tell you about him?"

117

"It's okay," he said, touching her hand. "It'll be okay. You never even met him. No one will judge you by him."

"Not even your father?" She sat down on one of the high stools next to the kitchen counter, looking at him very seriously.

"Especially not him. He says you are what you make of yourself." He raised and lowered his shoulders. "Unless you're his son. Then he indulges you even if you don't make anything of yourself."

"He indulges you?"

"Yes. My sister's like him, so she gets all the expectation. I get the pampering and the free passes."

"Do you mind that?"

"I mind a lot. And you're the first person to ever guess that might be the case."

She hooked her feet around the back of his legs and drew him to her. "I never held it against your father that he said what he did about mine. He was right — we were all better off without Adil Pasha. But now I mind. Because when I think about it, he comes across as unforgiving. I don't like the idea of you having a father who is unforgiving. I want to know he's different with you." She kept kissing him as she spoke, light kisses on his mouth, his neck, his jaw, slightly frantic.

He drew back, took her hands in his. "It's fine to talk about this. It's true, he can be unforgiving, particularly of people who betray his country."

"What if you were the one asking him to do the forgiving?"

"You want me to ask him to find out what he can about your father?" But she was shaking her head emphatically. No, she didn't want to know. Her father was nothing to her — it was her grandmother who had needed to know what had happened to her son; maybe her mother, maybe Isma. But not her, not Aneeka. She wanted to know about him, about Eamonn. She would like to have a picture of what it meant to be Karamat Lone's son beyond what the photo album revealed.

"He's one kind of person as a politician. Another kind as a father. There's nothing he wouldn't do for me."

"That's good," she said, a new note in her voice, one he couldn't place. "That's how it should be." She put her arms around him, and he tried to ignore how relieved he felt at knowing she didn't expect him to raise the issue of her father with the home secretary. Of course if this continued — and he desperately wanted it to — Eamonn would eventually have to tell his father that he was

119

involved with the daughter of a jihadi. Not now, though, not yet. Let Aneeka's game of secrecy allow things to remain simple for as long as they could.

The weeks went by. Life adjusted around the rules she set. In the hours when he knew Aneeka wouldn't visit, he went to the gym, did his shopping, dropped in on his mother to prevent her dropping in on him. He fired his cleaning lady, who also worked for his parents, claiming it was a temporary situation until he started earning again — then hired someone else, whose details he found in a corner shop window. In the time he had at home without her he started learning Urdu, the difficulty of it made worthwhile by her delight in his growing vocabulary, which she augmented with words no online tutorial would ever teach. She started e-mailing him surprisingly interesting articles related to contract law, and they were both pleased to discover that his short time in the working world had given him insights she wouldn't necessarily find in course reading. They cooked together, alternating roles of chef and sous-chef with perfect good cheer. Parallel to all this, his friends' teasing about his "double life" faded away — as did their invitations to join them on weekends in the country, Friday evenings in the pub, picnics in the park, and dinners within the two-mile radius in which they all lived. He knew it was a paramount failure of friendship to disappear into a relationship, but to be in his friends' company now felt like stepping back into the aimlessness that had characterized his life before Aneeka came along and became both focus and direction.

"When you're ready for reentry let us know," his ex-girlfriend, Alice, now engaged to his best friend, Max, said sympathetically one Wednesday evening when he was over at their place with the rest of the old school gaggle, the discomfort of the patio furniture dulled by Pimm's. A few glasses in he learned that his friends had decided he was in a slump brought on by unemployment, his feeling of failure exacerbated by his father's continued conquest of the world. This midweek gathering in Brook Green, consequence of Alice calling up and demanding a date from him, was an intervention. Helen recommended a doctor who would prescribe pills without making a fuss, Hari invited him to join a rowing club on the Thames, Will offered to set him up with a "fantastic" work colleague who wouldn't expect anything serious, Alice proffered a job in her family's PR company, and Max rested a hand on his shoulder and reminded Eamonn that he was as good at listening as he was at creating distractions.

"I love you all," he said, meaning it. He felt in love with everything: the Pimm's, the furniture, the ironic gnomes in the garden, the sky with its bands of sunset colors. "But I'm really fine. Just doing my own thing, under the radar."

"I don't know," Max said. "Twenty-something unemployed male from Muslim background exhibits rapidly altered pattern of behavior, cuts himself off from old friends, moves under the radar. Also, are we sure that's an evening shadow rather than an incipient beard? I think we may need to alert the authorities."

"Take it straight to the home secretary," Hari said. "At least he's drinking Pimm's, so we know we haven't lost him completely."

He hardly drank anymore. Aneeka hadn't told him not to, but the first time he'd moved in for a kiss with alcohol on his breath she'd recoiled. Even after he'd brushed his teeth, she said she could still smell it. "Sorry," she'd said. "We can do the other things, but just don't kiss me." That distilled the issue in a way that made only one outcome possible. He leaned back in his chair, looked at his friends and tried to imagine walking into this garden with Aneeka — the hijab, the refusal of alcohol, Wembley. Everyone would be perfectly polite, but at some point the following day, either Max or Alice would call him up to say, "Lovely girl. I hope she didn't mind our sense of humor?" No relationship had ever withstood "hope she didn't mind our sense of humor."

"What would you have done if I had walked in with a full beard?" he said, picking a piece of apple out of his Pimm's and chucking it at Max.

Alice made one of those annoying humming sounds of hers that was meant to, and did, stop Max from reacting, and came around to pull Eamonn's head to her stomach, stroking his hair as if he were a child.

"We'd hold you down and shave it off, my darling. Friends don't let friends become hipsters." It was the kind of glib answer he'd previously have found amusing, but now he was impatient with it, with her, with the stale dynamic of all of them. What was the point of surrounding yourself with other versions of yourself all the time?

He allowed Alice to hold his head against her almost concave stomach, so that his friends could exchange whatever glances they needed to, and all the while he was thinking, before Aneeka there was Alice. This body, these hands, this scent. Less than two months after it ended he had given his blessing when Max wanted all that for himself, and he'd meant it. How had he ever imagined what he'd felt was passion, let alone love? Before Aneeka, there was only the facade of feeling. And now he was in so deep that everyone but Aneeka was blurred and indistinct, poor creatures of the surface, their voices receding.

Every so often there were times she would switch out of the frequency of their relationship. That was the only way he knew to describe it to himself; a sudden transformation, as if an elbow had accidentally pressed against a radio button and, mid-note, jazz became static. She'd turn cold, or sad, sometimes angry, and any attempts to talk to her about it were futile. One particularly strange night he woke up in the early hours of the morning to see her standing at the foot of the bed, staring at him with one of her unreadable expressions. When he called to her she said, "Go back to sleep and tell yourself you dreamed it." He tried talking to her instead — demanding to know what was wrong, made angry by his own inexplicable fear — and she ended up leaving,

Eamonn following her on the street in boxers and flip-flops to make sure she was safe until a cab came along and she stepped into it.

Worse followed just a few days later. They were having a languorous afternoon, lying on a thick-pile rug, playing favorite songs from their childhood for each other, swapping stories of growing up. Aneeka was teasing him gently for thinking that his was the more "normal" life despite his millionaire parents, both of whom regularly appeared in the newspapers. The trace unpleasantness of that strange night had finally disappeared, and they were both grateful for this return to happiness, slightly silly with each other. Her mouth against his arm, blowing out to make trumpetlike noises in time with the music, when her phone announced an incoming Skype call. She always ignored calls, no matter who it was — from one particular expression of distaste he guessed it was often Isma — but even so, she had to check her screen when she heard the sound.

"You're not going to answer it. Stop with the Pavlovian response," he said, pretending to grab for her ankle as she scrambled to her feet. He was too lazy, though, to turn and watch her reach for the phone. The next track that came on was one he loved and hadn't heard in ages, and he turned up the volume and sang along. It was a few seconds before he realized she had left the room, and he went in search of her to apologize for raising the volume just as she answered the phone, which is what must have driven her away.

She wasn't in the hall or the bedroom, but the bathroom door was closed and through it he could hear sounds but not the words they formed. He stepped up to the door and put his ear to it.

"I'm making sure of things here," he heard her say.

At the end of the sentence her voice seemed to move closer to the door, and he backed away and quickly returned to the living room. It was a long time before she joined him there, and when she did her eyes were bloodshot, as if she'd been crying, but also glinting with a kind of frenzy that he'd only ever known in the manic or the high.

"Who were you talking to?" he said.

"One day you'll know," she replied. She burst into laughter and wrapped her arms around him. "Soon, please God, soon."

She was a weight against him, unwanted, clinging. In that moment he could imagine not loving her; he could imagine wanting her gone from his life, with her secrets and her strangeness, her swerves of mood, the sheer inconvenience of her. But then she pulled away, put a hand over her eyes, and when she looked at him again she was Aneeka once more.

"I'm acting a little crazy, aren't I?" she said. "I'm sorry. Please bear with me. Please." She rested the back of her hand against his cheek, a touch he'd never had from her before. He bowed his head and rested it against hers, a moment of love between them that made all obstacles surmountable, even the ones around her heart.

4

Cocooned in white sofa cushions and the sound of rain outside, Eamonn watched a man dancing on the top of a train, declaring in Urdu, with subtitles, that if your head is in the shade of love then surely your feet are in paradise. It was a sentiment Eamonn would have sung along with, trying to get the accent right by the time Aneeka arrived, but today the world was sitting a little too heavily on his shoulders. He clicked out of the video and returned to the clip of his father addressing the students at a predominantly Muslim school in Bradford, which counted among its alumni Karamat Lone himself and two twenty-year-olds who had been killed by American airstrikes in Syria earlier in the year. There he was, no notes in hand, the lectern ignored as he stood front and center on the stage, the old school tie drawing attention to how little he'd changed physically from the head boy whose image was projected onto the screen behind him, other than a graying around the temples, a deepening of character in his face. "There is nothing this country won't allow you to achieve — Olympic medals, captaincy of the cricket team, pop stardom, reality TV crowns. And if none of that works out, you can settle for being home secretary. You are, we are, British. Britain accepts this. So do most of you. But for those of you who are in some doubt about it, let me say this: Don't set yourself apart in the way you dress, the way you think, the outdated codes of behavior you cling to, the ideologies to which you attach your loyalties. Because if you do, you will be treated differently — not because of racism, though that does still exist, but because you insist on your difference from everyone else in this multiethnic, multireligious, multitudinous United Kingdom of ours. And look at all you miss out on because of it."

More than twenty-four hours after the speech that ended with those sentences, the media attention had barely died down. Across the political spectrum, except at its extreme edges, the home secretary was being lionized for his truth-telling, his passion, the fearlessness with which he was willing to take on both the antimigrant attitudes of his own party and the isolationist culture of the community he'd grown up in. #YouAreWeAreBritish was trending on social media, as were #Wolfpack and its Asian offshoot, #Wolfpak. The phrase "future prime minister" was everywhere.

The Eamonn of a month ago would have been proud. Now, he kept imagining a meme of his father's voice saying "Don't set yourself apart in the way you dress" played over a video of Aneeka standing up from her prayer mat and walking into his embrace, shedding her clothes along the way until only the hijab remained. The video wouldn't reveal the things that were most striking about her in those moments: the intensity of her concentration, how completely it could swerve from her God to him in the time she took those few footsteps, or her total lack of self-consciousness in everything she did — love and prayer, the covered head and the naked body. He heard the door open — Aneeka entered and called out from the hallway to say she was taking a shower.

He no longer had feelings of dread if she didn't turn up when he expected, or of relief when she did — he had come to accept that he was who she wanted to be with. The joy of that moved through the days with him, burnishing every moment, even this one in which he stretched out on his sofa, listening to the different tones of the rain — clattering against windows, slapping against leaves, pinging off bricks. In Aneeka's company he'd learned to listen to the sounds of the world. "Hear that," she used to say in the beginning, somewhere between a command and a question. Soon he learned the pleasure of being the one to say it to her, hear that, the London we never enter together: the lawn mower rattling against pebbles at the edges of the garden; the differing weight of vehicles on the street outside — the swoosh of the motorcycle, the trundle of the van; the voices of drunk English lovers, matched in pitch though not in tone by caffeinated Italian tourists. Hear that, the varied creaks of the bed frame: the short cry of disappointment when you leave, the long groan of pleasure when you return. Hear that, the quickening of my breath, my blood, when you touch me, just so. At her urging, he started to record snippets of the time he spent without her, playing them back and asking her to identify the sounds he linked together to form a narrative of life without her: tube barriers opening and closing, his mother's pruning shears cutting through stems in the rose garden, the heavy

131

thud of the door to the newly constructed panic room in his parents' house, a row of men on treadmills at the gym engaging in unacknowledged competitions of speed and stamina, conversations with the interactive Urdu learning tutorial, his hand bringing himself to climax while he thought of her. When he asked her why she didn't bring him the soundscape of her days, she shrugged and said he'd have to think up a game of his own for her to play, he couldn't simply borrow hers. But his mind didn't know how to do that.

"Caught in the rain?" he said, going over to kiss her when she entered the room in his blue-and-white-striped dressing gown, carrying an armload of wet clothes. She pulled away almost immediately, holding up the wet clothes as explanation. When she'd deposited them in the dryer, she sat down on one of the stools at the kitchen counter, and he walked over to dry her hair with a towel.

"Does anyone give you a hard time because of the hijab?" he said.

She tilted her head back to rest it against his chest and look up at him. "If you're nineteen and female you'll get some version of a hard time for whatever you wear. Mostly it's the kind of thing that's easy to shrug off. Sometimes things happen that make people more hostile. Terrorist attacks involving European victims. Home secretaries talking about people setting themselves apart in the way they dress. That kind of thing." He didn't say anything to that, just gripped a fistful of her hair and squeezed while moving his hand down along the length of it, water dripping onto the wood floor. "And no, I wasn't showering because I got caught in the rain. Some guy spat at me on the tube."

"Some guy what?"

She swiveled the stool around. "What do you say to your father when he makes a speech like that? Do you say, 'Dad, you're making it okay to stigmatize people for the way they dress'? Do you say, 'What kind of idiot stands in front of a group of teenagers and tells them to conform'? Do you say, 'Why didn't you mention that among the things this country will let you achieve if you're Muslim is torture, rendition, detention without trial, airport interrogations, spies in your mosques, teachers reporting your children to the authorities for wanting a world without British injustice'?"

"Wait, wait. Stop it. My father would never . . ." He had never heard her speak of any of this since the first time they met, when she'd made her Googling While Muslim comment, which he'd managed to put out of his mind until now. "Do you think he doesn't know what it is to face down racists? He wants people like you to suffer less from them, not more. That's why he said what he did, even if it wasn't the best way of phrasing it."

A small, sad smile. " 'People like you'?"

"That came out wrong."

"No, I don't think it did. There are people like me and people like you. I've always known it. Why do you think I did all this 'Let's be secret' stuff? I wouldn't have lasted five minutes in your life if you had to tell your family and friends about me."

"I know." The admission surprised them both. "But that was before. Now if the world wants to divide into Aneeka and everyone else, there's no question where I'm standing. Or kneeling, which is really what I'd like to do right now, but I don't know if you're anywhere near ready for me to do that."

"Do what?"

"I just proposed proposing to you."

For a moment he thought he'd made a terrible mistake, Aneeka looking at him as though he'd said the craziest thing in the world. And then her mouth was on his, his

134

hands on her shower-warm skin, everything he wanted in the world right here, right now, this woman, this life, this completeness.

Although they never went as far as the private communal garden, the flat roof jutting out a few feet from Eamonn's bedroom window, which he'd failed to turn into a terrace in the four years he'd lived here, had become a favorite retreat. With a little nudging from Aneeka, he had bought a variety of tall plants — cactus, chili, kumquat — which they placed along the edge of the roof, and although they shut out the view of the gardens below, they also made privacy possible while alfresco.

The morning after the "proposed proposal," as she enjoyed calling it, they sat outdoors pitting cherries for jam, the sun beating down almost as palpably as the previous day's rain. Eamonn in a pair of khaki shorts and Aneeka once again in the blue-and-white dressing gown, now hiked above her knees. The concrete warm on their skin as they sat cross-legged at the very edge of the janglingly colorful floor cushions that had been her way of objecting to the muted tones of Eamonn's flat. She'd carried them in a couple of weeks earlier, her

135

glare daring him to comment on the fact that she was claiming his space as hers, as he'd wanted her to do almost from the start. He placed a cherry in his mouth, considered kissing her, the cherry passing between them, but settled for watching her instead, enjoying her evident satisfaction at the clean workings of the cherry pitter she'd mocked not an hour earlier as an accessory of the rich who don't know what else to do with their money. *It's a cherry pitter. It pits cherries. How is that some wild extravagance?* In response she'd opened a kitchen drawer and held up one utensil after another: *A cherry pitter to pit cherries, a garlic peeler to peel garlic, a potato masher to mash potatoes, a lemon zester to zest lemons, an apple corer to core apples.* She'd grinned at him. *All you need is basic cutlery and a little know-how.* But here she was now, making a small satisfied noise with every cherry pit she neatly punched out using the gadget in her hand. She'd gathered up the dark weight of her hair and twisted it into a loose knot at the base of her neck. A temptation to tug just so and watch it tumble down.

"Whatever you're thinking, the answer is, not until we've finished with the cherries."

He grinned, stretched out a leg, laid it over her knee, part of her thigh, and picked up the knife he was using to cut into the cherries and flip out the stones with his thumb. "This reminds me of a summer holiday in Tuscany when I was ten or eleven. Cherries and gelato, that's all my sister and I ate the whole summer. At least in my memory."

"What do people do when they go away on holiday? Other than eat cherries and gelato."

"You've never . . . ?"

"There was a trip to Rome once, the year before my mother died. The travel agency she worked for gave her free tickets — but it felt more like a school trip than a holiday. She thought we should see as many sights and spend as little money as possible."

"What was she like, your mother?"

"Stressed. Always. It's what killed her. Isma said she used to be different — when my grandfather was alive and paying the bills, when my father wasn't yet a terrorist who could have us all driven out of our homes if any of us said the wrong thing to the wrong person."

"I really don't know how you survived your childhood."

"Didn't feel like it was something that needed surviving until she died. Everything else you can live around, but not death.

Death you have to live through." She smiled, shrugged. "But then again, no one told me I was missing out on holidays with cherries and gelato raining down. If I'd known that, I would have been much more disgruntled."

"Well, we should go somewhere together. As soon as your summer holidays start." She gave him the look of exasperation he was accustomed to receiving every time he suggested anything that involved leaving his flat. "Come on, it's time we entered the world together. We can start with Max and Alice rather than my parents if you want to ease into things. And isn't it time you told Isma? Maybe even that brother of yours?"

"Not yet," she said.

Exasperated, he threw a cherry pit into the bowl with such force that it bounced out and landed on the dressing gown, leaving a crimson stain on a white stripe.

"Let's go back to pretending it's a game," she said, flicking the stone onto his bare leg. "Who needs other people? Who needs to leave London on a vacation when everything we want is right here in this flat?"

"I'm not bloody spending my summer locked up in here. Neither are you. Come to Tuscany with me. Come to Bali. You don't want other people, fine. We'll find a remote island somewhere."

"If we try to leave the country together the people who work for your father will know." At his puzzled look: "MI5. They listen in on my phone calls, they monitor my messages, my Internet history. You think they'll think it's innocent if I board a plane to Bali with the home secretary's son?"

It was a mark of his love for her that he felt nothing other than protective about the Muslim paranoia she'd revealed the previous day. Gently he said, "My love, I promise you MI5 isn't watching you because of your father."

"I know. They're watching me because of my brother. Ever since he went to Syria, to Raqqa, last year."

"I don't understand," he said automatically.

"Yes you do."

He rubbed at the cherry mark on his leg. It was something to do while his brain sat inert in his skull, offering him nothing that would make this explicable.

"He's fighting there?"

"Parvaiz, fighting? God, no! He's with their media unit."

Their. The black-and-white flag, the British-accented men who stood beneath it and sliced men's heads off their shoulders. And the media unit, filming it all.

He stood up, walked to the edge of the roof. As far from her as it was possible to go. In his life he'd never known anything like this feeling — rage? fear? What is it, make it stop. He kicked out, knocked over the kumquat tree. Shoved with his hands, toppled the cactus plant. The kumquat fell straight, flower pot shattering as it hit the ground; for an instant the root-entangled soil held its shape, then the plant leaned forward and collapsed, orange fruit rolling around the garden patio. The cactus, by contrast, wheeled in the air, upturning itself as it fell, never before so anthropomorphized as with arms outstretched in a headfirst plummet, its neck snapping in two on impact.

He became aware of everyone in the communal garden looking up to see the madman on the terrace, the woman in a dressing gown stepping forward to take him by the hand and pull him toward the window. He allowed himself to be led, but once indoors he shook himself free of her, strode into the kitchen area, and opened a bottle of beer, which he downed in two long drafts, maintaining eye contact with her the whole while.

"Fight like a man, not a boy," she said.

"That the kind of advice that gets passed

140

down from father to son in your family?"

The words hung horribly in the beer-stenched air. He put down the bottle and hunched onto a stool, looking at the cherry stains on his hands. Through the open window he could hear the raised voice that was his neighbor coming outside to see the carnage on his patio. Aneeka sat down on the stool facing him, the long room with its tasteful decorations extending behind her, its track lighting in the ceiling, its expensive art. All of it his mother's handiwork. Every part fitting seamlessly together except this woman whom he'd allowed in.

"He wants to come back home," she said.

"Well, he can fuck off and stay in the desert he chose, can't he?"

"Please, Eamonn."

"Please, what? Oh, god." His thumb bit into the corrugated edge of the bottle cap, deep enough to draw blood. "Why did you get into the tube with the home secretary's son that day?"

She took his hand and placed his thumb in her mouth, drawing his blood into her. He pulled away with a *No.*

"I got into the tube because I thought you were beautiful."

"Don't lie to me." He slammed his hand on the kitchen counter, making the fruit

141

bowl jump, making Aneeka jump.

In a voice so low he could barely hear it she said, "I got into the tube because I thought the home secretary's son could help my brother come home and avoid charges."

No pain had ever felt quite like this. "That's what this has all been about?"

"No!" She tried to take his hand again, and this time he physically pushed her away from him. "I know you don't have reason to believe me, but the truth is . . . the truth is . . ."

"Give me enough respect to avoid the 'From the first time we kissed I fell in love with you' line. Do that much for me."

"You were hope," she said simply. "The world was dark and then there you were, blazing with light. How can anyone fail to love hope?"

"A love that's entirely contingent on what hope can do for your brother."

"I couldn't have done this, for all these weeks, if my feelings for you weren't real. You'll have to choose whether you believe that or not. No words I say here will convince you."

"Get out."

She went, without another word. He could hear her in their — his — bedroom, and could imagine too clearly her body as she unbelted the bathrobe and bent to open her drawer of silky underwear. He put on a shirt, walked downstairs with a dust pan and brush, and rapped on his neighbors' door. He had accidentally knocked over the plants, he said to Mrs. Rahimi, surprised to hear how ordinary his voice sounded, and yes, it was fortunate he hadn't fallen himself, and yes, she had warned him that he needed to build a proper terrace or this kind of accident could occur. Despite her protestations he insisted on helping her unprotesting husband clear up the mess on the patio. Even with his vigorous, concentrated sweeping it took longer than he expected, shards of pottery and clumps of soil everywhere. The kumquat plant was recoverable, Mr. Rahimi said, but the cactus, poor thing, was for the compost. There followed a conversation about the absurd smallness of the compost bin the council had provided, which Eamonn threw himself into with great verve. They moved on to kumquats after that — there was a Persian tangerine stew that might work very well with kumquats, Mrs. Rahimi said. Eamonn told her there was an old Notting Hill saying, "If you drop a tree on your neighbor's patio, all the fruit it ever bears is theirs by right — particularly if that stops them from suing you." Even Mr. Rahimi was won over by that, and Eamonn remembered how easy it was to be a social being, well liked, surrounded by uncomplicatedness.

Eventually Mr. Rahimi said he was returning to watch the test match, and would Eamonn care to join him. Eamonn said he would. He still hadn't heard the sounds telling him she'd left the flat.

"When I first arrived in England as a student I decided I had to understand cricket in order to come to grips with the subtlety of English character," Mr. Rahimi said, ushering Eamonn into the TV room. Holding a finger to his lips he withdrew two bottles of beer from a mini fridge, and handed one to Eamonn. "Then I encountered the figure of Ian Botham and discovered that the English aren't nearly as subtle as they want the world to believe. You Pakistanis, on the other hand, with your leg glances and your googlies."

Eamonn's response to statements like that had always been, "I've never even been to Pakistan." But he didn't want to say that now.

Mrs. Rahimi walked in, took the beer bottle out of her husband's hand, and replaced it with a glass of something yogurty. Mr. Rahimi said something in Farsi,

144

his tone one of affectionate protest. They'd married over thirty years earlier, despite the disapproval of their families — a difference of class, more insurmountable than any other difference in his family's eyes. Better you had married a Sunni from Iraq, Mr. Rahimi's mother had said, the same mother who now spent months in London, telling anyone who'd listen how all her other daughters-in-law took such little care of her compared to this one, whom she'd treated so badly at first.

Eamonn stood up, apologizing. He had to go, he said. He was sorry, he'd forgotten in the warmth of his neighbors' hospitality that he was expecting someone. He left the Rahimis sitting in front of the TV, Mr. Rahimi drinking from Eamonn's bottle of beer, Mrs. Rahimi sipping from the bottle she'd confiscated from her husband.

He took the stairs two at a time, calling Aneeka's name as he opened the door. When there was no answer he thought she'd left, but he found her sitting on the edge of their bed, still in the stained dressing gown.

He sat down next to her, for once not touching. She held her hand out to him. Within it, the phone with the factory-set picture for a home screen and security settings that ensured no one without the passcode could see who had called or texted. She tapped in the code and pulled up a photograph. A boy with headphones on turned toward the camera with an open smile and a thumbs-up gesture. He had Aneeka's skin tone and her fine bones — but while hers made her look fierce, like a panther, his gave him a breakable air. His eyes were sleepy, his shoulders narrow. If he was standing in a room with his sisters, your eyes would go straight over him to Aneeka's beauty, Isma's gravitas. "That's Parvaiz," she said unnecessarily, and leaned into him. "That's my twin. I've spent every day the last six months sick with worry about him. Now he wants to come home. But your father is unforgiving, particularly about people like him. So I'm not going to get my brother back. And I don't really know what to do . . . half of me is always there, wondering if he's alive, what he's doing, what he's done. I'm so tired of it. I want to be here, completely. With you."

It was what she'd say if she were still only trying to manipulate him. It was what she'd say if she'd really fallen in love with him.

You think marriage is in the large things, Mrs. Rahimi had once said. *It's in the small things. Can you survive the arguments about housework, can you learn to live with each*

146

other's different TV viewing habits. He thought of Aneeka opening his kitchen drawers, mocking the cherry pitter that pits cherries, the apple corer that cores apples. A life of small things forming between them.

"I've broken us, haven't I?" she said.

He put his arm around her and kissed the top of her head. "No," he said, and felt the relief go through her body, and his own. "Tell me everything about your brother."

His mother had warned him about increased security following the attention brought on by the Bradford speech, but that didn't make it any less strange to see SO1 officers where previously there'd been trees at the bottom of the garden. Makes it less likely for a terrorist to get in undetected, his mother had said on the phone when he asked if he could stop by for breakfast, and she told him the noise he was hearing in the background was his beloved childhood tree house and its support structure being sacrificed. She had sounded unbothered, but there were dark smudges around her hazel eyes, and she was crossing her arms with hands tucked beneath her armpits as she did when she wanted to hide her usually immaculate nails bitten down to stubs. She was the portrait to his father's Dorian

Gray — all the anxiety you'd expect him to feel was manifest in her.

Terry Lone, mistaking the uneasy looks her son was directing at the officers, turned her back on them and slipped a check into his pocket. When he shook his head and returned it to her, she raised her eyebrows. "You mean that's not why you've stopped by at this ungodly hour? That shouldn't have come out as an accusation — you know I'm happy to help."

He draped his jacket over his mother's shoulder, as a show of affection rather than a response to any sign of her feeling the early-morning cold. "You're magic. But some of the bonds you bought for me years ago just matured. And anyway, I'm going to get back to work soon. Alice thinks PR and I will be a good fit — she has a job waiting for me." He wasn't at all sure that was what he wanted to be doing, but he knew he couldn't turn up at Aunty Naseem's door as Aneeka's intended if he didn't have a job.

"Well, you know my thoughts on the matter of employment for the sake of employment. But your father will be pleased," his mother said, allowing him to ask where the man in question was.

"In his study, of course. See if you can drag him out, while I consider the roses."

148

He watched for a moment while she walked toward the rose bushes: Terry Lone, née O'Flynn, of Amherst, Massachusetts, one of Europe's most successful interior designers, with a chain of stores from Helsinki to Dubai bearing her name. When she was sixteen, her parents pulled her out of school a few weeks before the end of the semester to travel to London with them, hoping the visit to a city of "real culture" would cure her growing interest in the worrisome feminist movement that was so active on the nearby Smith College campus. They arrived to stay at the Savoy on April 29, 1978, and the next morning, while her parents slept off jet lag, she dutifully walked down to Trafalgar Square to see the National Gallery, and ran into the thousands gathered for a Rock Against Racism march, which was just setting off for Victoria Park to hear the Clash and other musicians raise their voices louder than the racist chants of the National Front. "You coming?" said a Spanish boy with dark hair falling around the shoulders of his black leather jacket covered in badges letting onlookers know NAZIS ARE NO FUN and RACISTS ARE BAD IN BED. They'd been marching awhile by the time she discovered his parents were from Pakistan, a country she'd never heard of. Considerably later that day, when the compliant side of her personality asserted itself and she said she had to return to her parents, he insisted on accompanying her all the way to the Savoy, even at the risk of missing the Clash, and when she burst into tears at the thought of saying good-bye to someone so thrilling, he vowed to marry her one day. For the next two years they communicated by letter, until she enrolled at Chelsea School of Art, by which point he'd left university and swapped his leather jacket for a banker's suit, which she found both a disappointment and a relief.

Terry Lone picked up a yellow petal, brushed the smoothness of it against the tip of her nose. It was only now that Eamonn understood how you could decide you wanted to marry someone in the course of an afternoon, and without drugs being the primary factor, as he and his sister had concluded many years ago. Did she ever wish she'd continued on to the National Gallery, he wondered. His parents weren't unhappy together, but there was a separateness to their lives. His mother winding down her daily involvement in her business just as his father became too busy for holidays or even breakfast — that seemed somehow apt for the state their marriage had reached.

Today particularly, he wished they were more like the Rahimis.

Glancing around the terrace, he tried to imagine an occasion later this summer when two families might be sitting out for dinner on a balmy evening. Karamat and Terry and Emily and Eamonn, Aneeka and Isma and Aunty Naseem, and maybe even Parvaiz. He acknowledged to himself he had no idea how the world might take him from this moment to that imagined one — he knew only that they all would have to find a way to make it happen.

He entered the house and made his way to his father's basement office, a room that lacked his mother's signature spare style and featured instead dark wood and solid lamps and windowlessness. Those years of nocturnal study had left their mark — Karamat Lone was at his most productive when there was no glimmer of natural sunlight.

"Since when does my son knock before entering?" he said, standing up to kiss and embrace Eamonn, a form of greeting that had embarrassed him for years, until one day it didn't.

"Since my father started bringing home top-secret documents. Do they actually have 'top-secret document' written on them?"

"No, they have 'If you aren't important

enough to have clearance for this, you'll be dead soon' written on them. In very, very small print, otherwise there wouldn't be room for anything else. Why are you awake, let alone here?"

"There's something I wanted to talk to you about. Can we sit a minute?" He gestured his father back to his worn leather chair and perched on the edge of the desk, facing him — the position in which he'd spent so much time in tense arguments with his father (his GCSE subjects, backpacking with Max, arrangements for his girlfriend's abortion) through that period of adolescence when Karamat Lone was a backbencher with more time for parenting than his wife had. Terry Lone was the one to whom Eamonn and his sister would turn when they wanted new gadgets, cars, and, later, a flat each of their own — the relationship's binary options of "yes/no," usually "yes," giving it solidity. But with father and son everything was more abstract, the baseline love threaded through with contradictory emotions that left the women of the family exhausted by the up-and-down of it all. *Who is this posh English boy with my face,* the father would say, sometimes with disappointment, sometimes with pride. Who *you made me, so blame yourself,* the son would

152

reply, and his father would respond with either *There is no blame, my jaan, my life* or *That was your mother's doing, not mine.*

"I'm seeing someone," he said, and watched his father's eyebrows lift. One morning, in the brief period when Eamonn was pining over Alice, the door of his bedroom had been kicked open and Karamat Lone had walked in, knees buckling slightly under the weight of the halibut in his arms, ice chips glinting on its skin. He had lowered the massive fish onto his son's bed, with the single word "replacement." It was the coarsest thing anyone in his family had ever known him to do, and Terry and Emily Lone were both horrified, words such as "misogynist" and "chauvinist pig" echoing around the house. Eamonn pretended to side with them, but he had been more amused than he'd ever admit, and the act put a decisive end to his pining. Though it was only since Aneeka that he'd come to agree, yes, Alice really had been a cold fish.

"Don't look at me like that," Eamonn said. "She's not like the others."

"How so?"

"For starters, she's not from around here."

"She's not British?"

"She's not West London."

This was received with his father's extrav-

153

agant snort, which his children were always amazed he could restrain from in public life. "Well, that is a change. Where's she from then? Cheltenham? Richmond — my god, not south of the river!"

"Wembley."

His father looked surprised, and pleased to be surprised. Eamonn picked up a paperweight with a lion and unicorn etched on it, turned it in his hands, a little shy, all the other concerns pushed to the side as he told the man he loved most in the world about the woman he loved most in the world. Aneeka, he said. Yes, Pakistan — her mother raised in Karachi, her father a second-generation Brit whose parents were originally from Gujranwala. An orphan at the age of twelve, raised by her sister. Preston Road. Beautiful, and so smart, Dad, on a scholarship to LSE for law. Only nineteen but far more mature than that. Yes, very serious. Yeh ishq hai. His father took his hand and squeezed it when Eamonn spoke the Urdu words, beaming at his son.

"Well, if it's love you'd better bring her around. Next Sunday?"

"There's one thing I should warn you about. She's a bit, well, Muslim."

"How 'well, Muslim,' exactly?"

"She prays. Not five times a day, but every

154

morning, first thing. Doesn't drink or eat pork. She fasts during Ramzan. Wears a hijab."

"Uh-huh. But she has no problem —" He brought the palms of his hands together and then separated them.

"What? Opening a book?"

"Sex."

"Dad! No, she has no problem with that. There is no problem with that at all. And if you want hand gestures for sex, try one of these."

"Those could be useful in Parliament, thank you. So, she's no halibut. Glad to hear it." He grinned in the way that had earned him the Wolf part of his nickname.

"You're taking all this much better than I thought."

"What? You think I have a problem with you dating a Muslim? I have a lot more trouble with all the double-barreled girls whose fathers don't waste a minute telling me of their family's long association with India — governor of this province, aide-de-camp to that viceroy. Helped quell the Mutiny. Helped quell the Mutiny! All delivered in a way that sounds perfectly polite, but everyone knows I'm being informed that my son isn't good enough for their daughter." Eamonn waited for the Chip to

155

play itself out. Alice's poor father would be mortified if he had any idea how much offense he'd caused with his "helped quell the Mutiny" line about his namesake. That's what Alice had said, and only Hari had rolled his eyes in response, but then Hari had a little version of the Chip himself. "Anyway, if she's only nineteen, I suspect she can be persuaded out of the hijab in time. Get your sister to take her off to the hair salon next time she comes to visit. I'm mostly joking. You know I grew up a believing Muslim. Didn't harm anyone but myself with it."

"I didn't know that, actually. I mean, I knew your parents made you go to the mosque and fast and stuff, but I didn't know you really believed."

"No? Well, I did. That's how I was raised. There are still moments of stress when I'll recite Ayat al-Kursi as a kind of reflex."

"Is that a prayer?"

"Yes. Ask your girlfriend about it. Actually, no, I'd prefer it if you didn't mention it to anyone."

"You shouldn't have to hide that kind of thing."

"I'd be nervous about a home secretary who's spoken openly about his atheism but secretly recites Muslim prayers. Wouldn't you?"

"Do I look nervous?"

"You've been looking nervous throughout this conversation. Son, she's your girlfriend. I'll be on my best behavior, as always. What I might say when you break up is another matter."

"There's one other thing. There's a boy she was close to at school. He's gone to Syria — I don't mean on humanitarian work."

"Parvaiz Pasha."

"How do you know?"

"I know all their names. Where they come from. Who they were before they went. There's only one from Preston Road. It's the last place in England I'd expect to find that kind of thing happening. But that one, he had exceptional circumstances. Terrorism as family trade. Illustrative of how much you need to do to root out this kind of thing. I mean, literally, grab by the very roots, and pull. Pull the children out of those environments before they're old enough for the poison to seep in."

"No, it's not like that."

"What's not like what?"

Eamonn stood up; it was warm in here, oppressive. Already the script he'd plotted in his head was beginning to unravel by the sheer fact of his being in his father's presence. *He knows he was wrong. He was brainwashed but now he understands, and he wants to come back. He didn't take part in the fighting, never actively recruited anyone. He's only nineteen. No reason to ruin his life over this. His name has never been in the papers, you can make it stay that way. He just needs a new passport, and to slip quietly back into the country without any charges against him. His friends all think he's been in Pakistan this whole time; no one will ever know. It's best for everyone — imagine the media storm if anyone finds out your son is planning to marry the sister of a boy who went to Raqqa. You'd never survive it.*

Trust me, he'd said to Aneeka. *I know my father. I know how to spin it so he'll agree.* But that wasn't spin, it was a threat. How could he possibly do that to this man who had always offered him the most unconditional of loves? And why was his father looking at him so strangely, as if he knew his son had come here with betrayal in his heart?

"Orphaned at the age of twelve, and raised by her sister?"

"Yes."

"Just like Parvaiz Pasha."

158

"All right, yes. She's his twin."

"Eamonn!" His father caught hold of him around the neck, half headlock, half embrace. "You stupid, stupid boy. My stupid boy."

Jaan, she had called him, kissing his eyes, his mouth, his cheeks, his nose, when he'd said he would speak to his father. Jaan, my life. A word his father was now saying as he held his son. And just as suddenly, Karamat Lone disengaged, stepped back, and wiped a hand across his face. Where there'd been a father, now there was a home secretary.

"You will have no more contact with this girl. I'm setting up a security detail for you."

"Dad! Look, just, meet her. All right? I'll bring her over. Tonight, this evening, and . . . what's so funny?"

"All this security around the house, and the nexus of al-Qaeda and the Islamic State is just going to waltz in on the arm of my son."

"Don't you ever refer to her in that way again. She's the woman I'm going to marry."

Nothing moved in his father's face. "Stay here."

"Or what, you'll arrest me?" But the home secretary was gone before the end of the sentence, door slamming behind him.

Eamonn sat down in his father's chair,

looked at the computer screen, which asked for a password. Riffled through the file of news clippings from this morning's papers. Wished he hadn't left his phone in his jacket — Aneeka was at his flat, waiting for him to call and tell her what had happened. She'd finally given him her number, but he hadn't thought to memorize it. If only he hadn't laughed off the suggestion when his mother said he should have a landline.

I could just leave, he kept telling himself. I could at least go up and eat something.

He had a small moment of satisfaction when he realized he could use his father's phone to call directory assistance and ask for the Rahimis' number.

"It's Eamonn," he said, his voice fissured, when Mrs. Rahimi answered. "Could you please do me a vast favor? There's a friend of mine upstairs, in my flat. Would you call her down. I really have to speak to her."

"The beautiful one in the hijab, you mean? I'm sorry, she just left. Almost knocked me over as I was taking the rubbish out. She seemed in a great hurry. Are you all right?"

He walked over to the sofa and lay down on it, curled up like an animal protecting its soft parts. A few minutes later, his mother entered the study and sat down beside him.

No, she wouldn't bring him his phone. No, he really should just stay in here until his father said otherwise. She told him to close his eyes, and stroked his back until he fell asleep. When he woke up, feeling he'd slept a long time, his father was sitting at his desk, watching him.

"My fault," his father said. Eamonn sat up, rubbed his hands across his eyes, tried to understand what that meant.

"My fault," his father repeated sadly. "I say it's your mother's doing, but I'm the one who never wanted you to know what it feels like to have doors closed in your face. To have to fight your way in. I didn't think it would make you so sure of yourself, so entitled, that you wouldn't stop to ask why a girl like that would have time for a public-school boy who lives off his mother because he can and has no ambition beyond beating his own high score in computer games."

"What have you done?"

"I haven't done anything. The officers who were called in when her brother left were concerned about her. They said she was clearly shocked by what he had done, but seemed more upset about being kept in the dark than the fact of his going. They thought she might be at risk of trying to join him. So there've been some people keeping an eye on her, for her own safety. But apparently there've been no phone calls, no texts, no communication of any kind that could be intercepted to suggest she was in touch with my son. Nothing to set off alarm bells. Which sets off alarm bells. And now, this." He placed Eamonn's phone on the desk. "Twenty-three missed calls from Aneeka Pasha."

Eamonn stood up. "Something's wrong."

"On that, at least, we agree."

■ ■ ■ ■

Parvaiz

■ ■ ■ ■

5

The two men walked into the electronics store in Istanbul with near-identical attitudes of ownership, though their South Asian features marked them as foreign. Their white robes, shoulder-length hair, and long beards further distinguished them as men whose attitude of ownership you don't contest. The younger of the two walked over to the wall of mics and scanned the empty display boxes. His companion leaned against the counter behind which the shopkeeper was standing and flipped his phone from hand to hand while looking at the other customers. They filed out quickly in response, leaving the two men and the shopkeeper alone in the cavernous store.

"Look at all this!" the younger man said. "The RØDE SVMX. The Sennheiser MKH 8040. The Neumann U 87."

"Uh-huh. Just get what Abu Raees asked for, and let's go. I'm starving."

The shopkeeper reached beneath the counter and pulled out a box. "The Sound Devices 788T. Didn't Abu Raees receive my message? I've had it for over two weeks."

"Should I tell Abu Raees he needs to dance in Raqqa when you snap your fingers in Istanbul?" The older man turned his muscular bulk toward the shopkeeper, who paled and started to stammer an apology that was cut short by the younger man's whoop of delight as he took the box containing the 788T into his hands, testing the weight of it.

"Sorry, Farooq. This will be a while. Abu Raees said I should try out some different mic combos with this to see which works best." He walked back to the wall of mics and started to pull empty boxes off the shelves, tossing them back toward the shopkeeper, who cried out, "Just tell me which ones you want! You're ruining my display."

Farooq made a noise of disgust. "I'm going to that café on the corner. You have half an hour before we go to the airport."

"Okay. Pick up some takeaway for the new recruits. You didn't give me anything to eat for hours after I arrived."

Farooq grinned. "What a baby you were, Parvaiz — afraid to ask for a slice of bread."

"I'm not Parvaiz anymore."

"Ma'ashallah," said the older man, his voice tinged with irony.

"Ma'ashallah," said the younger one, placing his hand on his heart.

His journey to the electronics store in Istanbul had started the night last autumn when Isma walked into the kitchen and said she was going to America and so it was time for all three of them to leave their home.

Nothing in the early part of that evening had suggested what it would become. It was just a few weeks after Aneeka had started university, and Parvaiz hadn't, but already the old routines of their lives had become a thing of the past, so there was a feeling of celebration about Aneeka being home to cook dinner for the first time that week, consulting the grease-stained recipe book with her usual intensity of concentration, as though a recipe might have changed between the forty-ninth time she followed it and the fiftieth. Parvaiz was sous-chef, cutting onions with his swimming goggles on to prevent tears. The playlist compiled by their guitarist cousin in Karachi streamed through the speakers — chimta and bass guitar, dholak and drums; overlaid onto it, the sound of Parvaiz's knife cutting through the yielding onions, hitting the hardness of the board beneath; two slim bracelets on Aneeka's wrist clinking together as she measured out ingredients; low hum from the refrigerator; a train pulling into Preston Road station almost precisely at the same moment another train pulled out; the banter of twins. Tonight's version centered around Aneeka pretending to craft Parvaiz's profile for an Asian marriage site: *Handsome Londoner who loves his sister* that sounds incestuous *ugly Londoner who loves his sister* that sounds desperate *handsome Londoner with strong family ties* why do you have to be in the first sentence how about broodingly handsome Londoner with *no, broodingly handsome is a euphemism for dark-skinned* how is it that *Heathcliff* he was also violent and a bit mad *yes but know your audience, dark-skinned is the real problem.*

Isma walked into all this, preceded by the smell of dry-cleaning solvent, and said, "A total lack of career prospects is the real problem." Parvaiz pushed the chopping board to a side, took off the goggles, and picked up his phone, its screen without message notifications from Preston Road friends, now scattered emotionally and geographically by the demands of post-school life. "Turn the volume down and listen to me," Isma said. She had a serious look about her that made him do as she asked even though ordinarily he would have turned the volume up in response. Aneeka saw it too, and reached out to put a hand on their sister's wrist: "Tell us," she said.

Isma had been issued her visa for America. She would leave for Massachusetts in mid-January. She announced all this in the way another woman would have announced an engagement — proud, shy, worried about her family's reaction to news no one had anticipated.

Aneeka stepped forward and wrapped her arms around her. "We'll miss you, but we're so pleased for you. And proud of you. Isn't that right, P?"

"America," Parvaiz said. The word felt strange in his mouth. "They really gave you the visa?"

"I know, I didn't think they would either."

When she'd first come to the twins to discuss the letter Dr. Shah had written to her, with its suggestion — almost a command — that she apply for the PhD program, Parvaiz had said, "What's the point?" And Isma had immediately agreed yes, he was right. Neither Parvaiz nor Isma had come right out and actually said it was the unlikelihood of a visa that made the whole thing futile, but they all recognized well enough when their father was subtext to a conversation. Still, Aneeka was adamant that she apply. "Sometimes the world surprises you," she said, "and more to the point, if you don't even try, you'll always wonder what might have happened." After enough of Aneeka's badgering, Isma finally said that it would seem ungrateful to Dr. Shah if she didn't at least try. She clearly had a greater capacity for hurling herself at disappointment than he'd known, Parvaiz had thought at the time with both irritation and regret.

"So," Aneeka said. "What are we going to do about the house?"

Parvaiz shoved his twin's shoulder. "I'm getting her bedroom. I need a studio, and you're not around nearly as much as I am anymore."

The sisters looked at each other and back at him. Isma said a number. It was the household's monthly expenditure. She invoked this number every time she wanted to remind Parvaiz that his earnings as a greengrocer's assistant were insufficient, that the time he spent building up his sound reel rather than chasing after job postings was wasteful. She didn't believe he was good enough to find work doing what he loved, didn't see that his sound reel was as much an investment in the future as Aneeka's law degree was. *She doesn't think our lives allow for dreaming,* Aneeka had said, in a way that rang as both indictment of and justification for Isma's position.

They'd been all right so far, Isma continued. But in America she would have only enough from the university to sustain herself, just as Aneeka had only enough from her scholarship for the most basic living expenses. The mortgage alone would become impossible.

"Don't go, then," he said. Aneeka threw a cube of potato at him, and he head-butted it back at her — reflex rather than play.

Isma opened the crockery cupboard and started unloading plates and glasses for dinner. She'd just stopped in across the road, she said; Aunty Naseem was getting older, she needed help around the house, and even though her daughters and grandchildren were often around to help out, she was struggling to keep up. Some extra hands about the place would be a huge assistance. That's how Aunty Naseem had presented the option.

"What option?" said Parvaiz.

"We'll move in with Aunty Naseem, and

sell the house." Aneeka said this as if it were a matter as small as buying a new set of towels. Now it was Isma who looked stricken; she said she was only thinking they'd rent it out. With the new French school opening in Wembley the following year, property values were going to go up and up, so it would be foolish to sell now. And anyway, in a few years, when she had her PhD and Aneeka was a lawyer, they'd be able to move back in. Ordinarily, Parvaiz would have felt the blade of being omitted from the conversation. But just then Aneeka shrugged in response, and he experienced one of those terrifying moments in which a person you thought you knew reveals a new aspect of their character that has taken hold while you weren't looking.

Aneeka would leave them. That's what the shrug said. After university she had no intention of continuing to live in this house and remain a sibling rather than anything else that a law degree made possible.

"You can't just decide this for us," Parvaiz said to Isma. But the "us" carried no weight with his twin helping her sister set the kitchen table, refusing to meet his eye.

"Traitor," he said, pushing away from the counter. He made enough of a production of looking for keys and phone and mic that

172

anyone who had wanted to stop him could have, but when they didn't, he had no option but to walk out, though the night looked less than inviting.

An autumn evening that carried more anticipation of winter than memory of summer. Cold seeped in through his badly chosen jacket, and his skin quickly speckled with goose bumps. The neighborhood lights captured by the clouds turned the sky a pale red. The sound of the world turned up just that little bit. One of the first occasions he'd become aware of the acuteness of his hearing was when he had asked a teacher why planes sounded louder on overcast days, and the teacher said they didn't, to the laughter of his classmates, only to return the next day to tell Parvaiz he'd been right.

His mother's old friend Gladys stopped him halfway down the street to talk about the ongoing library campaign, and to ask him if his doorbell had rung differently at any point today. Hers had — the usual chimes replaced by a gonglike sound. When she'd gone to answer the door there was no one there so she'd returned indoors, switched on the TV, and there was that psychic she liked to watch, saying that if ever your doorbell rings with a different sound that means it's the devil and you mustn't answer.

"Do you think the devil's in your house now, Glad?" he said, smiling. "Isma will know some exorcism prayers."

"I hope to find out when I go to bed tonight — keep that sister of yours away!" He held up three fingers in a Scout's sign and noticed the deepening lines around Gladys's eyes when she laughed. She and his mother had been only a few months apart in age.

Leaving Gladys to entertain the devil, he walked down to Preston Road, mostly shuttered and quiet. He dipped his head in acknowledgment at the curved spine of the stadium arch as he always did, and rapped his knuckles affectionately on the door of the notary's office, which had housed a pop-up library during one stage of the library campaign, before continuing on to the sports ground — it had rained for most of the day and perhaps he could improve on the "shoes on wet grass" segment of his sound reel, which he was overlaying on footage of a video game that had won sound awards. By early next year he'd start sending it out to both the big and the little gaming outfits, and — please God! — work offers would come in.

He was walking across the car park, at-

taching the mic and its homemade windscreen to his phone, paying no attention to
the lone car until its doors opened and three
boys he knew from football games on this
ground stepped out. Designer sneakers,
pristine white robes, ecosystem beards
(Aneeka had named them: *large enough to
support an ecosystem,* she'd said). They
hung around the neighborhood trying to
look troublesome, not understanding they'd
done themselves no favors with the name
they'd chosen: Us Thugz. A shortened form
of the Arabic astaghfirullah. What exactly
are you seeking Allah's forgiveness for, Isma
had asked them when they accosted her in
the street one day and told her that sisters
should cover up more. Their response made
it clear they had no idea what astaghfirullah
meant.

"Give it," one of them said, holding out
an upturned palm for Parvaiz's phone and
mic.

"I'll tell your mother," Parvaiz said.

The boy — Abdul, his childhood friend
— lowered his hand and mumbled something about Parvaiz's phone being too old
anyway, but the older boy standing next to
him, who wasn't from the neighborhood,
stepped forward, kneed Parvaiz in the groin,
and, when he doubled over in pain, took

the phone from his hand, tossing aside the expensive mic as if to prove his own stupidity.

Parvaiz lay on the ground of the car park, waiting for the pain to pass, as the boys' car screeched past him. The sound envelope: slow attack, short sustain, long decay. Nothing to hear that he hadn't heard before. How he hated his life, this neighborhood, the inevitability of everything.

Farooq found him the next morning, standing among empty crates around the back of the greengrocer's, trying to remove a splinter from his palm.

"Asalaamu Alaikum," said an unfamiliar voice in the faux-Arabicized accent of a non-Arab Muslim who is trying too hard, and Parvaiz looked up to see a compact but powerfully built man, muscles distorting the shape of his tightly fitting bomber jacket. Somewhere around thirty years old, with hair that fell in ringlets to his shoulders offsetting a beard neither hipster nor ecosystem but simply masculine. An instant glamor to him that excused all accents. He was holding out the tweezer component of his Swiss Army Knife, a surprising delicacy in the gesture. Parvaiz took it and tried to capture the splinter, but his left hand felt

176

clumsy, and he kept pinching his skin instead. Without saying anything, the man took the tweezers from him, rested his hand beneath Parvaiz's to steady it, and plucked out the splinter with a flourish and a wink. Then he pressed his thumb against the drop of blood that appeared, stanching the inconsequential wound.

"My kutta cousin took something of yours. I apologize. He didn't realize who you were." He reached into a pocket of his combat trousers and handed back the stolen phone. *Who am I?* Parvaiz wanted to ask, but he knew the answer already. He was Aneeka's brother. When older boys, the kind you would die to be friends with, paid attention to him, it was always because he was Aneeka's brother. Aneeka never liked the ones Parvaiz tried to nudge her toward, though; she preferred the quieter boys she could boss around.

"You know my sister?"

The man looked displeased. "What are sisters to do with me? I know of Abu Parvaiz."

"I'm Parvaiz. I don't know any Abu Parvaiz."

"Don't you know your own father's name?"

Parvaiz assembled his features into neutrality with a tinge of bewilderment. Who was this man — MI5? Special Branch? They too had seemed so friendly that time they'd come to the house in his childhood. One of them had entered his room and played racing cars with him on the track that took up all the space between his bed and Aneeka's — then he'd picked up the photograph album that Parvaiz's father had sent him and walked out with it. They'd returned most of the items they took, but not the pictures of Adil Pasha climbing a mountain, sitting beside a campfire, wading across a stream — sometimes alone, sometimes in the company of other men, always smiling, always with a gun slung over his shoulder or cradled in his lap. *When you're old enough, my son,* his father had inscribed inside it, which made Parvaiz's mother furious for reasons he didn't then understand. Although his grandmother had intervened to prevent her daughter-in-law from taking the album away from him when it had first arrived, he'd always suspected his mother had told the friendly man about it so he would remove those images of Adil Pasha from his son's life. It was discomforting to remember that and, with it, how early on he'd started to look at his always harried mother and think, *No wonder he left.*

"I never knew my father." This was what he'd been taught to say, over and over, by his mother and grandmother. There were whispers in the neighborhood about Adil Pasha, he knew, and one day in the school playground a group of boys had accosted him to ask if it was true his father was a jihadi who'd been killed in Guantánamo. *I never knew my father,* he had replied weakly. The boys walked over to Aneeka and asked the same question. She shrugged and turned away, disdain already perfected at the age of nine, but later she whispered to the most loose-lipped of her friends, *It makes him sound like someone in a movie, doesn't it? More interesting than a father who died of malaria in Karachi.*

"He regretted that," the stranger said. "That you never knew him. He fought with my father; I heard all the stories of the great warrior Abu Parvaiz."

"That wasn't my father's name. It was Adil Pasha."

"It was his —" the man said something that sounded like *numb digger.* "That's French for 'jihadi name.' Superhero name is how I think of it, though some of the brothers don't like that. But, yeah. Your dad. When he entered the fight for justice he called himself Father of Parvaiz. That was his way of keeping you close. So anytime someone said his name — his enemies, with fear; his brothers, with love; his comrades, with honor — they were saying your name too."

Horribly, Parvaiz felt tears come to his eyes in the company of a man who probably wouldn't cry if you drove a tank over his legs. But the man didn't seem to think any less of him for it. Instead he drew Parvaiz close, in a cologne-scented embrace, and said, "I'm glad I've found you, brother."

Parvaiz went home that evening with the incandescence of a beautiful secret in his heart. He did all the cooking, didn't take his plate off to the TV room while his sisters ate at the kitchen table, teased Isma about the American accent she would acquire in Massachusetts.

"What's happened to you?" Aneeka asked, and he had the satisfaction of having a hidden corner of his life that his sisters didn't know about.

Late that night, Farooq called.

"I've been thinking about you all day," he said. "I've been thinking, why does the son of Abu Parvaiz seem to know so little about his father?"

Parvaiz had no words with which to answer this. The question had never been a question before. He'd grown up knowing that his father was a shameful secret, one that must be kept from the world outside or else posters would appear around Preston Road with the line DO YOU KNOW WHO YOUR NEIGHBORS ARE? and rocks would be thrown through windows and he and his sisters wouldn't receive invitations to the homes of their classmates and no girl would ever say yes to him. The secrecy had lived inside the house too. His mother and Isma both carried an anger toward Adil Pasha too immense for words, and as for Aneeka, her complete lack of feeling or curiosity about their father had been the first definite sign that he and his twin were two, not one. His grandmother alone had wanted to talk about the absence in their lives, and part of their closeness came from how sometimes she would call him into her room and whisper stories about the high-spirited, good-looking, laughing-eyed boy she'd raised. But the stories were always of a boy, never of the man he became. *Oh, something happened, I don't know,* she'd say whenever Parvaiz tried to find out who his father had become by the time his son entered the world.

"Because no one ever told me," he said now.

"Do you want to know?"

"Of course."

"Don't answer so quickly. Once you know, you'll have to think about what it means to be that man's son. Maybe it's easier never to think about him."

He had always watched boys and their fathers with an avidity composed primarily of hunger. Whenever any of those fathers had made a certain kind of gesture toward him — a hand placed on the back of his neck, the word "son," an invitation to a football match — he'd retreat, ashamed and afraid in a jumbled way that only grew more so as the years passed and as the worlds of girls and boys grew more separate; there were times he was not a twin but rather the only male in a house that knew all the secrets women shared with one another but none that fathers taught their sons.

"I think about him every day," he said, whispering it.

"Good. Good man. What time are you done with work tomorrow?"

And so it began. At some point mid-morning, every morning, Farooq would text with a location: sometimes a kabab shop, sometimes a street corner — but more often than not, a betting shop on the High Road. That was usually where he was when Parvaiz finished work. Regardless of location, they'd talk and talk. Or Farooq would talk and Parvaiz would listen to those stories of his father for which he'd always yearned — not a footloose boy or feckless husband but a man of courage who fought injustice, saw beyond the lie of national boundaries, kept his comrades' spirits up through times of darkness. Here was Abu Parvaiz, the first to cross a bridge over a ravine after an earthquake despite continuing aftershocks, to deliver supplies to those stranded on the other side; here was Abu Parvaiz using the butt of his Kalashnikov as a weapon when the bullets ran out; here was Abu Parvaiz dipping his head into a mountain stream to perform his ablutions and coming up with a beard of icicles, which lead to dancing on the riverbank as if he were Adil Pasha at a discotheque rather than Abu Parvaiz in Chechnya, whose every shake of the head produced the sound of wind chimes. Of all the stories this was the one that most clearly evoked the father he'd never known: the rushing stream, the dancing icicles, the men around him similarly braving the cold water so they could provide the jester-warrior Abu

Parvaiz with an accompanying orchestra.

"The father every son wishes he had," Farooq said.

"But I never had him as a father," Parvaiz replied, tracing the lines of his own palm with the grenade pin — was it really? — Farooq had brought along to the kabab shop.

"Do you think he wanted the world to be as it is? No. But he saw it for what it is. And having seen it he understood that a man has larger responsibilities than the ones his wife and mother want to chain him to."

To help Parvaiz understand those responsibilities, Farooq talked to him of history: the terror with which Christendom had watched the ascent of Islam, the thousand years of Muslim supremacy, which was eventually squandered by eunuchlike Ottomans and Mughals who had lost sight of the moral path, and then the bloodlust with which the Christians had avenged themselves for their centuries of humiliation; imperialism, with its racist underpinnings of a "civilizing mission," followed by the cruel joke of pretending to "give" independence when really they were merely changing economic models via the creation of client states, their nonsensical boundaries designed to cause instability. There didn't seem to be any part of the Muslim world

184

Farooq didn't know about — Pakistan and India and Afghanistan and Algeria and Egypt and Jordan and Palestine and Turkey and Chechnya and Kashmir and Uzbekistan. If ever Parvaiz started to lose his concentration, Farooq would swerve the conversation toward football (he supported Real Madrid, Parvaiz Arsenal, but they agreed on the greatness of Özil) or the tiniest details of Parvaiz's life (*What did you have for dinner? Any interesting characters at the greengrocer's? Let me listen to another one of your recordings — this time, I'll guess what it is*) or the American reality TV show Farooq watched devotedly and that Parvaiz started watching too, in order to talk to him about it. But no matter what the topic of conversation, it always returned to the central preoccupation of Farooq's life, the heart of all his lessons: how to be a man.

"It's your sisters' fault," Farooq said one afternoon when they were sitting side by side in green bucket seats in the betting shop, watching a bank of screens with greyhounds racing around a track and sweating men in another time zone walloping a cricket ball in the direction of sponsors' billboards. The volume was off, allowing for some pleasing moments of synchresis, such as when the dogs were released from their cages just as the front door was hurled open by a drunk, or when the strip light overhead started to buzz and the on-field umpire batted midges away from his face. Farooq had placed three phones on Parvaiz's leg between knee and hip, and each time one pinged with a text message he'd glance down and go to the counter to place another bet. It was good training for Parvaiz to stop fidgeting, he said the first time he did it. Parvaiz always kept his legs so tensed up during those betting shop sessions he had trouble walking afterward. "They want you in the house, doing their shopping and mowing the garden, so they've tried to keep you a boy, a child in need of a mother. That older one particularly, you know what I mean? The one who claims to be a good Muslim, and thinks she has the right to decide whether or not you can live in your own house. Tell her it is written in the Quran, 'Men are in charge of women because Allah has made one of them to excel the other.' And by Allah's law, you, not your women, dispose of your property."

Your women. Parvaiz turned the phrase in his mouth while Farooq placed another bet. He liked how it felt. Though that didn't mean he'd be stupid enough to try to quote the Quran to Isma, particularly when it

186

came to the roles of men and women. He was a Muslim, of course; he believed in God, and went to the mosque for Eid prayers, and put aside 2.5 percent of his income for zakat, which he split between Islamic Relief and the library campaign, but beyond that, religion had, since early childhood, been a space he'd vacated rather than live in it in the shadow of Isma's superiority. But in Farooq's company he came to see there was such a thing as an "emasculated version of Islam, bankrolled in mosques by the British government, which wants to keep us all compliant," and there was more than a little satisfaction in knowing this.

"Where are you these days?" Aneeka asked him one night, climbing up the ladder he'd propped against the garden shed to get onto the roof with his phone, headphones, and pride and joy, the secondhand shotgun mic. A favorite perch since childhood that allowed a clear view of the trains pulling in and out of Preston Road. The bodies of the trains were shadows in the darkness but the long windows revealed illuminated snapshots of life passing by. Every so often there was a jagged break in the conventions of tube behavier: a man throwing a punch, a kiss so concentrated that train carriage or

187

gondola ride or bedroom were irrelevant details, someone pressing a palm against the glass, leaning toward the boy on the garden shed as though fate wanted them together but the wheels of plot weren't allowing it. Nearly two years ago he had started working on a project that would eventually be a 1,440-minute track that his ideal listener would play between midnight of one day and the next — a soundscape of every minute of a day from this perch.

He stopped the recording, took off his headphones, scribbled in his notepad. It might be nice to leave in that *Where are you these days* between 20:13 and 20:14. Aneeka's was the only human voice scattered through his audio files of *Preston Road Station Heard from the Garden Shed.*

"I'm here. You're the one who's hardly around."

"I meant where are you here?" She reached out to tap his head. "And here." She rested her hand on his wrist, at his pulse point, in the old childish way, but he didn't reciprocate. "Is this about moving to Aunty Naseem's? I know you're upset about losing this spot, but at least we'll still be in the neighborhood."

We, she said, but he wondered how often she'd be around. There was hardly a week

188

when she didn't spend at least one night at Gita's. He knew Aneeka well enough to recognize she was laying the groundwork for staying out more and more often — and it wouldn't always be with Gita either.

"This is our home," he said.

She clicked her tongue against the roof of her mouth. "Always so senti. You should join me in convincing Isma we should sell. You could afford to go to uni with the money we'd get. That'd make up for the loss of *More of the Same Heard from the Garden Shed,* wouldn't it?"

"They only gave you a scholarship because you tick their 'inclusive' and 'diverse' boxes," he said, wounded enough to vocalize a sentiment Farooq had recently dredged out of his unconscious.

"Since when are you so white?" She flicked his earlobe with her thumb and forefinger.

"Muslim women, particularly the beautiful ones, need to be saved from Muslim men. Muslim men need to be detained, harassed, pressed against the ground with a heel on our throat."

"None of these things has ever happened to you."

"How many times have I been stopped and searched by police? Compared to you?"

"Twice. Only twice, P. And you said yourself it was no big deal either time, so stop whining about it after the fact." She jumped down from the ladder, with that physical confidence that always made his breath stop in terror for her safety. "Isma's right, you know. It's time for you to grow up."

Previously he would have gone after her and turned it into a shouting match that would continue until they'd exhausted themselves into reconciliation. But now he remained where he was, watching all the lives within their narrow frames slide past on the tracks in the darkness, allowing the wound to fester so that tomorrow he could tell Farooq about it and receive the antiseptic of his new friend's indignation.

Farooq sent a text asking him to come to the flat in Wembley where he lived with two of his cousins, though not the one who had mugged Parvaiz. It felt momentous enough for Parvaiz to go home from the greengrocer's, scrub the dirt out from beneath his fingernails, and put on a fresh shirt.

When he pushed open the unlocked door at Farooq's address he smelled chicken grease from the fast-food joint downstairs, and familiar cologne. A window was rattling in its frame, not because of any breeze but as a consequence of the traffic on the street below. Farooq's baritone voice told him to stop waiting for a gold-plated invitation and come in.

The furnishings consisted of three mattresses piled on top of one another and pushed against a wall and two green plastic chairs, which faced a flat-screen TV hooked up to a video game console. The kitchen area had a microwave and an electric kettle, the open door of a cabinet offering a glimpse of rolled black T-shirts and black socks. A punching bag hung from a thick bolt in the ceiling, a slight creaking as it oscillated almost imperceptibly. There was a bolt in the floor, similar to the one in the ceiling, that didn't seem to serve any purpose. He remembered Farooq's texts — the ones he didn't know how to respond to — about wanting to chain up women from the American reality TV show, and looked away. An ironing board served as makeshift table for a lamp and a pair of boxing gloves. On the floor beside it, an iron rested on a base the size of a bread box.

"It's the Ferrari of irons," Farooq said, proudly, seeing Parvaiz looking at the appliance. "Only one setting so you never burn your clothes. You ever want to iron something, bring it here. Sit, sit, make yourself at home. You are at home. No, on the chair, on the chair."

Parvaiz sat down, tried to smooth the creases of his shirt. Farooq smiled, cuffed him on the side of the head, and handed him a mug of tea.

"Wait for me. I'll be back in a few minutes," he said, and walked out.

Parvaiz sipped the tea — too weak — and looked around the flat, trying to find any further clues to his yaar's life. The Urdu word came closer than "friend" to explaining how he thought of Farooq. Or even better, jigari dost — a friendship so deep it was lodged within you, could not be cut out without leaving a profound, perhaps fatal, wound.

A photograph was taped to the wall just above the ironing board. Three men with their arms around one another's shoulders under a DEPARTURES sign at an airport — Adil Pasha; Ahmed from the fabric shop, who had convinced Parvaiz's father to come with him to Bosnia in 1995; and a stocky third man. That must be Farooq's father. The man who fought for less than a week in Bosnia before running back home, a broken creature with night terrors who embarrassed his young son. Farooq had revealed all this only a few days ago — *Ahmed from the fabric shop would come to visit, and every time he brought more and more stories of the heroism of the man who had become Abu Parvaiz, which my father never wanted to hear, but I did.* Ahmed had moved away a few years ago — Parvaiz knew him only as the man his mother crossed the street to avoid.

He reached out to touch his father's arm in the photo, searched his face for signs of similarity. But he and Aneeka took after their mother's family; it was Isma, unfairly, who had their father's wider face, thinner lips. He leaned in closer to the photograph, the only one he'd ever seen of his father at the moment he set off on the path that would become his life. He looked excited. It was the first time in years Parvaiz had seen a photograph of his father that he hadn't already committed to memory. He found himself staring at the paler band of skin on his father's wrist. Where was his watch? Had he taken it off to go through the metal detector and failed to put it back on? Did they have metal detectors at airports back then? Perhaps at the moment the picture was taken he hadn't yet realized that he'd left his watch in the security screening area. Once he realized, he would have gone back, perhaps with the slightly anxious expression

Parvaiz knew from an Eid photograph, in which he looked off to the side, away from the camera. He thought of all the photographs of his father, the ones before Bosnia, and the very few ones after. Yes, he still had the watch with the silver band afterward. It was a triumph to remember this, to piece together this tiny truth.

It felt neither and both a long and a short time that he stood there, memorizing his father's image, before the door opened and two strangers entered, one of them bearing enough resemblance to Farooq for Parvaiz to work out that they were the cousins he lived with.

His words of greeting went unanswered. Instead the cousins walked over to the bolt in the floor and looped a chain through it.

"Come on," one of them said impatiently. Parvaiz approached them, uncertain what it was they needed his help with.

Then he was on the ground, one cousin straddling his legs, the other his chest. The one on his legs tied the chain around his ankles, the one on his chest slapped him to stop him from struggling, and then both of them maneuvered him into a squatting position and used the chain to shackle his wrists to his ankles. When he called out Farooq's name they laughed in a way that made him stop.

"What are you going to do to me?"

"We've done it already," one of the cousins replied.

They both stood up, walked over to the TV, and started to play a video game, the volume turned so high that even if he shouted again no one would hear. It didn't take long to understand what the cousin meant. The chain so short that it was impossible either to straighten up or topple over entirely, and he could only remain hunched in a squatting position, the pressure on his back increasing by the minute. What started as discomfort eventually became pain, shooting from his back down through his legs. When he tried to move — tried to find a way to roll onto his side — the chains cut into his flesh. Layered into the pain was the torment of not understanding why he deserved it and what he could do to make it stop. He heard his voice begging to be set free, but the two men didn't even look in his direction. The video game sound designer hadn't accounted for cheap speakers, and the crackling and distortion were more intolerable than the gunfire and death screams. He tried prayer but it did nothing.

Sunshine left the room. Clouds or evening, he couldn't tell. Even the relief of unconsciousness eluded him. Scorpions of fire were under his skin, frantic to escape — they raced from his shoulders to his calves, their stingers whiplike. Every crackle from the speakers was magnified until it became a physical force attacking his ears. He was screaming in pain, had been screaming in pain for a long time.

One of the cousins pressed pause.

The sounds of the everyday rushed to embrace him — rattling windows, traffic, his breath. The two men walked over, unshackled him. For a moment there was release, his body collapsing onto the ground, but then they picked him up, carried him to the kitchen sink, which was filled with water, and dunked his head in.

So, he was going to die. Here, above a chicken shop, just a mile or so from home. How would his sisters bear it, after all they'd lost? The men pulled his head out, he breathed in a lungful of air, they dunked him again. This went on. He told himself he wouldn't breathe in next time, but his body wanted to live. They pulled him out; the air had an increased concentration of Farooq's cologne in it; he braced himself for the next immersion, but instead they carried him over to the pile of mattresses and threw him facedown on it.

A hand touched his head, tenderly. "Now you begin to see," Farooq's voice said, full of sorrow.

The only response Parvaiz had was tears, and Farooq turned him over so that Parvaiz could see that the older man was crying too.

"They did this to your father for months," Farooq said.

The cousins had left the flat. There was only Farooq, stroking Parvaiz's arm, helping him into a sitting position. When Farooq stood up, Parvaiz reached out and held his leg.

"No, I won't leave you again," Farooq said. "I'm just getting something from the kitchen."

If he turned his head he'd be able to see what Farooq was doing, but all he could do was stay as he was, breathing in and out, feeling the stabbing, shooting pain move from back to lungs to legs. Farooq returned, held a hot water bottle to his back, handed him an ice cream stick wrapped in a chocolate shell. He bit down into it, felt sweetness spread through his mouth, remembered pleasure.

When he'd finished, licking every clinging bit of ice cream off the stick, Farooq took the photograph off the wall and placed it

197

into his hands.

"How much do you know about what they did to prisoners in Bagram?"

Parvaiz shook his head. It was all he was capable of doing.

"You've never tried to find out?"

A shorter shake of the head, ashamed now. It had always been there just out of the corner of his eye, the knowledge of "enhanced interrogation techniques," but he had never looked closely. Because he didn't want anyone to ask why he was so interested. That was the reason he'd always given himself.

Farooq rested a hand on his shoulder. "It's all right. You were a child, alone. You weren't ready for it. But that's changed now, hasn't it?"

A child, alone. He'd never been alone. There had always been Aneeka. Even when she was different, she was still there. He looked at the iron bolt in the floor, thought of Aneeka saying they should sell the house. She was unlinking the chains that held them together, casting him into darkness without the accompanying sound of her heartbeat for the first time since his heart had clenched in terror to find itself dividing into chambers, becoming an organ with the capacity to feel, then relaxed, knowing there was another heart experiencing every moment of fear, every second of wonder alongside it.

Legs still wobbly, he stood up. "I have to go."

Farooq stood with him and drew him into an embrace. "You're strong enough to bear this. You're his son, after all."

Parvaiz pulled away, walked out without saying anything. Please come home, he texted his twin while going down the stairs.

He was on the 79 bus home, just a few minutes later, when she texted back. Urgent? Class ends in 20.

He rested his temple against the window of the bus and watched the familiar world pass by. "Sicko," "creep" — those would be the words she'd use about Farooq, and she'd make him swear on their mother's grave never to see the man again. But the farther the bus took him from Farooq's flat the more he felt he was in the wrong place. The ache in his back had begun to recede and he remembered how, before the pain had become too unbearable for any thought beyond his own suffering, he had turned his head toward the wall, toward the photograph of his father, and there was this understanding, *I am you, for the first time.*

He texted back: Haha just testing your

devotion. Don't make me have another night of takeaway and Isma.

Idiot, you worried me, she responded. Paper due tomorrow so working late in the library. Will stay at Gita's tonight.

He slid the phone into his pocket. Near the front of the bus a man was tapping his wedding ring against a yellow handrail. The sound, metal on metal, was chains unlinking.

Parvaiz sat down on the stool near the till in the greengrocer's, wiping the back of his hand against his mouth, surrounded by a lie. Asparagus and plantains and okra and Scotch bonnet peppers and bird's-eye chilis and samphire and cabbage and bitter gourd. Nat, the green-grocer, said the world was divided into two kinds of people: those who regularly ate fresh food, and those who didn't. With each new influx of migrants to the neighborhood, he'd ask, What do they eat? and add to his stock accordingly. Pakistanis, West Indians, Albanians — they were all fine by Nat. His shelves bursting with freshness and color, the promise of family meals and welcoming neighbors.

Parvaiz set Nat's phone down on the weighing scale, surprised by how light it was. In his hands it had felt like an iron bar.

He'd taken it out of the pocket of Nat's winter coat, which hung in the back room, when Nat went to the café next door for his morning toast and tea. He'd switched the browser into private mode and typed "Bagram abuse" into the search bar. Then he'd read, and looked at images, until he'd had to run outside and throw up in an empty crate that smelled of cabbage.

He'd always told himself a story, which came from nowhere he could now recall, that said Guantánamo was the place where really bad things happened, and at least his father had been spared that. Such a clever little lie, neat as the piles of fruit and vegetables he'd so carefully arranged this morning, as if the placement of a pear were something that mattered.

Nat returned, took one look at him, and said, "What's happened?"

Parvaiz stood up. "Not feeling well. Can I go?"

"Of course. Should I call Isma? You need something from the pharmacy?"

He shook his head, unable to bear Nat's kindness.

A short while later he was at Farooq's flat. He walked over to the shackles, lifted their weight in his hand. The cool steel harmless in his palm, link clinking against link.

"Tie me again. I want to feel my father's pain."

"My brave warrior," Farooq said, as Parvaiz knelt down and waited for the agony to resume.

"Are you finally ready to tell me about her?" Aneeka said, perched on the arm of the sofa, her foot tapping against Parvaiz's ankle inquiringly as he lay prone beneath his favorite blue blanket, a hot water bottle against his back.

"Her who?"

"Really? You going to tell me you aren't lying here looking so wounded because of whoever you've been going off to meet every afternoon and texting deep into the night for — what — a couple of weeks now? Longer? Who is she? Why all the secrecy?"

"Why the law?"

"What?"

"Why is that what you've decided to do with your life? What does the law count for? How did the law help our father?"

She raised her eyebrows at him, unbothered. "You could just say you aren't ready to tell me who she is. Is she married? Oh god, she's not from one of those crazy honor-killing type families, is she?"

"Why are you pretending I'm not asking

you a valid question?"

"Well, you aren't, really. What has Adil Pasha ever had to do with our lives?"

He turned away from her, his face pressed against the sofa cushions. "You're just a girl. You don't understand."

She held his foot in her hands, pressing her thumbs into his sole. "Don't get your heart broken."

"Shut up. Leave me alone. You don't know anything."

A few days later there was a fund-raiser for the library campaign. Parvaiz had been involved with the campaign through his adolescence, ever since the council had announced that the local library, to which his mother had taken him and Aneeka after school at least once a week, would have to close. He'd handed out leaflets, written letters to the local newspaper, attended meetings with Gladys where strategies were discussed; when it became clear the council was going to go ahead with the closure he'd seamlessly moved into the next stage of the campaign, to set up and keep going a volunteer-run library. He'd sung carols outside the tube station to raise money, helped transport books local residents donated, volunteered at the library every

Sunday. But as the day of the fund-raiser drew closer, he became increasingly worried that one of the Us Thugz boys might see him at the cake stall with Gladys, selling Aneeka's chocolate brownies, Aunty Naseem's Victoria sponge, and Nat's apple pie, and report back to Farooq that with the world ablaze with injustice Parvaiz Pasha thought the cause to which he should devote his time was a local library. The only way to limit the damage was to break the news himself.

He found Farooq ironing in his underpants, the windows of the flat thrown open to allow in the sunshine of the unseasonably warm day and the chicken-grease-scented air. A pile of freshly laundered clothes lay in a basket near his feet. Squares of sunlight fell like epaulets on his chiseled shoulders. He was in a boisterous mood, instructing Parvaiz how to roll up the ironed clothes, asking him if he knew that was the best way to keep them from creasing, and deriding the "idiots" who chose to fold instead. Parvaiz found himself imagining Farooq working with Isma at the dry-cleaning store, swapping tips about stain removal.

Tentatively, Parvaiz mentioned the library campaign, which he described as a "habit" carried over from adolescence. Farooq upended the iron and pointed to a spot in the center of the ironing board.

"Put your hand there. Palm up. I'm going to press this iron on it."

Parvaiz looked from the hissing iron to Farooq's face, but there was no hint of a joke. Just a watchfulness, a judgment waiting to be made. He stepped forward, placed both palms on the ironing board, forced himself into stillness as Farooq lifted the iron, feinted, smiled when Parvaiz didn't flinch, then lightly touched the wedge-shaped weapon to Parvaiz's palms. It was hot but not unbearable.

"Uses steam pressure more than heat. It won't burn even the flimsiest silk," Farooq said, with the air of a salesman. He caught Parvaiz by the back of the neck and kissed his forehead. "My faithful warrior." He resumed his ironing, and Parvaiz jammed his hands into his pockets.

"The library," Farooq said. "Of course it matters. Same as what they're doing to the NHS, welfare benefits, all the rest of it. You know this country used to be great."

"When was that?"

"Not so long ago. When it understood that a welfare state was something you built up instead of tearing down, when it saw migrants as people to be welcomed not turned away. Imagine what it would be like to live in such a nation. No, don't just smile. I'm asking you to do something: imagine it."

Parvaiz shook his head uncertainly, not sure what he was being asked.

"There is a place like that we can go to now. A place where migrants coming in to join are treated like kings, given more in benefits than the locals to acknowledge all they've given up to reach there. A place where skin color doesn't matter. Where schools and hospitals are free, and rich and poor have the same facilities. Where men are men. Where no one has to enter haram gambling shops to earn a living, but can provide for his family with dignity. Where someone like you would find himself working in a state-of-the-art studio, living like a prince. Your own villa, your own car. Where you could speak openly about your father, with pride, not shame."

Parvaiz laughed. He'd never seen Farooq so light, so playful. "So what are we still doing here? Let's follow the yellow brick road, or is it the White Rabbit who takes us there?"

"What rabbit? What are you talking about rabbits for when I'm trying to tell you something serious."

"Sorry. You're talking about a real place?"

"You know where I'm talking about. The caliphate."

Parvaiz raised his hands defensively. "Come on, boss. Don't mess with me."

Farooq switched off the iron, stepped into cargo pants, pulled on his T-shirt. "I've been there. I'd just come back from there when we met. Who are you going to believe about what it's really like? The same people who said Iraq had weapons of mass destruction, the ones who tortured your father in the name of freedom, or me?"

Parvaiz's heart seemed to have taken up his entire chest cavity, hammering so furiously he was surprised his shirt wasn't moving. Farooq's expression became gentle.

"Believe the evidence of your eyes. Wait." He went into the kitchen area and came out a little while later with a tablet. "Don't worry, no one will know you're looking at this — it's all offline. I'm going to finish ironing. You have any questions, ask."

Parvaiz sat down on the piled-up mattresses, rested the tablet on his knee. Farooq had pulled up the photo browser to show him the image of the black-and-white flag he'd first seen only a few months ago and that he'd learned to glance quickly away from in newspapers on the tube so no one would think the Muslim boy looked too interested. He looked up at Farooq, who made a swiping gesture with his finger. Parvaiz flicked forward through the images. Men fishing together against the backdrop of a beautiful sunrise; children on swings in a playground; a man riding through a city on the back of a beautiful stallion, carts of fresh vegetables lining the street; an elderly but powerful-looking man beneath a canopy of green grapes, reaching up to pluck a bunch; young men of different ethnicities sitting together on a carpet laid out in a field; standing men pointing their guns at the heads of kneeling men; an aerial night-time view of a street thrumming with life, car headlamps and electric lights blazing; men and boys in a large swimming pool; boys and girls lined up outside a bouncy castle at an amusement park; a blood-donation clinic; smiling men sweeping an already clean street; a bird sanctuary; the bloodied corpse of a child.

Parvaiz didn't know he'd said anything in response to the last, but he must have, because Farooq asked, "What?" and came to see what he was looking at. "The Kurds, those heroes of the West, did that. Her name was Laila, three years old."

"And the men about to be executed in the

208

other picture?"

"The men who did that to her, or those just like them."

"These other images, are they real?"

"Of course they're real. Look!" He cycled back to the fishing image, and Parvaiz saw that one of the men — the one whose large muscles were straining with the weight of the catch he was trying to reel in — was Farooq.

"Okay, there's a little bit of a lie in there. That giant fish you think I've hooked — it was a waterlogged jacket. This is the Euphrates we're fishing in. You want to come and fish in the Euphrates with me? And with your other brothers? That's Abu Omar, that's Ilyas al-Russ, and this one is my sweet Abu Bakr, who was martyred by the FSA."

"So it's not true then? About all the violence? Only if they're enemy soldiers, is that what you're saying?"

Farooq sighed heavily and sat down beside him, hooking his arm around Parvaiz's neck. "What do they teach you in history?"

The French Revolution. That was Farooq's lesson of the day. The cradle, the bedrock, the foundation of enlightenment and liberalism and democracy and all the things that make the West so smugly superior to the rest of the world. Let us agree to

209

accept for a moment that the ideals that came from it were good. Liberty, equality, fraternity — who could argue against that? Well, Farooq could, but that was another day's lesson. For the moment, accept those ideals as ideal. But where would those ideals be without the Reign of Terror that nurtured and protected them with blood, eliminating all enemies, internal and external, that threatened the new utopia, and did so in full view of the public? It might have been regrettable — a man would rather fish with his friends than cut off the heads of his enemies — but it was necessary. Eventually the terror ends, having served its purpose of protecting a new — revolutionary — state of affairs that is besieged by enemies who are terrified of its moral power.

"So the question for you is this: Will you protect the new revolution? Will you do the work your father would have done if he'd lived?"

Parvaiz looked from Farooq back to the screen, flicking through the remaining images. A land of order and beauty and life and youth. A Kalashnikov resting on one shoulder, a brother's arm around the other. It was another planet, one on which he'd always be the boy from Earth whose lungs don't know how to breathe this wondrous, terrifying atmosphere.

But increasingly, his lungs didn't know how to breathe the air of London. MI5 officers were present at Bagram, Farooq told him, and showed him evidence to corroborate that. Your government, the one that took taxes from your family and claimed to represent the people, knew what was going on. How can you live in this place, accepting, after all that you now know? How can you live in this mirage of democracy and freedom? What kind of man are you, what kind of son are you?

The questions followed him through his days now. Everywhere he saw evidence of rot and corruption, lies and cover-ups. His two sisters had allowed themselves to become part of it too: one preparing to go to America, the nation that had killed their father and hundreds of thousands of other Muslim fathers; the other propping up the lie that theirs was a country where citizens had rights and courts of appeal.

At night, via the proxy servers Farooq said he could rely on, he went deeper and deeper into the Web, to stories of dogs raping prisoners at Bagram, pictures of tortured bodies, medical accounts of what the different forms of "enhanced interrogation techniques" could do to a body and mind. One night he lay in bed with his desk lamp directed straight at his eyes, his most powerful headphones blasting heavy metal into his ears — he managed for no more than twenty minutes before, whimpering, pathetic, he had to restore his room to darkness and silence. Increasingly, during the day he would stop in the middle of the smallest action — handing a bag of celery to a customer, waiting for a bus, raising a cup of tea to his mouth — and feel the wrongness of it all, the falseness of his life.

"You need to break up with her, she's no good for you," Aneeka kept saying, unable to imagine any pain in the world larger than a bad love affair. More than once he found her trying out different password combinations on his phone — he'd changed it from their joint birthday to the day he first met Farooq.

One day Farooq showed him a photograph that he recognized. A white man kneeling in the sand just prior to his execution, an image that encapsulated for the world the barbarity of the caliphate. When he'd first seen it he'd felt sorrow for the man with the courage to try to look brave with a blade at his throat, whose only crime was the nation he'd been born into. But this time what struck him most powerfully were the man's clothes, the same shade of orange as the prison jumpsuit in which his father had died. His vision expanded; he saw beyond the expression of the individual kneeling in the desert to the message the caliphate sent with his death: *What you do to ours we will do to yours.*

So this was how it felt to have a nation that wielded its sword on your behalf and told you acquiescence wasn't the only option. Dear God, the vein-flooding pleasure of it.

And then he found himself preparing to leave.

How exactly it happened he couldn't have said. He had been too busy changing to stop and chart the change. It had been a long time since he and Farooq had discussed football, reality shows, life at the greengrocer's. There was only one subject, and eventually he understood that the subject was a destination.

"You're sure I can come back if I don't like it?"

"Of course you can. I'm back here, aren't I?"

"You've never said why."

"Had to deal with family stuff. Then you

happened."

"What do you mean?"

"Should have left weeks ago. But thought if I waited, maybe you'd come too."

"You stayed for me?"

"Yes."

"And you'll really help me find people there who knew my father?"

"I really will."

"You're the best friend I've ever had."

"I'm your brother."

"Yes. I know. Thank you."

He called his cousin, the guitarist in Karachi — the one he'd hated because on the only occasion they'd met the other boy had said, "I'm a Pakistani and you're a Paki" — and said he was going to take up the offer, proffered by the guitarist's mother, to spend some months in Karachi working on a popular music show to build up his professional credentials. He sorted out his paperwork, one half of his brain believing he really would end up in Karachi, and booked a flight with a connection in Istanbul that would arrive in the old Ottoman capital soon after Farooq's flight. When Aneeka talked about meeting him in Karachi over Easter he enjoyed making travel plans with her, their heads bent together over maps of

Pakistan. Badshahi Mosque and Kim's Gun, the ruins of Taxila, the Peshawar Museum, with the world's largest Gandhara collection, and in Karachi the studio of the music show they'd been listening to since its inception a few years ago, where Parvaiz would soon be working.

"If I like it there, maybe I'll stay awhile and you can visit too," he said to Isma the December night before he was due to leave, the statement brought on by the smell of the masala omelet she was cooking for his final dinner at home.

The first weekend after their mother died, Parvaiz had stopped eating. He was unable to explain to himself why he was rejecting every item of food Aunty Naseem and her daughters and Aneeka offered him, and even Aneeka was at a loss to understand it. It was Isma, who disliked cooking above all other domestic chores, who had come into his room with a masala omelet such as their mother used to make for breakfast every Saturday. She had cut it into pieces and fed it to him, forkful by forkful.

Now she looked up in surprise and smiled in a way usually reserved for Aneeka. "I'd like that," she said.

Her smile sent him out the door into the cold December night, head tipped back to count the stars and keep the tears from falling. It was there that Aneeka found him a short while later.

"You're going to have to get rid of that growth on your face," she said, maybe or maybe not noticing the hand he quickly rubbed across his eyes at her approach. "The Heathrow officials might mistake what is fashionista for fundo and decide not to let you board the plane to Pakistan. Particularly if you're flying through Istanbul. Jihadi alert!"

He laughed too loudly, and his twin touched his arm. "You sure you want to go? You know I'm only allowing you to do it because you obviously have to get away from *her*. Will you never tell me who she is? I promise I won't beat her up too badly."

"I'm going in order to improve my career prospects for that Asian marriage site. Though the bio should still start *Handsome Londoner who loves his sister.*"

She stepped forward until there was almost no space between them, butted her head against his shoulder. "Both you and Isma leaving. What will I do all alone?"

He held her earlobe between thumb and finger. He knew she had wanted to say this since he first announced he was going. There was no living person for whom he'd leave her just weeks before she had to say good-bye to the older sister who had raised her — raised them both — as much as their mother ever had. But the dead made their own demands, impossible to refuse.

While the plane was taxiing he ignored the instructions to turn off his phone and listened, instead, to the audio track "Twin Heard from the Garden Shed."

These were the things her voice said:

It's getting late; even the birds have gone home.

Oh god, I'm interrupting you again.

Couldn't you have found a less solitary obsession?

Where are you these days?

Regardless, dinner's ready. Might as well come in.

The wheels left tarmac. He uploaded the track to her account on the Cloud and deleted her from his phone.

6

Parvaiz paid the man in the electronics store with the Turkish liras he was carrying in his knapsack, and then asked, as if it were an afterthought, if he sold phones with SIM cards that allowed international calls.

"The new arrivals will have to call home, and there's always one who weeps into the phone and covers it with snot. So they're not getting my phone again," he said.

"I don't need to know your business," said the shopkeeper, moving over to the glass-topped display case housing cell phones. "Here." He pulled out a bricklike handset that belonged to a time when calls and texts were all anyone expected from a phone, and that continued to exist, Parvaiz was sure, only because people in high-crime areas liked to carry around a decoy phone to hand over to muggers. "No charge," the man said expansively, as he slipped the SIM card into its compartment.

"Jazakallah khayr," Parvaiz said, scooping up the pile of boxed equipment for which he'd just paid a small fortune. "Do you have a back door? My car's parked behind your shop."

"Can you carry all that? Do you want to call your friend to help you? I would, but my back . . ."

"This is nothing after what they made us do in military training," he said.

"You're a fighter? I thought you were with Abu Raees in the studio."

"I am. But that doesn't mean they didn't teach me how to fight in the way of Allah in preparation for a time when I can be more useful that way. Why is it, my friend, that you're still living in Turkey?"

The man blanched. "I do my part from here. The back door — through there. I'll open it for you."

Parvaiz stepped out into the sunlight and started to walk toward the row of parked cars until he heard the door close. He turned, made sure the man had gone back inside, then set the pile of boxes down on the side of the road, placed his traceable smartphone on top of the pile, and began to run.

Six months earlier he had entered Raqqa in

the late afternoon, his stomach contracting with excitement and terror. A motorcycle backfired as it drove past an antiaircraft gun mounted on the back of a pickup truck; the soldier swiveled the weapon in the motorcyclist's direction. A joke, Farooq told him, relax! A row of palm trees slapped their fronds against one another in a breeze that wasn't felt at street level. The driver of the car, one of the two men who had picked Farooq and Parvaiz up at Istanbul airport, insisted you could hear the palm fronds whisper *Allah* if your ear was good enough. His ear was better than anyone else's in the car, Parvaiz said; he meant good as in "holy," Farooq explained. The colors of the buildings were sun-bleached, but there was a brightness in the call of the birds. A polyethylene bag caught in the electric wires strung across the street made shivering sounds. A man juggled a flattened loaf of bread the size of his arm that made all the saliva rush to Parvaiz's mouth; a *fwump!* sound as the oven-hot bread was dropped onto a table on the pavement. Bearded men stood around a cluster of motorcycles, two in long robes with bomber jackets, the others in jumpers and trousers, arguing in Arabic. Minarets reached high into the sky — at prayer time the azaan would bounce

220

between one slim tower and the next. A tank rumbled past a monument with two head-less statues. A very young girl in a green-and-yellow dress walked behind two women in black niqabs, even their eyes invisible beneath a face veil; Farooq hummed the music from a popular ninja video game until one of the men in the car warned him to stop disrespecting sisters or he'd have to report him to the Hisba — this was the first Parvaiz heard of the morality police, and he saw how mention of them strained Farooq's expression.

The soundscape changed around the central square, or perhaps Parvaiz stopped listening so acutely because of the distrac-tion of heads of enemy soldiers mounted on spiked railings. It was curiously unmoving, something you might see in a TV show. One day, inshallah, there would be no enemy and children would play in the square, Farooq said. In the company of the other men his English conversation had become peppered with Arabic, and perhaps this was what made his words sound false. Then a differ-ent part of town, more affluent: villa-like houses, tall apartment blocks, the yellow and white paint on the facades brighter here. The car pulled up in front of one of the double-storied villas, and Farooq said,

"This is our stop."

"Who lives here?" Parvaiz asked, stepping out of the car, taking in the sprawling luxury of the house, the size of three homes in his neighborhood put together.

"One of the perks of the media arm," Farooq said, nudging him, laughing at his disbelieving face.

Two men only a few years older than Parvaiz appeared in the doorway of the villa. One Scottish, one American. They introduced themselves by their noms de guerre, embraced him formally, greeted Farooq in the manner of friends. Cameramen, both of them, and yes, those were their SUVs in the driveway — another perk of the media arm.

Inside, the house had marble floors and faded places on the walls where once must have been photographs or artwork. There was a very large room with stiff-backed chairs and sofas with flower-patterned cushions, and beside it a formal dining room with a long table. Boxes lined the hallways — "our equipment," said one of the men, whose names he had already forgotten, so that he referred to them mentally as Abu Two Names and Abu Three Names. It was like an icebox, the lowered blinds adding to the mortuary atmosphere. But then the two men led him upstairs, saying this was the part they actually lived in. Here it was light and airy, pleasingly informal.

The American — Abu Two Names — ushered him onto a wraparound balcony that overlooked a garden dense with color. It was still afternoon, but he gratefully huddled into the shawl the Scotsman — Abu Three Names — offered him to counter the cold breeze, "from the Euphrates," that reached him as he sank down into the surprising blue beanbag. A man appeared from somewhere — "This is Ismail, he came with the house" — and offered him tea and biscuits on a silver tray. From up here you could make out the sounds of motorcycles and cars, hammering, birdsong, the wind through the branches of trees, fallen bougainvillea flowers dancing in the breeze along the balustrade of the balcony. Despite his disquiet at the spiked heads and veiled women, the blue skies and camaraderie of the men slumped in beanbags promised the better world he'd come in search of.

"One day you'll tell us the story behind your name," the American said. He was black, very tall, and had a wide smile. His friend was quieter, bespectacled, mixed-race Pakistani-Scottish. The name he meant was Parvaiz's nom de guerre — Mohammad bin

Bagram. Farooq had written it onto Parvaiz's registration form at the first checkpoint with an air of pride at having chosen it for his friend. It was both a reminder of what his father had suffered and an acknowledgment that this new Parvaiz was born out of vengeance and justice, Farooq said — which made it impossible for him to say he hated it. And anyway he'd quickly been distracted from questions of naming when Farooq had reached into Parvaiz's knapsack, taken out his passport, and handed it to the man at the registration desk, who had the soulless look of bureaucrats everywhere. *Relax,* Farooq said. *If you ever need it back I'll get it for you. But you won't need it back. You're now a citizen of al-Dawla — the State.*

Parvaiz tried not to think about the passport and asked the cameramen how long they'd been living here. They said they'd been sharing this house for over two months, though their friendship had assumed an instant depth that told them their souls must have met in Jannah well before the will of Allah brought them back together in Raqqa. They touched each other's arms and shoulders, unself-consciously affectionate, which made the whole thing moving instead of absurd.

"It was the same with this young warrior and me," Farooq said, ruffling Parvaiz's hair. "It'll be strange not seeing him every day."

"Where you going?"

"To the front. I'm a fighter, aren't I?"

"You won't be living in Raqqa?" He saw the American shake his head in that school-yard way boys signaled to each other that too much emotion was being revealed, usually around a girl, and Parvaiz attempted to undercut the pleading tone of his voice with a chin-jut that said *Huh, interesting, why didn't you say before?*

"I'm mostly away fighting the kafir bastards so you boys can be safe in your air-conditioned studios."

"Big-talking man. If you fighters are so important, why do we get paid more?" the American said.

The Scotsman put up a hand to stop the conversation. "Alhamdulillah, we all play our part in the way of Allah. Who is better or worse is judged only by the quality of his faith."

"Brother, you can always be relied on to remind us what's important, Ma'ashallah," Farooq said, in a tone that managed to sound genuine. "No, man. I'll mostly be gone. And when I'm here, I've got my wife and kid, haven't I?"

"You have?"

"Of course. They gave me a wife almost right away — these two highly paid men are still waiting to be approved by the marriage bureau."

"You just got here earlier, that's all," the American said. "The waiting time is up to six months these days. Anyway, I'm talking to a girl in France. She's almost ready to come over."

"No, but —" He heard his own voice coming out in a whine, but he couldn't help it. "You said you'd help me find people who knew my father."

Farooq shrugged. "You'll run into some of the old jihadis at the training camp. Tell them who you father was, and they'll hook you up with people who knew him."

"What training camp?"

"Didn't you tell him anything?" the Scotsman said.

What Farooq hadn't told him was that all new arrivals were required to undergo ten days of Shariah camp ("It would have been longer, but I put down your level of Shariah knowledge as 'intermediate' when I filled out your form"), followed by six weeks of military training. After that, assuming he was accepted into the media wing ("And of course you will be," said Farooq, but the other two were quiet), there'd be another month of media training. It all sounded a little overwhelming, Farooq knew, but soon enough he'd be placed in a studio, earning a salary, and would have his own SUV and portion of a house — maybe he'd even have a share of this villa if the marriage bureau or the French girl saw fit to move either or both of its present occupants into married quarters by then.

It would have been stupid to say he thought he'd been brought to this house because this was where he was going to live right away, un-Muslim to say he didn't want to go to Shariah camp, unmanly to say he didn't want military training, petulant to accuse Farooq of anything when he had been the one who hadn't thought to ask the practical questions about the life he was entering. He shrugged and said that was fine by him, although no one had asked.

"And once you're settled in you can put in a request with the marriage bureau too," the American said. "Though my advice is, try and find a European girl online. They know how to do more things than the Arabs, if you get my drift, though my bonnie friend here doesn't like it when I speak that way."

227

"Speaking of talking to girls, should we tell your sisters where you are?" The cascading noise from the beanbag was Farooq shifting his weight, reaching for the phone in his back pocket.

Parvaiz had sent Aneeka a series of texts since his arrival in Istanbul the previous afternoon. Cheerful lying messages about sightseeing during his daylong stopover en route to Karachi. Near the Syria–Turkey border he said his battery was dying, it hadn't charged overnight, so she might not hear from him for a while. Then Farooq had taken the phone from him, jerked his wrist, and sent the phone flying out of the car window. He knew Farooq's tests well enough by now to merely smile, shrug, and think of the new phone he'd buy in Raqqa with the income he'd receive for his work as a sound designer.

He took the phone from Farooq, was surprised by the time on the home screen — later than he'd thought. The flight from Istanbul to Karachi would be en route; soon his cousin would call Aneeka to say he was at the airport, the passengers had exited, but there was no sign of Parvaiz.

"Stay here while you speak to her," Farooq said when Parvaiz started to get up.

He logged on to Skype and called Aneeka,

imagining the bubbling sound of an incoming call bouncing around the interior of her tan-colored handbag slung on the handle of the door leading into the living area. He wiped the palms of his hands on his trousers, waited.

When Aneeka answered, his first thought was that her strange expression could be explained by the fact that she expected him to still be on a flight. "Where are you?" she said, voice catching.

"Hey. Before I answer that, promise you'll . . ."

"Who's Farooq?"

He glanced at Farooq, who took hold of his wrist and seemed about to pivot the phone toward himself, but the Scotsman quickly caught his shoulder. "Not if she's unveiled," he said.

"Who are you with? P, where are you?" she said.

"Why are you asking about Farooq?"

"You should be on a plane. The plane left on time. I checked. Why aren't you on the plane?"

"Calm down, it's okay. Why are you asking about Farooq?"

"Abdul told his mother you've gone with his friend's cousin Farooq. To Raqqa. Where are you really?"

"Can't even trust your own family to keep secrets anymore," Farooq said, but without looking unduly displeased.

"I would never go to the place you think Raqqa is. But it's not that place."

Something was squeezing his voice box, making the words come out funny. The American was giving him that look again, that shake of the head. Aneeka's face was unfamiliar to him for the first time in his life — an expression there he hadn't seen before and didn't know how to interpret. Her mouth a strange shape, pursed, as though she were eating something awful that she could neither spit out nor swallow. Then she vanished, and Isma was there.

"You selfish idiot," she said. This was easier to contend with — he rolled his eyes at Farooq, placed two fingers against his temples to mime a gun firing into his brain. "Watch your manners, brother. We have company." She swiveled the phone, and two men were standing in their living room, everything surrounding them as familiar as his own heartbeat. "Say hello to the men from the Met," Isma's voice continued, conversational. "They're going to turn our house and our lives upside down. Again. Do you have anything you want to say to them?"

He was conscious of the three men on the balcony watching him, waiting to see his response to the news that the police knew where he was and now there was no going back.

"My sisters didn't know anything," he said to the men from the Met whose faces were made of stone.

Farooq took the phone from him. "I will plant the flag of the caliphate on Buckingham Palace myself," he said, and jabbed the phone to end the call. "What?" he said, in response to Parvaiz's cry of outrage. "I should've said Downing Street instead?"

The Scotsman leaned forward, touched Parvaiz's knee sympathetically. "It's all right. Allah will protect them while you're here doing His work. Inshallah."

Parvaiz looked at the man's shining eyes, his certainty, and lowered his head as if in prayer so that the others couldn't see his panic.

Panic was a familiar companion, months later, of the man who sat at the back of the café, where the bright light of the June afternoon couldn't reach. Every so often he reminded himself to look down at the tourist guidebook, sip the apple-flavored tea.

The open-fronted café allowed him to

observe life along the narrow Istanbul street that carried tourists and residents between Galata Tower and the Golden Horn. The tiniest things seemed exceptional: a silver bracelet catching the light on a woman's wrist; a woman's wrist itself. Voices speaking over the azaan from the city's mosques, the sounds of trade continuing undisturbed, as though muezzins demanded as little attention as car horns.

The tray on the table provided a reflective surface, allowing him to see the slight, unremarkable boy from Preston Road whom the barber a few streets away had sheared back into existence. His face was deceptive now with its promise of familiarity to those who had known him when he still was that boy. He ran his hand along the clean-shaven chin, its contrast to the rest of his skin tone worrying him, pulled the baseball cap lower over his close-cropped hair, hunched. *Take me somewhere far from here where I can buy clothes,* he'd said to the cabdriver he'd frantically hailed after running away from the electronics shop. Then he'd phoned Aneeka.

A voice from the outdoor table, raised, spoke excitedly of "the meeting point of Asia and Europe." Such outmoded concepts, why did people still think they meant anything? The language of violence, spoken by the powerful of all nations, erased the distinctions beneath the surface. Two girls walked past, laughing, uninhibited. The sound — continuing on, burrowing down from the girls' throats to their bellies — was more remarkable than bracelets or wrists. Perhaps surface was all there was to fight for. He remembered how it felt to float on a surface of freedom and safety, to feel himself buoyed up by it, and longing tugged at his heart.

He looked down at his book again. The words on the page, dimly lit by the overhead lamp, made no sense. *Leave Nizam Caddesi to head down to the shore via Hamlacı Sokağı and eventually you will come to Leon Trotsky's house, standing ruined in its wild garden.* How was it possible, this invitation to a world in which you might spend an afternoon meandering toward a shore, stopping at a ruined house in which someone important once lived. No, not an invitation; the words assumed you already were of that world: *you will come to Leon Trotsky's house.* That promise, that certainty. Had there ever been a time when he could have slipped into such a life — a cheap flight, a youth hostel? Why not? In the company of Aneeka he could have left Nizam Caddesi to head down to the shore. But no, Isma would have stopped it. *I gave up my life to work in a dry-cleaning store and put food on this table; now it's your turn. If you can't get yourself a scholarship, at least pay some bills.* The depth of his homesickness announced itself with the realization that he was looking forward to sparring with Isma in the familiar, inconsequential way. If they allowed him back, that is, instead of handing him over to their allies in a prison somewhere outside the law. Perhaps they were better at keeping people alive now; or perhaps life and death weren't outcomes of any interest. They cared only about information, of which he had too little for anyone to believe he didn't have more. Or perhaps they cared only about inflicting pain. The one thing that the violent respect is more violence, Farooq had said last autumn, in those weeks when every word that tripped off his lips was wisdom and beauty. He pressed the soles of his feet into the carpet. Stillness — external stillness — was one of Farooq's lessons too.

Just when he felt he would have to scream to relieve the pressure in his chest, there was Aneeka, lighting up the screen of the phone:

HAVE PASSPORT AND TICKET. FLIGHT IN THREE HOURS. RUSHING TO AIRPORT.

Turn off your CAPS LOCK, Shouty.

DON'T THINK YOU CAN START BOSSING ME AROUND, IDIOT.

Love you too.

Until soon, Senti.

Until soon, Mental.

He ordered a coffee, some bread. Perhaps when she arrived there'd be time to go look for the ruined house in the wild garden. A bearded, broad-shouldered man appeared in the doorway, his shadow extending deep into the café. Someone asking the waiter for directions. There were houses and gardens enough in London. The British consulate, the airport: that was all he wanted to see of Istanbul. Tomorrow at this time he'd be back in Preston Road. Inshallah.

His phone buzzed again, making him smile. Aneeka the Anxious. He raised himself off the seat, pulled the phone out of his back pocket, read:

You're a dead man, my little warrior.

The man knelt in the sand, motionless except for the movement of his lips.

"Find something to gag him with," said Abu Raees, the head of the Raqqa sound studio. "We don't want that interference."

Parvaiz ran back to the SUV in which he and Abu Raees had only minutes ago driven up to this scene out of a movie. Blue winter sky, a day so still not a single speck of sand moved in the desert landscape, no sign of life other than the kneeling man and the executioner sitting a few feet away, turning his sword this way and that so it caught the sun and became a dancing beam of light. Parvaiz opened the passenger door of the SUV and ducked inside. Hidden from view, he rested his head against the leather interior, tried to stop the shaking of his hands that had started the moment they stepped out of the SUV and he understood what was going to happen.

It was late March. He had survived the tedium and affront of Shariah classes, in which he learned that everyone he loved was either an infidel or an apostate, and that both categories deserved to die, and that it was against Allah's will to wear T-shirts with slogans on them, or to give anyone the wrong directions, or to allow your women to sit down in public. He had survived military training, during which he learned that fear can drive your body to impossible feats, and that the men of his father's generation who fought jihad in Bosnia, Chechnya, Kashmir, all went home to their families for the winter months. That piece of information had made him blubber into his pillow at night, not because it made him understand that his father had never loved him (though he did understand that) but because he finally saw that he was his father's son in his abandonment of a family who had always deserved better than him. He had survived all that, and even though he knew by then the nature of the joyless, heartless, unforgiving hell-hole for which he'd left his life, he believed he had survived the worst. The media wing had accepted him, trained him (and he had found pleasure in the learning), and now he had a position at the Raqqa sound studio and had taken the Scotsman's place in the villa (the marriage bureau had found him a wife, but the American's French girl had backed out of coming — the only piece of news that had actually made Parvaiz feel happy in the last three months). In his two weeks at the sound studio he'd been assigned mainly low-level tasks — editing distortions out of speeches, cataloging Abu Raees's haphazard sound files — but today Abu Raees, a man who was known to prefer working alone, had asked him to come along and help set up an important field recording. He had felt proud, even though after Farooq — whom he hadn't seen since that first day in Raqqa — he'd learned to mistrust his need for an approving father figure.

He heard Abu Raees calling the name he'd learned to answer to, and pulled a cloth out of the glove compartment. The sand shifted beneath his feet as he trudged back, hands fisted in pockets. The executioner lifted his blade, brought it down onto the kneeling man's neck. Parvaiz bent over, stomach emptying. When he straightened, wiping the back of his hand across his mouth, the executioner was lifting the blade again, bringing it down to within a few inches of the man's neck again. Abu Raees, headphones on, was checking the DAT levels. The executioner pointed off to the side and Abu Raees walked in the direction he was gesturing, just a few feet away. They were anticipating the trajectory of the man's head when it left his shoulders. Working out where to place the mics.

He reached the kneeling man, bent down

238

to place the cloth in his mouth. The man's lips still moving, the words now discernible. He was praying. Ayat al-Kursi, the prayer Parvaiz's grandmother had taught him to say in times of distress. The prayer he too had been whispering on the walk from the SUV to the kneeling man. The man looked up. Parvaiz wouldn't remember anything of the man's face afterward, only his expressive eyes.

"Come here, listen to this," Abu Raees said, holding out his headphones. Parvaiz reached for them, dropped them. "What's wrong with your hands?"

He shook his head, picked up the headphones again, and managed to fit them onto his head. Abu Raees, eyes narrowed, handed him a mic. What he heard through the headphones was the sound of the mic juddering in his hand. The tremors had moved all the way up to his elbow.

"I can't stop it," he said. And then, "I'm not feeling so well."

"Go and lie down in the SUV," Abu Raees said, turning away.

He did as commanded, lay sealed up in the back of the car, imagining it again and again: the blade cutting through air, cutting through flesh and bone, the body slumping, the head bouncing on the sand, rolling to a stop. The eyes still open, not afraid but accusing.

How long does it take to cut off a man's head?

When Abu Raees finally returned to the car, Parvaiz said, "I don't know why Allah made that happen. My will was in one direction, but my hands couldn't follow. I must have failed Him in some way."

Abu Raees gave him a long, considered look as he invoked the will of Allah as explanation for his failure. A lapse in loyalty could see a man stripped of his privileges and sent to dig trenches on the outskirts of town, where he would be an easy target for aerial bombing. "You should stay up all night praying for forgiveness," Abu Raees said.

"I will," he answered. It was unclear if the taciturn Iraqi believed him or just didn't want to do without such an efficient worker. Impossible here to know who was a true believer and who was playing along for any of a host of reasons, from terror to avarice. The price of letting your mask slip was far too high for anyone to risk it.

For days and days after that, he worked in the studio on sound effects of beheadings, crucifixions, whipping. This was both a test and a punishment. In the studio, he had control of himself. Abstracting himself to that place where nothing but getting the sound right mattered. The fascination of discovering the different pitch and timbre of a nail through flesh, a blade through flesh. Some men were men in their dying screams, some were animals. He, Mohammad bin Bagram, now numbered himself among the animals.

And that's why, although he'd been given his own phone since joining the studio and could finally speak to his sister without a minder standing within earshot, he hadn't called her. Just daily chat messages to let her know he was alive, then he'd log off. Conversation had become unimaginable. What have you been up to? How was your day? How are you doing?

But then, in the early days of April, he logged onto Skype to quickly send his daily message and there was one from her: Call me. I'm working on a plan to get you home.

Home. A place from a past he'd turned his back on, and to which MI5 would make sure he never returned.

I'm fine here, he wrote back.

And she replied, Liar.

He left the café, head bent, walk altered. Keeping watch for Farooq's white SUV, he

241

shuffled past Galata Tower to the broad pedestrianized İstiklal Caddesi, where the presence of a clothing shop he knew from London was a comfort. He entered, bought a pair of blue jeans, a gray T-shirt, a black baseball cap with the shop's name stitched on it. Changed into the new set of clothes, left the ones he had bought just a couple of hours earlier in the changing room, and walked out.

The next shop he went into sold cell phones. He'd destroyed the SIM card from the brick handset in case it could be used to locate him, but buying a new SIM card required identification. Or, he discovered, part of the large wad of Turkish liras left over from his shopping spree in the electronics store. He fitted the SIM card into the brick and texted Aneeka to let her know how to contact him. Her flight would be leaving soon.

Doing something other than waiting for Farooq to walk into the café and find him made him feel briefly in control, and for a few minutes he walked unconcernedly among the camouflage of crowds of people, looking at the elegant facades of the buildings lining the street. The bookshop tempted him, as did the movie theater, but it felt safer to be in public, among people, with more than one direction in which he could run. From the corner of his eye he caught a flash of white sleeve and his legs turned to water before his gaze traveled up the arm to an unfamiliar face.

He sat down on a step leading into a shop. Closed his eyes, forced himself to remember the song playing in the kitchen the day Aneeka joked with him about Asian wedding sites. Chimta and bass guitar, dholak and drums, a man's voice carrying a song that arose from a place deeper than the currents of history. He drew his knees up to his chest. Just across the street was a narrow road. If he cut down it he would be at the British consulate. Perhaps he should just do it. Why wait for Aneeka, why embroil her in this? He could simply present himself there: I made a mistake. I'm prepared to face trial if I've broken laws. Just let me go to London. But he was the terrorist son of a terrorist father. He rested his head on his knees. He didn't know how to break out of these currents of history, how to shake free of the demons he had attached to his own heels.

The MiG dropped its payload close enough to rattle the windows and the plates in the studio's communal lunch room.

"Go," Abu Raees said. "Hurry. Take this." He pulled the Zoom H2 out of his pocket, but Parvaiz was already on his feet, reaching into his own pocket to demonstrate he hadn't forgotten the most basic lesson: always have a portable recorder on you. "Good! Now go."

He drove in the direction of the plume of smoke, one hand pressing the horn to move other vehicles out of the way. Before he reached the place where the smoke was densest — a market — he slowed, switched off the air-conditioning, and rolled down the windows to let in the blast of hot May air and the sounds of the city. Across Raqqa, the roar of power generators provided an aural map of where the members of the State lived and worked, but he was too accustomed to the inequality between the locals and those who ruled over them to pay it much attention anymore. Before long he heard a loud, repeated cry that came from a street so narrow he had to park his SUV around the corner and enter on foot. There were men standing on the corner, facing away from the street. All locals, who knew him at a glance by his foreign features, his white robes, as a member of the State. They looked at him, a couple seemed about to speak, but he brushed past them. By now he could make out the word "help" in a woman's voice.

The narrow street was deserted, even the shops along it empty. Parvaiz ran, able now to see the collapsed section of a wall even though he couldn't see what was pinned beneath it.

A voice called out sharply. The door opened to a van he'd assumed empty, one he now identified by the writing on its side as belonging to the Hisba, the morality police. The man who emerged — only a little older than Parvaiz — spoke to him first in Arabic and then, seeing he didn't understand, English.

"She has taken off her face veil. You can't approach her. We've called the women's brigade." He was holding his hand against the side of his face so that no inadvertent movement of his eye muscle might cause him to look upon an unveiled woman.

"Please," she called out. "Please, please help me." Oh god, a Londoner's voice. A young voice, maybe his age, Aneeka's age.

"If we go to her to help, surely that isn't a greater sin than leaving a sister to suffer?"

"She is being left to suffer because she removed her face veil."

"She may have needed to do it to breathe properly."

Could she hear him, he wondered, as he raised his voice? Could she hear the London in him? "Please," she was still crying out, "please help, it hurts." And then, jolting his heart, "Mum! Mum, I'm sorry."

A memory then of arms lifting him up when he fell off the garden shed, a cheek pressed against his. His mother. Or Isma. There was a woman without a face veil just a few feet from him. A woman's face, the softness of her cheek. She might have bad teeth, a crooked nose, chickenpox scars, and she would still be the most remarkable, the most dangerous thing in the world.

"Brother, watch yourself."

There were a great many things he could say right then, and all but one of them would get him killed. "Jazakallah khayr, brother. Thank you for correcting me. And for preserving our sister's modesty from the gaze of strangers."

The man took his hand, squeezed it. "Are you married? No? You should be. We will find you a wife. Alhamdullillah."

"Alhamdulillah," he replied, disengaging his hand as soon as, but not before, it seemed inoffensive to do so.

"Please don't go," she called after him. "Please, brother. Why won't you help me?"

Oh, to be deaf. Allah, take away my hearing. Take away the memory of that voice.

What was in his face that made the men on the street corner back away, frightened? At nineteen he was terrifying to grown men. He was the State.

He strode onward to the SUV. Once inside he rolled up the windows he'd left open, knowing no one would dare touch what belonged to a man like him. These were the kinds of things he'd learned to take for granted, the small privileges he enjoyed. Whispering a prayer, he logged onto Skype. Her status was DO NOT DISTURB, but that was never meant for him. It would have to be a voice call rather than a video call so that no one might look in through the window and see him talking to an unveiled woman.

"P! Thank god. Oh, thank god."

Her voice, so long unheard, broke him open. He leaned his forehead on the steering wheel so that no one could see the tears he thought he'd stopped being able to cry.

"What's happened? Are you in trouble?"

The things you forget. How it feels to hear someone speak to you with love.

"No, I just. I can't stay here. I can't do it. They're taken my passport so I have to but I can't. I thought if I learned the rules . . .

but I can't. I can't. I just want to come home."

He could hear her exhale on the other end, understood that she had been waiting for this admission since he'd left, and that failing to make it had been just another way he'd caused her pain. He started to apologize but she cut him short, her voice taking on the brisk efficiency of the women of his family, which he loved, which he missed, which he should never have left.

"You have to get to Istanbul. Can you do that?"

"I don't know. Maybe. Yes, eventually. When they trust you enough you can get a pass if you have a reason."

"Find a reason. And then go to the British consulate and tell them to give you a passport."

"Aneeka, I'm the enemy. You know what they do to the enemy. Do you? Do you know? You said you had a plan — please tell me you have a plan."

"What happened to our father won't happen to you."

"You don't know that."

"I'm making sure of things here."

"What does that mean?"

"Explain when I see you. Some things

need to be explained face-to-face. But trust me."

"What are you up to?"

"It's funny. I thought I was doing something for you. But it's turned out nice for me. Remember that when I explain it to you, okay?"

"Oh god, what? You shagging the head of MI5?"

The joy of teasing her, of finding that voice still lived in his throat.

"Shut up. Come home."

"Okay."

People were beginning to look at the man with the trembling hands sitting on a step while everyone else on İstiklal Caddesi was moving. He stood, walked a short distance, and crossed into a shop that had books and old maps in its windows. Inside, an old man behind the counter looked up, nodded, looked down again at his newspaper. There was a quiet inside here of the sort other people would call "atmosphere," but he knew it was all about the way the carpet muffled footsteps, and the closed door blocked out noise from the outside, and the tiny hum of the air conditioner. He walked over to the wooden map display cabinet with four drawers, each containing dozens

249

of old maps. The Ottoman Empire, Konstantinopel, La Turquie en Asie, Asia Minor, Egypt and Carthago, The Dardanelles, The Abbasid Caliphate in the Ninth Century.

He handled the maps with one hand, the other holding tightly to the brick handset. Aneeka should have texted back by now. Something was wrong at her end, he didn't know what, but when he'd called as his cab sped away from the electronics shop and said he was in Istanbul she sounded first incredulous, then irate. *Why didn't you give me any advance warning?* I didn't want to get your hopes up in case something went wrong. *Today of all days!* Why, what's so special about today? *Nothing, never mind, it'll be fine. Today is perfect. Just, it's all being sorted out right now. It'll be fine.* Which one of us are you trying to convince? What's going on? *Look, I need to call someone, I'll call you back.*

But when she called back a few minutes later she was anxious, didn't directly answer his question about whether she'd arranged whatever she was trying to arrange. He'd said perhaps he'd be safest returning to Farooq, maybe trying this again some other time. *No, just go to the consulate.* I can't. I'm scared of what they'll do to me. *No,*

wait, give me five minutes, I'll call you back.
No — if I'm going back I have to go back
now, before he realizes I've run away. *No,
no, no. Don't. I'll come to you. I'll get the next
flight. Just find someplace he won't find you,
and stay there until I arrive. We'll go to the
consulate together.* And all he could think
was at least that way he'd see her. Whatever
they did to him once he arrived at the
consulate, at least he would see her first. He
could bear anything else, as long as he saw
her first.

A little space of clarity opened up in his
brain. Of course they wouldn't allow her to
board a flight to the very place from which
her twin had disappeared into the world of
the enemy. She was probably still arguing
the point, refusing to leave the airport until
they gave her a boarding pass. Isma's voice
in his head calling him selfish, irresponsible,
and she was right.

He wrote to her: You don't need to come
here and hold my hand. It'll be ok. I'm going
to the consulate now. Will be home soon —
biryani when I get there? Page 131 of the
recipe book.

He pressed send, his hands steady.

It was Farooq, in the end, who was his
means of escape. He turned up at the villa-

cum-studio one afternoon, catching Parvaiz in a headlock as he stepped off the prayer mat in the covered veranda at the end of Zuhr prayers, and kissing him hard on the temple.

"My little warrior's grown up," he said. "Do you get a lunch break?"

Abu Raees, who had been praying alongside Parvaiz, tapped Farooq on the arm. "Who are you? What are you doing here?"

"I'm a fighter," Farooq said, moving his shoulders back, his chest forward in a way Parvaiz had once thought of as impressive and now saw as ridiculous. "And I'm his sponsor."

Abu Raees looked as uninterested in this as he did in all conversations suggesting any of his employees had a life beyond the studio. "Early for lunch," was all he said.

"I'm driving out soon," Farooq said, with a tone of self-importance. "Picking up new recruits in Istanbul tomorrow." Glancing at Parvaiz, he said, "The cousins are getting good at it."

Parvaiz forced his face into a look of appreciation. A few weeks earlier, during a dinner of kebabs at a restaurant overlooking the Euphrates, the Scotsman confirmed what Parvaiz already half knew: when they'd met, Farooq had been in London to train his cousins as recruiters. Parvaiz had appeared at just the right time to serve as guinea pig. The Scotsman hadn't really said "guinea pig." The word "pig" was too haram to pass his lips. Instead, he'd found some other way of expressing it that made Parvaiz out to be an instrument of Allah's will. From Farooq's manner now it seemed this was a line Parvaiz was expected to have taken too. Parvaiz imagined running a sword through Farooq's throat, hearing the gurgle of blood.

"Take him with you," Abu Raees said, jerking a thumb at Parvaiz. "I need some equipment for the studio."

"If you can organize a pass before I leave," Farooq said doubtfully, looking at his watch.

"Of course I can," Abu Raees said.

That easy.

He stood on the pavement of Meşrutiyet Caddesi, looking at the brick wall with black spikes rising from it that allowed only a partial glimpse of the facade of the consulate. But the view of the red, white, and blue flag that fluttered from the roof, cheerful in all its colors, was uninterrupted. Mo Farah at the Olympics, Aunty Naseem's commemorative cake tin from the Queen's

Golden Jubilee.
London. Home.

254

■ ■ ■ ■
Aneeka
■ ■ ■ ■

7

i.

It was not a possibility her mind knew how to contain. Everyone else in the world, yes. Everyone else in the world, inescapably. Some in stages: their grandfather, for weeks half paralyzed, unable to speak, even his breath unfamiliar. Some in a thunderclap: their mother, dropping dead on the floor of the travel agency where she worked, leaving behind the morning's teacup with her lipstick on the rim, treasured until the day one of the twins stood up in a rage and swung the cup by its handle, smashing their mother's mouth (Aneeka thought it was her; Parvaiz insisted it was him). Some in a sleight of hand: their grandmother, awaiting the test results that they had already decided would be presented as a death sentence, crossing the road as a drunk driver took a turn too fast; the doctor called two weeks later with the good news that the tumor was benign. Some as abstraction: their father, never a living presence in their life, dead for years before they knew to attach that word to him. Everyone died, everyone but the twins, who looked at each other to understand their own grief.

Grief manifested itself in ways that felt like anything but grief; grief obliterated all feelings but grief; grief made a twin wear the same shirt for days on end to preserve the morning on which the dead were still living; grief made a twin peel stars off the ceiling and lie in bed with glowing points adhered to fingertips; grief was bad-tempered, grief was kind; grief saw nothing but itself, grief saw every speck of pain in the world; grief spread its wings large like an eagle, grief huddled small like a porcupine; grief needed company, grief craved solitude; grief wanted to remember, wanted to forget; grief raged, grief whimpered; grief made time compress and contract; grief tasted like hunger, felt like numbness, sounded like silence; grief tasted like bile, felt like blades, sounded like all the noise of the world. Grief was a shape-shifter, and invisible too; grief could be captured as reflection in a twin's eye. Grief heard its death sentence the morning you both woke up and one was singing and the other caught the song.

When she received the words that made her singular for the first time in her life, she pushed them away. It was not true, they meant someone else, it wasn't him. Where was the proof, bring him to me. No, they couldn't do these things because it was not him. If it had been him it wouldn't be this man sitting in Aunty Naseem's living room bringing the news, a plastic comb sticking out of his breast pocket. He wasn't one of yours, she told the man; we aren't yours. Then she left him downstairs, went to her room to catch up on the reading for class she had neglected since her brother had called earlier that day. And now he was sulking because she hadn't come to him though she promised she would. She locked her door against Aunty Naseem's knocking and entreating. It wasn't her fault, they hadn't let her through. *For your own protection,* they'd said, taking her passport away, refusing to say when she could get it back. Or no, he wasn't sulking, he was on his way to her, the texts he had sent stuck somewhere in a foreign network, this happened sometimes, a logjam of communication unable to cross borders for hours or days at a time and then the onslaught of pinging that was every message arriving in triplicate. It had happened with her aunt texting from Karachi six months ago: Where is he? When is he coming? He could at least call to explain, don't they teach manners in England? He was on his way to her, flying home, watching the stars from his window seat — Castor and Pollux holding hands through the cold, dark night.

She fell asleep and at some point there were arms around her in that childhood familial way. It wasn't a surprise, but that made it no less a pleasure to curl into the warmth of a twin and slip deeper into that level of sleep where nightmares can't reach, held fast by love, a foretaste of heaven.

ii.

The sunlight across her eyes was late morning. She turned in bed, her body heavy with sleep and anticipation. No one there but an indentation on the pillow. Out of bed and down the stairs she went, to the voices of Aunty Naseem and her two daughters and sons-in-law, all of whom had skipped work to come over and welcome home the boy whose absence they'd carried as a secret these past six months when everyone else thought he was in Karachi. Kaleem Bhai — Aunty Naseem's older son-in-law — had even given Aneeka the handset he used on trips to Pakistan so she could send occasional messages seemingly from Parvaiz to his friends missing home not missing the weather camels look so surly because they can never escape their own smell sorry trying to stay off the grid — exploring my inner ascetic. *Someone will find out eventually,* Kaleem Bhai had said, but she'd known from the start that her brother would never stay away very long.

But why was it Isma coming toward her — liar, betrayer, but now that Parvaiz was home she could be forgiven. But even so, why was it Isma catching her in a familiar familial embrace, and why the face she knew too well the one that had said Ama's dead

261

Dadi's dead, why her voice heavy with tears saying, "I took the first flight when Aunty Naseem called," and "We'll always have each other," when Isma had never been "always"; "always" stretched both forward and back, womb to tomb, "always" was only Parvaiz.

And why was he back, the man with the plastic comb in his pocket, the representative of the Pakistan High Commission, holding his hands up as she entered the room, apologizing for yesterday, which should have meant apologizing for bringing them someone else's grief but instead meant apologizing that he'd failed to lift his cupped hands and recite Inna lillahi wa inna ilayhi raji'un — We surely belong to Allah and to him we return.

"No," she said to the man. "You're confusing him with someone else. He's a British citizen; he has nothing to do with you."

"I'm sorry," the man said, miserably, looking at Isma, who had taken Aneeka's hand as if one of them were a child in need of help crossing the road. "You're obviously a good, pious family. You don't deserve this treatment from your government. This home secretary has a point to prove about Muslims, no?"

She'd been so preoccupied with waiting

262

to hear from Parvaiz she'd failed to notice
Eamonn hadn't called back.

[CLOSED CAPTIONING]

The Turkish government confirmed this morning that the man killed in a drive-by shooting outside the British consulate in Istanbul yesterday was Wembley-born Pervys Pasha, the latest name in the string of Muslims from Britain who have joined ISIS. Intelligence officials were aware that Pasha crossed into Syria last December, but as yet have no information about why he was approaching the British consulate. A terror attack has not been ruled out. The man in the white SUV who shot Pasha has not been identified, but security analysts suggest he could have belonged to a rival jihadi group. The home secretary spoke just minutes ago to our political correspondent, Nick Rippons, about Pervys Pasha:

— So we have yet another case of a British citizen who

— I'm going to cut you off there, Nick. As you know, the day I assumed office I revoked the citizenship of all dual nationals who have left Britain to join our enemies. My predecessor only used these powers selectively, which, as I have said repeatedly, was a mistake.

— And Pervys Pasha was a dual national?

— That's correct. Of Britain and Pakistan.

— Practically speaking, does this have any consequences now that he's dead?

— His body will be repatriated to his home nation, Pakistan.

— He won't be buried here?

— No. We will not let those who turn against the soil of Britain in their lifetime sully that very soil in death.

— Has his family in London been informed?

— That's a matter for the Pakistan High Commission. Excuse me, Nick, that's all I have time for.

iv.

#WOLFPACK
Just started trending

#PERVYPASHA
Just started trending

#DONTSULLYOURSOIL
Just started trending

#GOBACKWHEREYOUCAMEFROM
Just started trending

V.

The kitchen filled with food for mourners who didn't come.

Only Gladys phoned. Her daughter had arrived in the afternoon to bundle her in the car and take her to Hastings, where she wasn't supposed to leave the house until the news cycle stopped replaying the woman with mascara-stained cheeks telling news cameras: "He was a beautiful, gentle boy. Don't you try to tell me who he was. I knew him from the day he was born. Shame on you, Mr. Home Secretary. Shame on you! Give us our boy to bury, give his mother the company of her son in the grave."

vi.

@gladysinraqqa

Tweets 2 Following 0 Followers 2,452

Ooh such beautiful boys, let me lift my veil to see them better — oh, I'm being gently #crucified.

Come on boys, look at me, I can do things those 72 virgins don't know about. #MaybeThisIsntHeaven

vii.

What was this? Not grief. Grief she knew. Grief was the stepsibling they'd grown up with, unwanted and inevitable. Grief the amniotic fluid of their lives. Grief she could look in the eyes while her twin stared over its shoulder and told her of the world that lay beyond. Grief changed its shape to fit your contours — enveloping you as a second skin you eventually learned to slip into and resume your life. Grief was the deal God struck with the angel of death, who wanted an unpassable river to separate the living from the dead; grief the bridge that would allow the dead to flit among the living, their footsteps overhead, their laughter around the corner, their posture recognizable in the bodies of strangers you would follow down the street, willing them never to turn around. Grief was what you owed the dead for the necessary crime of living on without them.

But this was not grief. It did not cleave to her, it flayed her. It did not envelop her, it leaked into her pores and bloated her beyond recognition. She did not hear his footsteps or his laughter, she no longer knew how to hunch down and inhabit his posture, she couldn't look into a mirror and see his eyes looking back at her.

This was not grief. It was rage. It was his rage, the boy who allowed himself every emotion but rage, so it was the unfamiliar part of him, that was all he was allowing her now, it was all she had left of him. She held it to her breast, she fed it, she stroked its mane, she whispered love to it under the starless sky, and sharpened her teeth on its gleaming claws.

viii.

The police came around, notepads on knee, recorders in hand, received as their due Isma's thanks for not insisting on an interview at Scotland Yard.

"Why won't you let him come home? He wanted to come home, he was trying to come home."

They weren't there to talk about Parvaiz, they were SO1, Specialist Protection, assigned to the home secretary.

"Oh. This is about Eamonn?"

Isma had lifted the teapot to pour a cup for the policemen and seemed to forget what she intended to do with it, holding it motionless just a few inches off the table, looking at her sister, color rising from her throat to her face.

"I was with him because I thought he could help. Ask him, he'll tell you, I wanted my brother to be able to come back. It's all I want now. Why the secrecy? Why do you think? Because of men like you with your notepads and your recorders. Because I wanted him to want to do anything for me before I asked him to do something for my brother. Why shouldn't I admit it? What would you stop at to help the people you love most? Well, you obviously don't love anyone very much if your love is contingent

271

on them always staying the same."

Watching Isma, who had set the teapot down without pouring it and was staring at her. Suspecting something that had never occurred to her before. What might she have felt about it were there space for other feelings?

"There's no need for any such warning. What good would it do me to contact him now?"

When they left there was Isma, wounded and appalled.

"Don't look at me like that. If you liked him you should have done it yourself. Why didn't you love our brother enough to do it yourself?"

"Aneeka. Can I come up?"

"Why? I don't want to see you, and now you know about Eamonn you don't want to see me either."

"You're the only family I have left. There's nothing bigger than that."

"What's that noise?"

"The movers packing up inside."

"Have they left? The Migrants?"

"Yes. We have their expensive blinds and an electric kettle with four heat settings in place of next month's rent."

"You're blaming him, aren't you? For the loss of your posh tenants."

"Stop acting as if you're the only one whose heart is broken. He was my baby boy."

"And Eamonn? What was he? I think you mind about him more than Parvaiz."

"Why do you want to be so hurtful? He was five minutes of my life. You two were my life. I'm coming up."

"You never did when he was sitting here."

"Move up a little, won't you?"

"I don't think he wants you here."

"He's beyond wanting now."

"I don't want you here. You betrayed him."

"That isn't why he's dead. That has nothing to do with why he's dead. You have to forgive me. Please, I'm sorry, forgive me."

"Do you believe in heaven and hell?"

"Only as parables. A god of mercy wouldn't condemn any of his creation to eternal suffering."

"So what happens after death?"

"I don't know. Something. Our dead watch over us, I know that. They're trying to speak to me today, to tell me what I can do for you."

"Nothing. There is nothing to do for me. What are you willing to do for him?"

"I pray for him, for his soul."

"What about his body?"

"That's just a shell."

"Hold a shell up to your ear and you can still hear the ocean it came from."

"Hmm. So, what do you believe happens after death?"

"I don't know the things you know. Life, death, heaven, hell, god, soul. I only know Parvaiz."

"What does he want?"

"He wants to come home. He wants me to bring him home, even in the form of a shell."

"You can't."

"That isn't reason not to try."

"How?"

"Will you help me?"

"Why can you never understand the position we're in? We can't even say the kinds of things Gladys said, we don't have that liberty. Remember him in your heart and your prayers, as our grandmother remembered her only son. Go back to uni, study the law. Accept the law, even when it's unjust."

"You don't love either justice or our brother if you can say that."

"Well, I love you too much to see anything else right now."

"Your love is useless to me if you won't help."

"Your love is useless to him now he's dead."

"Get off his shed. Your voice doesn't belong here."

"Aneeka. I need my sister — how can either of us bear this alone?"

Isma's hand stroking her hair, trying to take her away from Parvaiz.

"Go."

"SHATTERED AND HORRIFIED":
SISTER OF PARVAIZ PASHA SPEAKS

Early this morning, Isma Pasha, the 28-year-old sister of London-born terrorist Parvaiz Pasha, who was killed in Istanbul on Monday, read a statement to journalists outside her family home in Wembley. She said, "My sister and I were shattered and horrified last year when we heard that our brother, Parvaiz, had gone to join people we regard as the enemies of both Britain and Islam. We informed Counter Terrorism Command immediately, as Commissioner Janet Stephens has already said. We wish to thank the Pakistan High Commission in Turkey for the efforts they're making to have our brother's body sent to Pakistan, where relatives will make plans for his burial, as an act of remembrance to our late mother. My sister and I have no plans to travel to Pakistan for the funeral."

Pasha's local mosque has also issued a statement to clarify it does not intend to hold funeral prayers for the dead man, and condemned rumors to the contrary as "part of a campaign of hatred against law-abiding British Muslims."

Pasha's body is in a mortuary in Istanbul, and sources say it could be several days before it is released for repatriation to Pakistan.

Istanbul police have said the dead man was not carrying any weapons at the time of his death. His reasons for approaching the British consulate when he was killed remain unknown, as does the identity of his killer — described by eye witnesses as an Asian male in his 30s. Commissioner Janet Stephens has said Pasha was working with the media wing of ISIS, which is responsible for the recruitment of fighters and of so-called "jihadi brides." Tower Hamlets resident Mobashir Hoque, whose daughter, Romana, left for Syria in January to marry an ISIS fighter, told reporters, "My daughter was tricked into going by the lies and propaganda of men such as Parvaiz Pasha. My only disagreement with the Home Secretary's decision is that it deprives me of the chance to spit on the terrorist's grave."

Sources in the Home Office say the Immigration Bill due to go before Parliament in the next session will introduce a clause to make it possible to strip any British passport holders of their citizenship in cases where they have acted against the vital interests of the UK. Under present rules only dual nationals or naturalized citizens with a claim to another nationality can have their citizenship revoked. The Home Secretary has repeatedly expanded on his predecessor's claim that "citizenship is a privilege not a right" to say "citizenship is a privilege not a right or birthright." The human rights campaign group Liberty issued a statement to say: "Removing the right to have rights is a new low. Washing our hands of potential terrorists is dangerously shortsighted and statelessness is a tool of despots not democrats."

Woke up to rain gusting in through the windows broken by rocks. Isma had said at least it meant they spared Aunty Naseem's house. Isma, shattered and horrified, playing the good citizen even now, dragging her sister's name into that shameful act. Isma, traitor, betrayer.

Alone now in the house they'd grown up in, empty, the Migrants gone with all their furniture, only a mattress for furnishing, which Kaleem Bhai and Isma dragged across the street, *since you insist on sleeping here,* a double mattress for both sisters but this house was for the twins only now. Made Isma leave with a shrieking flapping of arms, madwoman behavior that finally drove her away. Downstairs a pounding sound, what? Someone trying to break in, to break the house from inside for the crime of having been a roof over the terrorist's head. Picked up the electric kettle with four heat settings the closest thing to a weapon that remained. Opened the door to David Beckham, the Queen, Zayn Malik boarding up the broken windows. Beckham almost hammered his thumb in surprise. "Didn't think anyone was here," he said from behind the mask with the voice of Abdul.

"Better go inside there may still be journos lurking," said Zayn Malik, who was really David Beckham's father.

"Cuppa would be lovely, though," said the Queen aka Nat the greengrocer, jerking her tiaraed head toward the kettle.

xii.

Countless hours of recording, and never his own voice. As though he'd started to practice disappearing long ago. Now he wouldn't even enter her dreams. Too angry.

HOW MANY PARVAIZ PASHAS WILL IT TAKE FOR THE GOVERNMENT TO WAKE UP?

The revelation that Adil Pasha, the father of recently dead terrorist Parvaiz Pasha, abandoned his family in order to take up jihad has not entirely come as a surprise to one former classmate of the Preston Road resident.

"There was a rumor that his father had been a jihadi in Afghanistan who died in Guantánamo," said the classmate, who wished to remain unnamed. "His sisters always denied it and said he'd died of malaria while abroad, but Parvaiz never did. I didn't think anything of it at the time, but looking back it's obvious he thought jihad was something to boast about when he was still just a little kid."

Sources at the Met say Adil Pasha fought with jihadi groups in Bosnia and Chechnya in the '90s, and traveled to Afghanistan in 2001 to fight with the Taliban. He is believed to have died soon after. "We have no idea if he was killed in a battle or died of malaria or from other causes. But if he'd ever been in Guantánamo there would have been records, and there simply aren't," said a retired Special Branch officer who interviewed the Pasha family in 2002. "I remember the son, Parvaiz. He was very young but was already being allowed to idolize the father who fought with Britain's enemies. I took away the photograph album he had with pictures of his dad holding a Kalashnikov, and an inscription saying 'One day you'll join me in jihad.' I recommended CPS keep a close eye on him, but unfortunately this recommendation was never taken up."

It's a cause of profound concern that the children of jihadis, many of them British-born, are not closely watched by the state. How many more Parvaiz Pashas will it take for things to change?

He'd returned from the Pakistan High Commission that day to say he didn't have to pay the exorbitant visa fees for British nationals or go through bureaucratic processes in order to work in Karachi because turns out he had something called a NICOP.

"Oh yes," Isma said, "I got them for all of us when I was planning that trip to Pakistan which never happened, remember?"

Up to the attic Parvaiz went, and down he came triumphant. One for you and one for me, he said, handing Aneeka the laminated card with NATIONAL IDENTITY CARD FOR OVERSEAS PAKISTANI printed on it. She glanced at the picture, remembered then how sullenly she had accompanied her sister to the High Commission to have the card issued, hating the idea of missing a summer in London, to spend it in a country teeming with relatives who thought blood ties gave them the right to interrogate and lecture and point to the sisters' hijabs as proof that British Pakistanis were "caught in the past" then point to their jeans to prove they were "mixed up." It didn't improve her mood to see that the card insisted on listing NAME OF FATHER. In the end, though, something in the phone conversations with the rich relatives who had promised to fund the trip had gotten Isma's back up, and the cards were dispatched to the filing cabinet in the attic along with birth certificates and NHS cards and X-rays of broken bones.

"What is an Overseas Pakistani, exactly?" she asked.

Parvaiz shrugged. "Think it just means your family's from there so you're exempt from visas. Anyway, that's the only part that's relevant to me."

"To us," she said. "I'll need it when I come to visit you. Put it in my purse, would you? I don't want to have to go up to the spidery attic to find it when you're gone." She had no memory of his expression as he did as she asked.

Now the laminated card with her sullen fourteen-year-old self sat on the desk at the High Commission while the man with the plastic comb in his pocket looked sadly down on it.

"You should do what your older sister says, and stay away," he said. "Ladies don't go for the burial anyway, so you would only be praying at home, which you can do just as well in London as in Karachi — Allah would hear even a prayer whispered by a mute from the bottom of the world's deepest ocean."

"Am I or am I not entitled to a Pakistani

passport?"

"Yes."

"I have a bank draft for the urgent-processing fee. Please tell me who I should give it to."

HO-JABI! PERVY PASHA'S TWIN SISTER ENGINEERED SEX TRYSTS WITH HOME SECRETARY'S SON

Aneeka "Knickers" Pasha, the 19-year-old twin sister of Muslim fanatic Parvaiz "Pervy" Pasha has been revealed as her brother's accomplice. She hunted down the Home Secretary's son, Eamonn, 24, and used sex to try and brainwash him into convincing his father to allow her terrorist brother back into England.

"Knickers" kept her true identity hidden from her lover until hours before her twin brother was fortunately killed while trying to enter the British consulate in Istanbul. Eamonn Lone quickly informed the Home Secretary that the woman he had allowed into his bed wanted him to use his influence with his father to bring her evil brother back into Britain. Karamat Lone immediately contacted the security services, but before any actions could be taken Pervy Pasha was killed.

The brave Home Secretary, who has taken a strong stand against extremists at risk to his own life, had kept quiet while a police investigation was taking place. This morning his office issued a short statement revealing the sordid affair and promised "full transparency." Although the terrorist's Twisted Sister cannot be proved to have broken any laws, she has been told to keep her distance from the Home Secretary's son, who is understood to be staying with friends in Norfolk. "She was barking up the wrong tree. The Home Secretary would never compromise this nation's security for any reason," say sources close to the Lone family.

INSIDE: DAUGHTER AND SISTER
OF MUSLIM TERRORISTS, WITH
HISTORY OF SECRET SEX LIFE —
THE EXCLUSIVE STORY OF
"KNICKERS" PASHA

xvi.

He looked like a taunt
tasted like a world apart
felt like barriers dissolving

He looked like opportunity
tasted like hope
felt like love

He looked like a miracle
tasted like a miracle
felt like a miracle

A real
actual
straight from God
prostrate yourself in prayer
as you hadn't done since your brother left
miracle.

xvii.

Packed a suitcase, wheeled it outside, the first time leaving the house in days, cameras, microphones, police holding them back. Isma rushing out from Aunty Naseem's house across the road "where are you going." Isma not someone she ever had to answer to again.

Kept walking, police flanking her "miss please go back inside" stepped into the waiting car, Dame Edna this time aka Abdul who had become chief protector, ally, jumping garden walls to enter her house unseen by the press outside. Abdul, who had taken her token and picked up the passport, booked her ticket, paid for it so that Isma wouldn't receive an alert from the credit card company.

Joined quickly by a police escort, TV vans following, never mind, nothing to hide, better this way.

"Why are you helping me, Abdul?"

"Something about me you don't know."

"I've known you're gay since before you did, probably."

"Not that but thank you for never mentioning. I told that Farooq's cousin who Parvaiz was, the rumors about your father, I mean. I think that's why Farooq came for him."

"It's not your fault he went."

"Why did he go?"

"I don't know exactly. I stopped asking it. He wanted to return home, that's what mattered."

"If he comes back, Farooq, I'll kill him."

"No, don't kill him. Take his skin off with the world's smallest scalpel, remove his eyes with an ice cream scoop, drip slow-working acid on his tongue."

"You've thought about this, I guess."

"It's one of the few things I can concentrate on."

"I don't think I could do any of that."

"I know. It's okay."

"One other thing you don't know."

"What's that?"

"Really fancied your brother." Said in a Dame Edna voice.

"Thank you, Abdul. I'd forgotten what it felt like to smile."

At the airport she expected the interrogation room again, but the man at the security checkpoint looked over her shoulder at the police, then down at her new passport and the boarding card to Karachi, and nodded her through.

"Why are you going?" one of the journalists called out from across the barrier, just before she walked into the departure lounge.

"For justice," she said.

xviii.

Karachi: colorful buses, colorless buildings, graffitied walls, billboards advertising cell phones and soft drinks and ice cream, birds circling in the white-hot sky. Parvaiz would have wanted the windows down to listen to every new sound, but she sat back in the car in silence disrupted only by the rattling vents of the air conditioner, a silence not of her own devising but of her cousin's, the guitarist, who refused to explain why she had been escorted off the plane by airport officials who drove her to the cargo terminal where he was waiting to pick her up in a beige car with a sticker on its windscreen announcing its membership to a golf club; it looked more suited to a businessman than a musician.

"Take off the hijab and put these on," was the only thing he'd said, passing her a pair of oversize glasses. She refused, but eventually the sun's glare made her change her mind about the glasses.

The silence continued until he turned into the driveway of a tall white hotel, cleared an ineffectual security check, and pulled over, waving away the valet who came around to take his keys.

"You can get out here," he said.

"For what?"

"Entrance to the hotel is through there. I've checked you in for three days. Under the name Mrs. Gul Khan. His body arrives tomorrow, he'll be buried by the evening. We've arranged a funeral plot, I'll send a car to take you there the next morning. Nine a.m. You can pray over the grave, and leave. Okay? Do not call me. Do not call my mother. You understand?"

"You're the one who needs to understand. He isn't going to be buried. I've come to take him home."

The cousin held his hands up. "I don't want to know. Crazy girl. I don't want to know anything. My sister lives in America, she's about to have a child there — did you or your bhenchod brother stop to think about those of us with passports that look like toilet paper to the rest of the world who spend our whole lives being so careful we don't give anyone a reason to reject our visa applications? Don't stand next to this guy, don't follow that guy on Twitter, don't download that Noam Chomsky book. And then first your brother uses us as a cover to join some psycho killers, and then your government thinks this country can be a dumping ground for its unwanted corpses and your family just expects us to jump up and organize a funeral for this week's face of terrorism. And now you've come along, Miss Hojabi Knickers, and I have to pull strings I don't want to pull to get you out of the airport without the whole world's press seeing you, and it turns out you're here to try some stunt I don't even know what but my family will have nothing to do with it, nothing to do with you."

"I don't want you or your family to have anything to do with it. Just tell me what time tomorrow he's arriving, and who to speak to about where to bring him."

"What do you mean, where to bring him? You planning on checking a corpse into your hotel room?"

"You really want to know?"

"No. Get out."

"Who do I speak to about where to bring him?"

He reached into his wallet, pulled out a business card, and threw it at her.

"Thank you. By the way, how far are we from the British Deputy High Commission?"

"Look at a map," he said, leaning across to open her door.

xix.

The British Deputy High Commission compound was surrounded by barbed wire, vans bristling with guns, and roadblocks to prevent any stranger's approach. But just a few minutes' walk away there was a park lined with banyan trees, their ancient overground roots more enduring than wire rusting in the sea air or guns that jammed with dust or the calculations made today by politicians looking to the next elections.

Here she would sit with her brother until the world changed or both of them crumbled into the soil around them.

■ ■ ■ ■

KARAMAT

■ ■ ■ ■

8

Karamat Lone ignored the unusual twitchiness of the shadow stretched out alongside his on the Thames path and poured a second shot of coffee from the thermos into a paper cup. On two separate occasions Eamonn had given him one of those insulated mugs as a birthday present, well intentioned but oblivious to the mug's inability to keep a man's hands warm while doing the same for the coffee. When it came to his son, Karamat had always treated "well intentioned" as good enough. With his daughter, the only other possible candidate for such preferential treatment, there'd never been any need. Poor fellow, he used to think, considering the gap in abilities and achievements between Eamonn and his younger sister. It had never occurred to him that Eamonn alone was blind to his own — the word hurt in relation to a man's only son, but nothing else would do — inadequacy. All the good cheer Karamat had admired as a front became an embarrassment when revealed to be a genuine attitude. *She loves me!* he had continued to insist in the face of all evidence to the contrary. *Why is that so impossible to believe?* A question Karamat had hated answering. He held the paper cup to his face, allowing the steam to enter his nostrils, warm his cheeks. There was a precise calibration to how long you could do this before the coffee dipped below optimum drinking temperature.

He gulped down the coffee, felt it burn its way pleasingly through him while he continued to look at the Palace of Westminster and its watery reflection, the yellow stone pink-gold in the interlude of sunrise. The heart of tradition, everyone agreed, but few understood Britain as well as Karamat Lone and knew that within the deepest chamber of that heart of tradition was the engine of radical change. Here Britain whittled down the powers of the monarchy, here Britain agreed to leave its empire, here Britain instituted universal suffrage, here Britain would see the grandson of the colonized take his place as prime minister. The most constant criticism against Karamat Lone was that his positions flip-flopped between

300

traditionalist and reformer — but the critics learned nothing from their own inability to know which was which. Take, for instance, his intention to expand the home secretary's power to revoke British citizenship so that it applied to British-born single passport holders. It was, clearly, the sensible fulfillment of a law that was so far only half made. You had to determine someone's fitness for citizenship based on actions, not accidents of birth. An increase in draconian powers! said one set of his opponents on the left; a renewed assault on true Englishmen and -women by Britain's migrant population, said another set on the far right. Both sets probably drank coffee out of insulated mugs.

You're doing the contemptuous thing again, Terry would say.

It was one of his wife's few remaining misconceptions about him. Contempt, disdain, scorn: these emotions were stops along a closed loop that originated and terminated in a sense of superiority. In their preservation of the status quo they were of no use to Karamat Lone. A man needed fire in his veins to burn through the world, not ice to freeze everything in place. He'd thought he had mastered the art of directing the fire, but yesterday, with TV cameras on him, he'd heard the girl's one-line

301

explanation for leaving England and hadn't been able to stop himself from responding: "She's going to look for justice in *Pakistan*?" That final word spoken with all the disgust of a child of migrants who understands how much his parents gave up — family, context, language, familiarity — because the nation to which they first belonged had proven itself inadequate to the task of allowing them to live with dignity. At some point, he'd have to respond to the foreign secretary's irate message about his comment. Or not, if the PM kept up his silence — a silence Karamat worried had less to do with favoring his home secretary than with the PM's irritation at how Pakistan's prime minister was trying to make political capital of the situation. He'd sanctimoniously explained that Pakistan, as a matter of state policy, shouldered the cost of repatriating its citizens while the UK government expected the bereaved to pay thousands of pounds to have the remains of their loved ones returned to them.

A Lycra-covered runner approached, swerved skin-scrapingly close to the Thames path barrier as soon as he was close enough to recognize the home secretary, and held up a hand to the officers to indicate he wasn't a threat. Brown skinned. Karamat clicked his tongue against the back of his teeth.

He twisted off the thermos cap again, shook the container gently, considered the liquid swishing around the glass-lined interior. He didn't seem to need it despite his total lack of sleep the previous night. The wonders of adrenaline — it had been a long time since he'd stayed up all night wondering what his opponent was going to do. People were usually so predictable.

"Sir," cautioned Suarez behind him.

"That one too Muslim for comfort?"

"That one was Latino."

"You always insist the good-looking ones are your cousins rather than mine."

"We really should go, sir."

Karamat turned to look at the head of his security detail. From the start, Suarez had understood the home secretary's insistence that he didn't want to know anything at all about the threats against him; *You do your job and let me do mine,* Karamat had said. Of course when they cut down trees in his garden and put officers in their place it was obvious there'd been some "development," but Suarez maintained an air of calm through everything. Today, though, he was visibly anxious, and although Karamat had managed to insist on this riverside coffee, a

303

post-sleepless-night tradition stretching back to his earliest days as a backbencher, it was clear that he wouldn't win the argument twice.

He was about to stand up when his phone rang, and the screen told him it was his son. He cradled the phone in his hands for a moment, found the old empty habits forming the word "Bismillah" before he answered.

"Hi, Dad. Thought you'd be up." Eamonn's voice was calm, affectionate, nothing like that of the crazed thing who'd had to be physically restrained from returning to the arms of that manipulative whore. Well, "arms" wasn't really the bit of her he wanted to return to, was it? Though Karamat probably shouldn't have said so at the time.

"You okay?" He hadn't spoken to Eamonn since Terry had arranged for Max and Alice to take him away to one of Alice's family estates after he'd moved from hysteria to a listless resignation — the press assumed the estate was the one in Norfolk, though it could just as well be Normandy. Karamat hadn't asked Terry not to tell him where their son was, but she knew well enough that it was information better kept from him in case someone asked him a direct question, which he'd have to answer honestly.

His wife had always had a perfectly judged sense of who he was, who he had to be, as a public figure, which made it all the more mystifying when she packed up a segment of his wardrobe and moved it down to the basement bedroom in response to his office's breaking the story of Eamonn's involvement with the girl. *You could have protected him,* she'd said, as if her husband were the kind of man either stupid or unethical enough to try to organize a cover-up. She hadn't relented when most of the newspapers correctly portrayed Eamonn as a dupe, and some even managed to suggest he'd turned on the girl as soon as he'd realized what she wanted.

"Yes. I'm sorry how I behaved the other day."

Karamat crossed a foot over his knee, considered the openmouthed sturgeons with bulging eyes and entwined tails at the base of the nearby lamppost. Usually grotesque, they now appeared winningly comical to his benevolent gaze. "I'm sorry you're going to have a rough ride for a bit. Perhaps that move to New York your sister suggested might not be the worst idea."

"I worry about you more than me."

Karamat stood up and walked to the lamppost, leaned against it, and turned away from his security detail. "That's nice to hear, but unnecessary."

"It's just that from where you're sitting it may not be clear how this looks. A government that sends its citizens to some other country when they act in ways we don't like. Doesn't that say we can't deal with our own problems? And stopping a family from burying its own — that never looks good. That's what people are beginning to say around me. If your advisers won't tell you this, your son will."

"My son, schooling me in politics from his vantage point among the landed gentry," he said, pressing his knuckles into the bulging eyes of the fish.

"I'm saying this because your reputation matters to me. More than you know."

"She told you to say all this, didn't she?"

"I haven't heard from her. You know that. I've done what you asked. I haven't called or texted. You said if I agreed, you would help her. How have you helped her?"

"She's had police protection stationed outside her house. I haven't let the world see the kinds of videos her beloved brother worked on. She hasn't been locked up in an interrogation room for fourteen days without charge, not even after admitting that she seduced my son in order to help a terrorist. You saw that transcript, didn't you? She admitted it."

"Of course she said that once she thought I'd abandoned her."

"Do you hear yourself?"

"Do you hear yourself? You think you're doing someone a favor by not locking them up for fourteen days without reason?"

"Please don't try to develop a spine. You weren't built for it. Did she give you your first really great blow job, Eamonn? Is that what this is about? Because trust me, there are better ones out there."

A pause, and then his son's voice at its most cuttingly posh: "I think we're done here, Father."

The call went dead and Karamat turned around, crumpling the empty paper cup in his fist. Suarez stepped forward and extended his palm to take the cup, teeth marks visible on his thumb. He saw Karamat's eyes on the indentations and folded his thumb over his palm to hide the visual reminder of Eamonn kicking wildly at the air, teeth clamped on Suarez's gag-hand.

Pivoting away from Suarez, he sent the paper cup flying in the direction of the garbage can. It hit the rim, bounced up, plummeted into the receptacle.

Take out the trash. Keep Britain clean.

■ ■ ■ ■

Mid-morning in London, mid-afternoon Karachi, someone called @CricketBoyzzzz uploaded pictures of a woman in the white of mourning, sitting cross-legged on a white sheet covered in rose petals. The sun-singed grass and the patches of damp on her kameez conveyed an extraordinary heat despite the banyan tree under whose spreading branches and beardlike aerial roots she'd arranged herself. #Knickers #Found-Her

All the press assigned to the Pasha story, scattered among upscale hotels and graveyards and family homes and airport terminals, descended on the park, only to be met by the blank stare and silence of a girl whom Karamat was beginning to suspect of being as unhinged as she was manipulative.

"Find out where the body is," Karamat instructed his assistant, James, eyes moving between the two TV screens in his Marsham Street office, one tuned to a Pakistani news channel, the other to an international one.

The Pakistani channel had a split screen. One side showed scenes from the park, as increasing numbers of onlookers arrived to cluster around the girl, as if she were the site of an accident; the other showed a studio in which the urbane host of a religious discussion program explained what Shariah law had to say about the Pasha case. The man had slicked-back hair and a black mark on his forehead — the latter a sign of piety, helped along by banging one's head against a stone or rough surface during the daily prostration of prayer. Karamat picked up a lion-and-unicorn paperweight, pressed it to his forehead. First, said the man, the boy had joined those modern-day Khajarites who were a greater enemy of Islam than even America or Israel, and so he should never be described as a "jihadi." Second, he should have been buried before sunset on the day he died, no matter how far from home he was, and anything else was un-Islamic. Third, by her own admission to the UK police, the girl was a sinner, a fornicator, and should be flogged.

Karamat made a note of the man's name and turned his attention to the international channel, where the anchor had pulled up a digital 3-D map of the area surrounding the park and was describing the location as "significant" as red circles appeared on the map identifying the gas station next to the park, the convent school and Italian consulate across the street, and the busy roundabout a stone's throw away. The 3-D models of buildings and trees collapsed into the ground as if from a powerful detonation, and what remained was the figure of a girl facing the British Deputy High Commission.

Karamat pressed the mute button and watched the doe-eyed girl in white, head covered, surrounded by bloodred rose petals, the park railings looking like a backdrop of prison bars in close-up shots of her. Nothing accidental in any of it, but what was all the iconography of suffering meant to achieve?

James returned to say the Turkish embassy could confirm only that the body had arrived in Islamabad, but had no details of how or when it would be transported to Karachi, and the Pakistan High Commission had made it clear they expected an apology from the home secretary before they would reveal any information about their citizens to him. Karamat handed him the piece of paper with the urbane host's name and said, "If he has a UK visa, find a reason to cancel it."

"There are some people who think you're wanting a reason to strip her of her citizenship too," James said, indicating the girl on the screen, his accent turning more pronouncedly Scottish and working-class, as it always did when he thought he might be about to enter into a disagreement with Karamat. It was a tic James was almost certainly unaware of, but Karamat had always found it winning that the young man's unconscious played his outsider status up rather than down when he challenged the home secretary.

"And what do you think of that?"

"I think it's a terrible idea. Everyone will think it's because of Eamonn."

"Everyone should know better," Karamat said. He stood up and approached the split screen. "Damned if I know what she's planning next. Would you be standing as near her as all those people in the park?"

"You think she's wearing a suicide vest under those clothes?"

"No, I think she turns everything around her toxic. Look, it's all gone a bit yellow around her, hasn't it?"

"Must be something wrong with the camera lens. I'm sorry, sir, about the suicide vest comment."

"Don't be silly, James. These are the times we live in."

The girl stood up fluidly from her cross-legged posture and stepped off the sheet. A single rose petal adhered to the top of her slim, bare foot. He imagined his son's mouth pressed where the petal was, made a flicking-away motion with his hand. Both TV channels were showing the same scene, from slightly different angles, the air clearly yellow with an impending dust storm. The park — no more than twice the size of the Lone family garden — was bound in by railings and banyan trees, with an open gate toward which she was walking. A van had pulled up outside — an ambulance.

"No. Oh, come on, no."

The driver of the ambulance opened the back doors, called out for some of the onlookers to help him. Far more men than was necessary lifted out the unadorned casket and carried it on their shoulders behind the girl, who, pale but composed, led them back to the white sheet and rose petals — the scene of martyrdom now complete. The men laid the casket down, but the girl wanted something more from them. She spoke to the man who had driven the ambulance; he shook his head vigorously, pointed to the hazy sky — indicating either the Almighty or the afternoon sun. She knelt beside the casket, placed the palms of her hands, one on top of the other, against the lid, near the corner, and pressed down with all her weight, her knees lifting off the ground with the effort.

"Move the cameras away," he heard himself say.

The wood buckled, splintered.

"Jesus," James said. "Jesus, no."

The dupatta had fallen from her head, long hair whipping across her face as the wind picked up. The casket revealed its flimsy construction, nails ripping out of wood as the girl set to dismantling it with her bare hands. One by one she collapsed the sides until what remained was a shape sandwiched between the coffin's base and a top layer of plywood. The girl sat back on her heels, as if only now, at this moment, had she stopped to consider what she was asking her own eyes to look at. Or maybe she was waiting for what happened next: the yellow-brown wind picked up the plywood and flung it into the air with a whipping sound.

The girl lowered herself to her knees, placed her hands on the ground on either side of her, and leaned forward, as a child might examine some unknown animal found in the garden. Her brother, embalmed, looked *not right.* How else to say it? Dead.

She lifted a hand, looked at it as if she wasn't sure what it was about to do, and watched as her palm came to rest on the forehead of what had once been her twin. The hand jerked away, settled back down, slid along his skin toward his temple. Karamat and the cameras saw the stitches before she felt them, the place where death entered him. Her expression when she touched the thread was irritated, as if objecting to the untidiness, nothing more. The hand lifted again, moved down to the corpse's wrist, two fingers pressed against what would have been a pulse point. Her mouth opened and a small word or sound may have come out, nothing the mics could pick up.

James said the words "broadcast regulations" with nothing around them. Every phone in the room was ringing. Someone was knocking on the door. "Shut up," Karamat shouted, to everything.

The dust storm that had sent its advance guard now arrived in a hurtling, pelting wind. The white sheet flew up at its corners, tossing aside the rectangles of wood that had weighed it down; rose petals pitched up into the air, came down muddied; leaves were ripped from the banyan trees; the world tilted this way and that; the women wound their dupattas around their faces, the men made themselves small. One camera recorded only the flattened grass through a cracked lens. The other, moving

314

closer to the girl, showed her dupatta fly toward it, a close-up of the tiny embroidered flowers on the white cloth, and then a battering darkness.

For a few moments there was only a howling noise, the wind raging, and then a hand plucked away the white cloth and the howl was the girl, a dust mask on her face, her dark hair a cascade of mud, her fingers interlaced over the face of her brother. A howl deeper than a girl, a howl that came out of the earth and through her and into the office of the home secretary, who took a step back. As if that were the only thing the entire spectacle had been designed to achieve, the wind dropped as suddenly as buildings collapse in 3-D models, and the girl stopped her noise, unlaced her fingers. The cameras panned, then zoomed. In the whole apocalyptic mess of the park the only thing that remained unburied was the face of the dead boy.

"Impressive," said the home secretary.

The girl licked her thumb, ran it over her mouth, painting lips onto the dust mask. Then she looked directly at the home secretary and spoke:

"In the stories of wicked tyrants, men and women are punished with exile, bodies are kept from their families — their heads impaled on spikes, their corpses thrown into unmarked graves. All these things happen according to the law, but not according to justice. I am here to ask for justice. I appeal to the prime minister: Let me take my brother home."

Karamat spun the paperweight on the desk, watched the lion and unicorn animate, smiled. After all the noise and spectacle, she was just a silly girl.

Prime Minister's Questions was usually an embarrassment. Childish jeering and taunts, the PM parading his ability at that facile talent, the put-down, the chancellor — or "chancer," as Karamat preferred to think of him — sitting beside him with an expression both obsequious and smug close up but that managed to look just the right degree of supportive on camera. Parliament reduced to a playground. Karamat had been particularly dreading today — the first PMQs since the Pasha affair began. The PM, who had been abroad and out of touch the last few days, had been worryingly quiet on the whole matter, and any withholding of support from his home secretary would be a victory for the chancer and his leadership bid. But then the girl had opened her mouth.

"Heads impaled on spikes. Bodies thrown into unmarked graves. There are people who follow these practices. Her brother left Britain to join them."

The PM rose above party politics; the leader of the opposition rose to join him. There were "hear, hears" on either side of the aisle. The home secretary was lauded for the difficult decisions he had to make and the personal trials he'd undergone that had in no way affected his judgment or commitment to doing the right thing. Even the chancer had to lean across the space vacated by the PM as he stood at the dispatch box and pat Karamat appreciatively on the shoulder, a tiny nerve pulsing near his eye, which he saw Karamat recognize as defeat.

James was waiting for him in his room behind the Speaker's Chair, mimicking some awful footballer's goal celebrations as he entered, the right mix of genuine and ironic. Not for the first time, Karamat wished his daughter and James would get together. But that set him off thinking about his children and their choice of partners — you could see Aneeka Pasha was the kind of

317

girl who would do anything. A girl who looked like that and was willing to do anything. His poor boy never stood a chance. He sat down heavily in his chair, missed his wife — not in the ways he used to miss her when he was Eamonn's age but in the way that only one parent can miss another, when their child is in pain.

He nodded at James to make the required call, and chose to speak in Urdu when his assistant handed him the phone, purely because he knew that puffer fish in human form who was the Pakistan high commissioner would assume it meant the home secretary believed his English was inadequate.

"What mischief are you people up to now?" Karamat asked.

"That's a strange way to start off an apology," the HC replied, in English.

"I'm not the one who has to apologize. That body would never have made it to the park if your government hadn't agreed to it. Or engineered it."

"Come, come," the HC said, unconvincingly. "The closest living relative asked for the body to be brought to a particular spot — on what grounds should the driver have refused? As for my government, it has bigger things to worry about than the logistics of a corpse."

"I assume someone is going to remove the body from the park. On the grounds of hygiene, if nothing else."

"I'm my nation's representative to the Court of St. James's. Do you think I go around talking to municipal councils in Karachi? But maybe things are different in Britain, in which case please tell my bin man not to make such a clanging noise when he comes round in the morning."

"How's your son's student visa application coming along?"

"Actually, he's decided to go with Harvard rather than Oxford. The girl made some interesting points, don't you think?"

It was beginning to stop being enjoyable, so he switched to English. "Fine, I spoke out of turn. Pakistan's judiciary is a credit to your nation."

"Bunch of bastards," the high commissioner said unexpectedly. And then he was the one to switch languages — not to Urdu but Punjabi. "Listen, I'm a father too. I would want her off the news as well."

"It's not that."

"Oh shut up, friend, I'm being sympathetic." Punjabi allowed this breach of etiquette, and Karamat felt something in his whole body shift, become looser. He tightened his shoulders against it. "The issue is, my government has no reason to intervene."

"Intervene on decency's behalf. What kind of madness makes someone leave a corpse out in the heat to putrefy?"

"The madness of love. Remember your Laila-Majnu, Karamat? The lover so grief-stricken at the loss of the beautiful beloved that he wanders, in madness, in the desert. This beautiful girl in a dust storm has managed to become Laila and Majnu combined in the nation's consciousness. Or Sassi and Punnu in parts of the nation — same story, except it's the girl who runs grief-crazed through the desert in search of her love."

"This nation, which has decided to cast her as a romantic heroine, is the same one that wants her flogged?"

"Oh, people are already saying your government made up the whole story about her relationship with your son to discredit her, though opinion is divided whether it was you or one of your enemies who was behind it. Either way, for us to act against her now is difficult."

"For god's sake, man, do you really expect me to believe your government makes decisions based on a combination of folktales and conspiracy theories?"

"You really are as British as they say you are. Let me put it in language you'll understand: The people, and several opposition parties, have decided to embrace a woman who has stood up to a powerful government, and not just any powerful government but one that has very bad PR in the matter of Muslims and as recently as yesterday insulted us directly. So, now it's political suicide for my government to get involved. I hope we'll see you at our Eid reception. Until then, Allah hafiz."

The door swung open. The expected supporters, and some unexpected ones too, entered, bowing and throwing imaginary hats in the air. Karamat rubbed the back of his hand against his mouth, tasting dust.

He was in a coffin made of slabs of ice, a prince in a fairy tale. The owner of the city's largest ice factory said he would supply his product free of charge, a truck driver said he would transport it as a religious duty. Everyone who had gathered in the park took turns unloading the ice slabs and passing them along a conveyer belt of human hands to the white sheet, now soaked through. When the ice left their hands they touched their red palms to their faces, the burn of cold against the burn of heat. Those nearest the corpse wrapped their faces in cloth. The translucency of the ice made it possible for the news channels to continue their live coverage without worrying about meeting broadcast standards: the corpse was little more than a blurry outline. The girl didn't assist with the continual rebuilding of the melting ice coffin, nor did she stop it. Her only insistence was that his face should remain uncovered. Now, as sunset bruised the sky, she stood with her back pressed against the banyan tree, her eyes never moving from that face.

"Is This the Face of Evil?" a tabloid asked, illustrating the question with a picture of the girl howling as dust flew around her. "Slag," "terrorist spawn," "enemy of Britain." Those were the words being used to describe her, the paper reported, placing inverted commas around the words as proof. Would the home secretary strip her of her citizenship for acting against the vital interests of the UK, as surely she had done by giving ammunition to the enemies of Britain?

The home secretary set the paper aside with a sound of irritation and resumed looking at Aneeka Pasha. Even when there was nothing new to report there was always someone new to interview, and so the TV journalists were thrusting microphones into the faces of the "representatives of civil society" who had shown up in support of the bereaved girl and were now starting to light candles in the deepening twilight.

There was no need to do anything so dramatic as strip her of her citizenship, a move that could be traced back to personal motivations. She couldn't return to the UK on her Pakistani passport without applying for a visa, which she was certainly welcome to do if she wanted to waste her time and money. As for her British passport, which had been confiscated by the security services when she tried to join her brother in Istanbul, it was neither lost nor stolen nor expired and therefore there were no grounds for her to apply for a new one. Let her continue to be British; but let her be British outside Britain.

The candles threw their reflections onto the ice coffin. Flames trembled along its length, creating the impression of something stirring inside. Karamat walked over to the blinds, opened them to let in the afternoon sunlight, and looked down at the familiar scene of Marsham Street, suddenly so moving in all its quotidian details, cars parked in parking spots, a woman walking by with shopping bags braided around her wrists, trees with thin trunks standing side by side. His London, everyone's London, everyone except those who wanted to harm it. He touched a vein in his neck, felt the reassuring warmth of his own blood.

He returned home to Holland Park after *Newsnight,* a tough interview as expected, but he'd maintained his calm, clarified that he had never made a decision about a corpse — his decision had been about a living "enemy of Britain" (he used the expression three times, which seemed just right, though he might have been able to get away with a fourth). The very word "repatriation," which is what the girl wanted for her brother's corpse, rested on a fact of citizenship that had ceased to exist the day he, Karamat Lone, took office and sent an unequivocal message to those who treated the privilege of British citizenship as something that could be betrayed without consequences. No, he didn't think it was harsh to send that message even to the girls who went as so-called jihadi brides. It was well past the point when anyone could pretend they didn't know exactly what kind of death cult they were joining. The British people supported him, and that included the majority of British Muslims. The news anchor had raised his eyebrows at that.

Are you sure? he'd said. *There seems to be a common view, repeated on this program just yesterday by a representative of the Muslim Association of Britain, that you hate Muslims.*

I hate the Muslims who make people hate Muslims, he'd replied quietly.

Up the stairs he went to the bedroom he'd been exiled from. Terry would have been watching, and she'd know how much that question wounded him. He was aware she would still be angry about what she saw as his failure to protect Eamonn, but even so, she would have softened toward him. All he asked for was to be allowed to lie down next to her, not quite touching — unforgiven but not unwanted. At some point in the night she'd touch her foot to his — the once involved rituals of making up pared down to this single gesture over their more than three decades together. *Our love is almost middle-aged now,* she'd said to him a few weeks earlier, at the anniversary of their first meeting, trying to hide how much she minded that he'd returned home very late from Marsham Street having forgotten the date they always celebrated privately, unlike the wedding anniversary, which was generally a family, or more widely social, affair.

His memory lapse was particularly blundering given that it came just months after she'd moved herself to a ceremonial role in her business, something she'd often talked about but that he didn't think she'd ever do. *One of us has to be a fixed point in the universe, otherwise we'll keep missing each other,* she'd said when she announced the decision, the only indication that she'd done it because his promotion to home secretary was imminent. The least he could have done in exchange was to remember the damn anniversary. He was generally a man to acknowledge a mistake the moment it was made, correct it (he had brought her breakfast in bed the next morning, and before leaving for work was attentive in other ways that pleased her), and never think of it again — this raking over a past failure was disquieting, adding to the wrongness of every part of the day, from Suarez's jumpiness to the conversation with his son to the question about hating Muslims to the girl, that fucking girl.

"No," Terry said when he pushed the door open. "No. Out."

"I'll sit there," he said, pointing to the stool next to her dressing table.

"I spoke to our son. He told me what you said. About the blow job. Are you an expert on the better ones out there?"

"Whatever my failings are you know that isn't one of them," he said, loosening his tie, kicking off his shoes.

"Karamat, I mean it. Out."

There was no arguing with her in this mood. Unbelievable that his son should have repeated that part of the conversation to his mother — did he know nothing about the rules between men? Down the stairs he went again to the consolations of a laughably expensive bottle of red wine, a gift that Terry had been saving for a special occasion. The ground floor was the place for formal entertaining, the basement the space in which he shut himself away from his family — each as alienating as the other, in the circumstances. He took the wine outside to the patio, where the moving shadows made him drop into a squat to offer as small a target as possible before he realized they were there for his protection. He finally ended up in the kitchen, sitting on the counter, swinging his legs as his children used to do when he would prepare breakfast for them while his wife was on a business trip somewhere. The kitchen table had long since been removed and a gleaming chrome island was in its place to allow more space for cheese boards, platters of canapés, glasses — sorry, children, "flutes" — of champagne. He rolled up his sleeves, picked up the wineglass. The first Indian cricketer to be loved by the English, Ranjitsinhji, always wore his sleeves buttoned at the wrist to hide his dark skin — something about holding an expensive glass of wine made Karamat understand how he'd felt. He let the wine sit in his mouth before it slid down with all the languor of the overpriced.

There was a gentle knock on the door leading outside, and a moment later Suarez entered.

"You're supposed to be off duty."

"My men called. There's someone who's been walking repeatedly up and down the street. Jones finally asked her what she wanted and she said she knew you lived on this street but didn't know which house, and thought if she loitered long enough your security detail would identify themselves."

Karamat grunted in amusement. "Who is she?"

"Isma Pasha. The sister —"

"I know who that is. Bring her in."

"In here, sir?"

"My mother didn't raise me to turn women out onto the street at midnight. And Suarez, there are only male officers tonight, aren't there? Keep the pat-down minimal."

"Too late for that, sir. Your security comes first."

When she entered her eyes scanned the dimensions of the kitchen and Karamat could already feel a judgment being passed. He poured wine into a second glass and slid it across the chrome island toward her.

"No thank you," she said, instead of the expected purse-lipped *I don't drink*. She looked nothing like the girl — not just a matter of coloring and features but also the way she was holding in her body, as if aware enough to understand she was in the presence of a man who had all the power and might just choose to exercise it. *Probably a virgin,* he thought, and wondered when he'd become the kind of man who reacted in this way to the sight of a woman with a covered head who made no effort to look anything but plain.

"It may just be worth going to hell for," he said, taking a long sip.

She picked up the glass with both hands and sniffed its contents. "Smells like petrol."

There had been a moment, experienced in the pit of his stomach, in which he'd thought she was going to take a sip because she believed he was demanding it as the price of listening to whatever she had to say. "What do you want?" he said, the tone of his voice making Suarez step forward from his post near the door to see what the girl had done.

"I want to fly to Karachi in the morning without anyone at the airport stopping me from going."

He took her glass and poured it into his. "Your statement to the press was exactly as it should have been. It made me think you were reasonable."

"She's my sister. Almost my child."

"She doesn't show much concern for you, though, does she?"

"Do you love your children based on how much concern they show for you?"

"Watch yourself." Not a girl, this one. An adult, far more dangerous than that banshee in the dust.

"Eamonn worships you. And you've allowed the world to think he's a fool."

"That was his doing, not mine. A girl that obsessed with her brother never said anything about him that should have raised suspicions? Or about her father?"

She leaned back against the fridge, her elbow pressing a button on the LED panel that smoothly ejected two cubes of ice from the dispenser before she jerked away. The noiseless efficiency had always been a disappointment — in his childhood he coveted the rattling, groaning ice dispenser in the fridge door of one of the Wembley relatives. Isma Pasha of Preston Road, the upmarket end of Wembley, picked up one of the ice cubes from the grille onto which it had been deposited and briefly became the embodiment of all his childhood ambitions. Surely she was among those who could be saved, despite the wreckage of her family.

"Eamonn knew about our father all along. I told him, before he even met Aneeka."

She was standing there with an ice cube melting between her fingers, not knowing what to do with it now that she'd picked it up. A picture of harmless awkwardness. A wolf in lamb's clothing.

"You've been sensible so far. Keep being sensible," he said, swirling the wine in his glass, looking contemplatively into the miniature blood ocean.

"What? No, I didn't mean . . ." She placed the ice in the empty wineglass, where it soaked up the color of the remaining droplets of red. "Do you think I'd try to make it my word against the office of the home secretary? Or that I'd try to make things worse for Eamonn? I only meant to suggest your son has more character than you give him credit for. There's strength where you think there's weakness."

"You're very impassioned on the subject of my son. Pity he didn't end up with you instead of that sister of yours. You I'd accept."

"He didn't want to end up with me," she said, her tone flat.

He raised his eyebrows at her over his wineglass. "Was that an option?"

"No."

"There are interesting shades of 'yes' in that 'no.' We may have to return to it one day. But first let's deal with the situation in which we find ourselves. You're here to ask a favor. All right. Let's see how sensible you are. Will you convince her to let the body be buried, in Karachi? No airline would carry it in the state it's now in anyway." He couldn't take his eyes off the ice cube in the glass, now pinkly melting.

"There's no convincing her. I want to be with her, that's all."

Those were almost exactly the words Eamonn had used. *I only want to be with her.* Meaningless words from a weak boy. He had been repeating that word to himself endlessly about his son: "weak." He took hold of the almost-emptied glass on the chrome island, swallowed the numbingly cold water with its tinge of something else.

A foreign body in ice.

"Suarez, where is my son?"

"Normandy, sir. On Miss Alice's estate."

"Is someone watching him?"

"Sir, no. I thought it would be enough to watch his . . . Aneeka Pasha . . . to ensure there was no further contact, as you asked. Would you like me to —"

"No, no. You've done the right thing. Well, thank you, Suarez, for coming out so late. You can leave me here with her. I'm closer to the knife block than she is."

When the door closed behind Suarez, Isma Pasha said, "Eamonn has your sense of humor."

"He's funnier."

"Yes."

He took his phone out of his pocket, texted James: Find out if my son's used his passport in the last few days. Discreetly.

He folded his arms, leaned back. He heard a tiny sigh from Isma Pasha and tilted his head forward to see her replicating his posture, the fridge her headrest. Curious woman. She was quite clearly besotted with Eamonn, but that seemed to make no difference to her devotion to her sister.

"Why sociology?" he said. He shouldn't have opened the wine — it would only make Terry angrier. There was never anything to

333

be gained from pettiness.

"I wanted to understand why the world is so unfair."

"Shouldn't your God give you those answers?" he said, surprised by the slight teasing of his own tone.

"Our God did, in a roundabout way."

"How's that?" he said. She was pretty when her face was at rest, wiped clean of the encroachment of anxiety.

"For starters, He created Marx."

"So you have a sense of humor too."

"Only assuming I meant that to be a joke." She looked directly at him, and something passed between them — it wasn't about sex, but something that felt more dangerous. She was familiar to him, a reminder of a world he'd lost.

He flexed his shoulders, trying to loosen them, looked at the microwave clock, wondered how it was still today. "You must have seen what was happening to your brother. Why didn't you say something? How do I get people like you to say something when it's still early enough to act?"

"We saw something was happening, my sister and I. We thought it was some kind of secret affair, his first time in love. In a way, it was. What else explains a person being turned inside out in the space of just a few weeks? Did you see what was happening with your son?"

He could feel the muscles of his face contract. "Let me tell you this: If it turns out you're right, and I'm wrong. If there is an Almighty and He sends His angel Jibreel to lift up your brother — and your sister — in his arms and fly them back to London on his wings of fire, I will not let him enter. Do you understand? Not Jibreel himself."

"A pair of nineteen-year-olds, one of them dead," was all she said.

The quietness of her tone made his rhetoric of angels and wings of fire — the language of his parents — sound exactly as hysterical as it had been. He touched his tongue to his incisor to help him formulate a response that would decimate both Isma Pasha and his own momentary lapse, but was distracted by James calling. He answered the call, said "Yes" and "Thank you." Hanging up, he poured the contents of his wineglass back into the bottle without wasting a drop. He'd need a clear head in the morning.

"Will you allow me to leave tomorrow?" she said.

"You won't matter tomorrow. Do what you want."

He left the kitchen, headed down to the

basement. Along the way he passed a console table with a smiling picture of Eamonn. He picked it up and kissed his son's cheek. *My beautiful boy.* One final lingering moment in which he allowed himself the luxury of being a father to a son — a son who was moving in the opposite direction of home, burning bridges in his wake, a trail of fire in the sky.

9

Karamat never remembered the tiniest shred of his dreams, so when he was awakened in the middle of the night his first thought was that it must have been some unwanted presence making his heart race so fast it woke the rest of him up. But the silence of the spare bedroom in the basement was so complete it was obvious nothing had disturbed it. The sliding glass door with its rolled-up blinds looked onto a light well composed of a glass platform overhead and carefully angled mirrors that were reflecting a confusing, cold light into the bedroom. In his pajamas he walked out into the light well. The moon was full and low overhead. He lay down on the wooden bench built into the wall at the insistence of his heat-seeking boy, who used this space as a sunroom. But now it was cold — the light cold, his skin cold, the emptiness cold. He stood up on the bench, on the tips of his toes, pressed his palm flat against the glass platform. A subterranean creature reaching for the moon. He shuddered, felt a terrible loneliness. "Terry," he said, in the way that as a child he had mouthed prayers to ward off the darkness of the world.

A short while later he was climbing into bed with his wife, traversing the sheets to fit himself to her as she lay on her side. He hiked up her silk nightdress so he could rest his hand on the warmth of her inner thigh, a place he particularly loved, heard her breathing change to tell him she was near enough waking to know he was there. "Let me stay, jaan," he whispered. She relented, as she almost always did when he used that tone of need, shifting against him, a minor adjustment that increased their points of contact. Her foot pressing against his. Tomorrow he would have to tell her that Eamonn had gone to Karachi to prove to his father he had a spine. He inhaled the scent of his wife, slid his hand up to the source of her heat. After tonight, who knew when she'd allow him to do this again? He touched his mouth to Terry's bare shoulder, rolled away, and got out of bed, ignoring her muffled noise of protest. Too distracting. He needed to keep his mind clear.

He went back to sleep in the basement, and when he woke there really was an unwanted presence in the room, and it was James, a mug of coffee in his hand. Karamat sat up. It wasn't yet light outside.

"Eamonn's landed?" he said.

"Just boarded the connecting flight," James said, handing Karamat the coffee. "Someone recognized him at the boarding gate and tweeted a picture, so the media will probably get it soon. Have you spoken to the ambassador yet?"

"About what?"

"I thought you might have asked the Pakistanis to put him on a plane back home when he arrives."

"Would I do that if he weren't my son?" He wondered if Eamonn was counting on this — the father watching over him, not allowing things to go too far.

"With respect, sir, he is your son."

"With respect, James, he's a British national who made a choice and has to face the consequences. As any other British national would."

"There's something else the media will get soon. It went online just a few minutes ago." The little folder James was carrying under his arm turned out to be his tablet. He proffered it to Karamat, who shook his head and got out of bed, reaching for his dressing gown. A man couldn't be prone in his pajamas when something important happened. James followed him into his office, and although there was a desktop computer with a large monitor he set up his tablet on a stand on Karamat's desk.

"So bad I shouldn't look at it in large scale?" Karamat said, and James didn't meet his eye.

In that way the mind has of focusing on trivial details to avoid the enormity of what it has to bear, Karamat spent the first seconds of the video feeling irritated that his son hadn't sat down with a journalist but had decided instead to speak directly to a camera and upload the whole thing to a website. It was the kind of choice that wanted to come across as honest and direct but was really just controlling. Or lazy.

"There's been some speculation about my whereabouts these last few days," Eamonn said, handsome and well rested. The close-up shot showed nothing of his surroundings, only a white wall behind him, his shoulders broad and trustworthy in a button-down navy blue shirt. His eyes moved — to whom? — then settled back on the camera lens. "I admit, I've been paralyzed by indecision" — he made it sound like an actual ailment — "caught between the two people I love most in the world: my father and my fiancée."

"Ah, no," said James, moved beyond expletives by the damaging awfulness of the word "fiancée."

"I had hoped my father would change his thinking about this, but I understand now that won't happen. Let me clear something up. Aneeka Pasha didn't come looking for me. I went to her house looking for her. While carrying a gift of M&M's from her sister, who I had had the privilege of spending some time with in America."

Nice touch there, the M&M's. Who was it behind the camera whom Eamonn just looked at again?

"It's true I didn't know right away about her brother, but I did know that her father had been a jihadi, that he'd gone to Afghanistan to fight with the Taliban, was held — and possibly tortured — at Bagram, and died on his way to Guantánamo. Like almost any other Brit, I despise the choices Adil Pasha made, and I despise the manner of his dying. But the indefensible facts of his life and death make Aneeka and her sister, Isma, extraordinary women. In the face of tremendous difficulties — including the death of their mother when they were very young . . ."

How earnest he looked, how *good,* as he continued to speak of the trials and glories of the Pasha sisters. Faith in human nature positively rolling off him. Silly clot, as if this were a time in which anyone would trust the idealistic.

"We fell in love. God, all my friends are going to have a go at me for that — we don't just come out and say things like that in public, do we? But there we are. It's my truth."

When had this phrase become so popular, "my truth"? Hateful expression, something so egocentric in it. And something so cynical, also, about all those absolute truths in the world.

"I don't know why I was lucky enough for her to feel that way about me — my father, who knows me well enough to know that I don't deserve a woman that wonderful, tells me she must have been pretending —"

"Ouch," said James under his breath.

"— but there was never any pretense between us. And that's why she told me about her brother when she agreed to spend her life with me. I can't tell you how hideous

342

it's been to see how that admission — which took so much courage for her to make, and showed such trust in me — has made people paint her as . . . as . . . I can't really say the words."

Embarrassing. That's all this was. "How much more of this is there, James?"

"Don't know, sir. Didn't seem right to watch it before you did," said James, furiously examining the pattern on the carpet.

"It's true that I went to my father, the home secretary, almost immediately to talk to him about Parvaiz Pasha. Not because my fiancée had asked for any favors but because, as a son, I felt honor-bound to tell my father that my personal life and his professional life were bound to collide. You see, I knew Parvaiz Pasha was trying to get to the British consulate in Istanbul — not for some act of terrorism, but because he wanted a new passport that would allow him to return home. I have shared this information with Counter Terrorism officials — I'm sure Aneeka has done the same — and it's unclear to me why the British public has been allowed to continue thinking that terrorism was his motive for being where he was at the time of his murder — which I'm sure was carried out by those he almost succeeded in escaping."

Oh don't, son, don't make him out to be a hero. They'll never forgive you that.

"But Parvaiz Pasha is not my concern. I never met him and it's true, I don't know what he did, what crimes he might have committed while in Syria. I do, though, know his sister. The woman you've been watching on your TV screens is a woman who has endured terrible trials, whose country, whose government, and whose fiancée turned away from her at a moment of profound personal loss. She has been abused for the crime of daring to love while covering her head, vilified for believing that she had the right to want a life with someone whose history is at odds with hers, denounced for wanting to bury her brother beside her mother, reviled for her completely legal protests against a decision by the home secretary that suggests personal animus. Is Britain really a nation that turns people into figures of hate because they love unconditionally? Unconditionally but not uncritically. While her brother was alive that love was turned toward convincing him to return home; now he's dead it's turned to convincing the government to return his body home. Where is the crime in this? Dad, please tell me, where is the crime?"

So this was what heartbreak felt like.

Karamat acknowledged it, allowed it, arms dangling helplessly from his side. *Personal animus.* That was an arrow dipped in a poison only those closest to him could know to use. Whoever was standing behind the camera, whoever had honed Eamonn's words, whoever had chosen that particular shade of blue that the color psychologists insisted instilled confidence and trust — it didn't matter. It was Eamonn who mixed the poison, fired the arrow. He knew it to be a lie, he knew that of all lies it was the one that would hurt his father the most, he knew that once he'd said it he gave carte blanche to every one of Karamat Lone's political opponents to repeat the claim. If a son doesn't recognize personal animus, who does? Fathers and sons, sons and fathers. An Asian family drama dragged into Parliament. He clenched his fists, pulled them up to rest on the arms of his chair, muscles taut along his back and shoulders. Where the body leads, the mind learns how to follow. He breathed in slowly, pacing his thoughts along with his breath, the chess player in him seeing the move just made then examining the whole board.

James waited silently until the home secretary turned to look at him. "What do we do now, sir?"

"We do nothing. He's, excuse the expression, digging his own grave." He looked at his watch. "Let's go to the office and watch it unfold."

"Will you be wanting a few minutes with your wife before we leave?"

"James, until this thing is over I don't have a son and I don't have a wife. I have a great office of state. Are we clear?"

"Yes, sir. Sorry, sir."

Karamat returned to his room, opened the cupboard, and looked at his tie rack. There were more blues than any other color, but today his hand reached for a matte red — strong but subtle, the tie of a man assured of his own power.

He arrived at Marsham Street along with the first editions of the morning papers, which he still insisted on reading in print. His face, half in light, half in darkness, like some comic book villain, was above the fold of the newspaper most closely allied to his party. NATIONAL INTEREST OR PERSONAL ANIMUS? asked the headline.

"Someone must have leaked the video to them ahead of time," James said unnecessarily.

"Stand outside the door and don't let anyone in. I don't care if it's the Queen

346

herself." The building was empty, most of London asleep. He simply wanted to be left alone.

The first paragraph gave him the phrase "anonymous cabinet member," which, when put together with the name of the journalist, almost certainly meant the chancer. The anonymous cabinet member reflected on the irreversible damage to the home secretary if his son had been seen attending the funeral of a terrorist — "of course he'd do everything in his power to prevent that from happening." Such a simple line of attack, as the most effective ones always were.

Piece by piece the article dismantled yesterday's principled man of action and remade him: an ambitious son of migrants who married money and class and social contacts in order to transform himself into an influential party donor, which allowed him to be selected ahead of more deserving candidates to run in his first election. He used his identity as a Muslim to win, then jettisoned it when it started to damage him. It remained a mystery how he had had the privilege of running in a by-election for a safe seat after his constituents threw him out following Mosquegate; it had led to resignations within the party. Rather than fully address the questions regarding his connections to known terrorists in the mosque he frequented, he'd taken on a new role as the loudest voice of criticism against the community that had voted him out. Working-class or millionaire, Muslim or ex-Muslim, proud son of migrants or antimigrant, modernizer or traditionalist? Will the real Karamat Lone please stand up? And the final blow, again from Anonymous Cabinet Member: "He would sell out anyone, even his own son, if he thought it would move him closer to number 10."

It escalated from there. Britain woke up to a chorus of tweets, hastily written online columns, and morning TV interviews all placing the home secretary on trial. "Personal animus" the phrase they all picked up on, which one wit turned into #PersonalEnemas.

A professional, coordinated effort, all in all. Why had it taken him so long to work out who was behind the camera?

"Alice, you've never liked me, have you?" he said, when the Halibut deigned to answer her phone on the fifth ring.

"Mr. Lone, your son hired my family's PR firm," she said, in a tone of warm honey dripped onto cold fish scales. "This is purely professional. No personal animus."

He hung up, laughing, and unbuttoned

his cuffs. "Hold your nerve, marshal your forces," he said to James. It wasn't quite eight a.m. yet. Plenty of day yet to come, and there was only so much the Halibut could spin.

He clicked on the video file on his desktop. A shadow on the desert sand of a man kneeling, a curved sword like a crescent moon above his head. Exceptional production values, the work of people who cared about camera angles and light and — he pressed a key repeatedly to increase the volume of God's name being sung in praise — sound. This came from the media unit for which Parvaiz Pasha had been working. He didn't want to release it to the British public — barbaric, nightmare-inducing stuff. He shouldn't have to. If he had gauged the situation correctly — and he was sure he had — it would take only the sight of Eamonn walking into that most un-British spectacle in the park to switch the conversation from personal animus to Eamonn Lone's clear lack of judgment. But just in case it didn't work that way, it was useful to have a backup plan to remind the public that the only story here was that of a British citizen who had turned his back on his nation in favor of a place of crucifixions, beheadings, floggings, heads on spikes, child

349

soldiers, slavery, and rape. And did Karamat Lone take this personally? By god, yes, he did! He thumped his hand on the desk, practicing, wondered if "by god" was a good idea, as a head rolled in the desert sand.

The first time he'd watched the video he had been unable to eat meat the rest of the week. Had barely been able to shave without thinking of that blade on flesh. Now it was his weapon. He looked up from the computer screen to the television, which he'd switched on as soon as he'd entered the office. The girl was cross-legged beside the ice coffin, hair still caked with mud, once white clothes soiled, everything about her older and more tired. *Do you even know the man you're mourning?* he wondered.

His phone buzzed with a text message from Terry: Get home now or the next news headline with your name in it will have the story of your wife moving out to a hotel.

He ran his hands through his hair, not knowing whether to be admiring or despairing that she'd written to the politician rather than the father or husband. Not even a video of a beheading would shift the story away from the Asian family drama if Terry Lone, celebrity interior designer, style icon, the most admired of Westminster wives by a mile, according to a recent poll, backed up her son's story of personal animus.

Checkmated, Teresa. I'm on my way.

Terry's signature aesthetic was muted colors, sleek-lined furniture, and wooden floors, on display in every room of the house except her husband's lair and the family room with its red walls, deep carpet and sofas, and white bookshelves filled with the family's best-loved books. As Karamat approached this room he heard an unexpected voice telling him his footsteps had started to sound more portentous since he'd become home secretary.

He covered the remaining distance in the largest possible strides and held his arms out to his second-born, Emily the Uncomplicated, the son he'd never had.

"I'm here to find out if any of that racist, misogynistic ho-jabi nonsense is coming from your office, and to fire whoever is responsible," she said, pulling away and beaming at her father. Beautiful Emily, physically her mother's child, with the light brown hair and hazel eyes, the delicate hands with their quick gestures.

"Oh and here I thought you had come to support your old man," he said, tugging at her nose.

"My old man will be fine. He always is.

351

But my brother's turned a little loopy, hasn't he?" She threw herself down on a sofa and resumed attacking a half-eaten croissant. "Still, he is my brother. And he is your son. I thought I'd come and remind you what parental feeling feels like. And then I can whisk him off to New York until this whole thing goes away."

He was aware of Terry in her dressing gown with her back toward them, her fingers moving along the spine of the children's books as though they were piano keys. It was cowardly, but easier, to talk through Emily. He sat down next to his daughter, took a sip from her teacup, and wrinkled his nose at the lack of sugar.

"You know what he's done, don't you?"

"Mum just showed me the video. That was stupid of him. How are you going to fix it?"

Astonishingly, the story about Eamonn traveling to Karachi hadn't yet become public knowledge. Whoever had tweeted the picture of him at the departure gate had since taken it down — whichever branch of the security services was responsible for that, Karamat was grateful. He must remember to thank James, the only one to notice it because he was the only one who had thought to include among his Google Alerts the misspelling #EamonLone. Not that it mattered very much — everyone would know soon enough. But at least he could be the one to tell his wife, who had finally turned around, her expression making it clear what a terrible idea it had been to leave the house this morning without waking her up first. "Get some rest while I talk to your father," she said.

Emily sat up straight, looked from one parent to the other. "Sorry," she said, kissing her father's cheek.

When she had gone Terry walked over to the balcony doors and opened them. Her fresh-air mania undeterred by the early-morning cold. Some irritations dissipate in a marriage, some accumulate.

"Sometimes I forget how much like you she is," she said.

"Only compared to her brother, who's nothing like either of us."

"That's not true. He's who I was. Before you. Before I concentrated my life on making myself good enough for you."

He had to laugh at that. "I think you have that the wrong way round, my blue-blooded East Coast heiress. Remember the first time I took you out for dinner?"

But she shook her head, wanting to be alone in some distorted version of their life together. He tossed the remnants of Emily's tea into the flowerpot with the money plant and poured himself another cup. No sugar in sight so he dropped in a teaspoon of jam and stirred vigorously. But not even that outrage reached her. Instead she stayed at her end of the room, gnawing at whatever remained of her thumbnail.

"You used to ask me what I thought," she said. "Every campaign, every bill, every speech."

This, again. In all the times she'd brought it up he'd always stopped himself from pointing out that in the early days it was her because there was no one else. He was the boy from Bradford who'd made his millions and bought his way into the party no one expected someone like him to join. "Is it so terrible that I want my home to be a haven away from the noise of Westminster?"

"Don't you talk to me as if I'm some housewife here to bring you your slippers at the end of your working day. Have you even stopped to wonder what I think about this business with the boy?"

He watched the bits of jam bobbing in the tea, felt mildly revolted, but took a sip rather than admit it. "You want to protect your son. Of course you do. It's your job. But it can't be mine, not in these circumstances."

"I'm not talking about Eamonn, you self-important idiot. I'm talking about a nineteen-year-old, rotting in the sun while his sister watches, out of her mind with grief. He's dead already; can't you leave him alone?"

His family. His goddamned family and they were the ones least able to understand. "This isn't about him. It isn't about her. It isn't about Eamonn. Perhaps I don't ask your advice anymore because your political mind isn't as sharp as it was. And close those doors — my tea's turned to ice already." A way to stop drinking the jammy liquid and make it her fault. Satisfying, that, even though she seemed entirely oblivious to the whole thing.

"Sharp enough still to see what you don't. That within the party you have enemies rather than rivals, backers rather than supporters. That brown skin isn't made of Teflon. Why do you think I really stepped away from my business?"

The question was a surprise, and he followed it back along the thread of conversation to understand its logic rather than admit as much. Oh. "To spend your energies being — which one of us first came up with the phrase? — the silk draped over my too-dark, street-fighting muscles. As you did at the start." He held out his hand to her,

355

prepared to be indulgent. "It's true I wouldn't be here without you. That's never forgotten."

She finally closed the balcony doors but only, it seemed, in order to slam something. "You arrogant idiot. You arrived at the foothills and your mind catapulted you to the summit. You're the one person who doesn't realize the article this morning was the beginning of an avalanche that it's already too late to stop." She finally came over to him, but it was to pick up the remote and point it at the television. There she was, the girl, still cross-legged, no change since he'd left the office. He looked at the clock on the mantelpiece. Eamonn would be landing soon.

"A few days ago your greatest rival was a man born with a diamond-encrusted spoon in his mouth, a party insider for years. And now it's this orphaned student, who wants for her brother what she never had for her father: a grave beside which she can sit and weep for the awful, pitiable mess of her family life. Look at her, Karamat: look at this sad child you've raised to your enemy, and see how far you've lowered yourself in doing that."

The ice coffin was sealed up now, slabs laid on top of the corpse, the face no longer

356

uncovered. What state of decay had it reached for her to allow that? Where before there were people nearby, now she seemed to be alone with the body, in the singed grass, beneath the banyan tree, rose petals desiccated around her. The smell, Karamat guessed. It had pushed everyone to the periphery. Soon his son would walk into this park, into the stench of death, the woman he loved at its center.

"Oh, god," he said, seeing it — his boy surrounded by the rot-drenched horror.

"And you've lost your son too," Terry said. She placed her hand over his eyes, and her touch made something in him stop, something else in him start. He bent his head forward, resting the too-great weight of it against his wife's palm. Once, on an afternoon when rain beat on the windows, he'd sat here with his arm around his son's shoulder, comforting him through his first heartbreak. Eamonn all of thirteen, just the age at which he'd stopped allowing a father's embrace, except in this moment of pain. The elements raging fierce outside, and Karamat helpless with love for the boy weeping into his shirt. He knew he should tell him to be a man, to take it on the chin, but instead he pulled him closer, grateful beyond measure that it wasn't mother or sister or best friend that Eamonn had turned to but his father, who loved him best, and always would.

Terry removed her hand. "Be human. Fix it."

A flutter of silk and she was gone. Now there was only him and the girl who reached out to touch the ice. He bunched his hands together, blew on his cold fingertips. The night his mother had died he'd kept vigil over her body until the morning, reading the Quran out loud because she'd have wanted him to although it touched nothing in his heart. How important it had seemed to do everything with unwavering devotion — not because he believed there was anything left of her to know either way but because it was the last thing he could do for her as a son.

It felt like an effort to reach into his jacket pocket and pull out the phone to call James.

"Thanks for having the tweet about Eamonn taken down, and get me the number of the British deputy high commissioner in Karachi," he said.

"It wasn't us who took it down, sir. I'll text you the number in a minute."

Hanging up, he considered going to his wife. No, he would fix it, for his son, for the girl, and then he would tell Terry. He stretched out on the sofa, arms crossed over his chest, eyes open. Who would keep vigil over his dead body, who would hold his hand in his final moments?

Thunder in the house, on the stairs, in the hall. He stood to meet it just as three men from his security detail charged into the room, a human wall around him, a moving wall running him down the stairs, lifting him off his feet and carrying him like a mannequin when he tried to veer away to find his wife, his daughter. Calling out their names, "Terry, Emily," the only two words in the world that mattered. "Behind you," his wife's voice, rapid footsteps following him down. "I have them, sir." Good man, Suarez! Sirens outside, the human wall moving away from the front door down toward the basement. Guns out, voices coming through the walkie-talkies, Suarez commanding: "Lock the door, don't let anyone in until we give you the all-clear." Into the safe room, wife and daughter behind, door pulled shut, Terry turning the multipoint lock.

"Why are we in the bathroom?" Emily said.

It took Karamat a moment to remember his daughter hadn't been back since he'd become home secretary. She was a visitor from the past, a reminder of a life before. "It's a safe room now."

"Oh my god we're going to die."

His daughter's face something he couldn't bear to look at so he busied himself running his hands along the doorframe. As if he were a father capable of finding a point of vulnerability and fixing it. "Suarez," he shouted, banging on the door. "What the hell is going on?"

A voice on the other side — Jones, was it? — said, "We'll get you out as soon as possible," as though the home secretary and his wife and daughter were in a malfunctioning elevator. The English, sometimes. Even when they were Welsh. He reached into his pocket, but the phone wasn't there. On the table waiting for James's text. Emily and Terry didn't have theirs either. Banged on the door again. "I'm going to need something more than that."

"Sir, we picked up chatter. About an imminent attack."

"This isn't helpful," Terry said, her arms around their daughter. He should go over to join them, think of something comforting to say, but instead he sat down, back to the tiled wall. What could he say? That they would be all right?

"I'm sorry," he said, and waited for one of them to tell him it wasn't his fault.

Terry turned her face away from him, started speaking in a clear, practical tone to their daughter, explaining security protocols, the safety features of this room, the likelihood that chatter meant nothing was going to happen because why would anyone broadcast plans of an attack that they actually intended to carry out? "Blast-proof" . . . "bulletproof" . . . "air supply." These were the words with which she reassured their child.

How beautiful they both were, his wife and daughter. While his enemies were out there playing politics to bring him down — leaks and innuendos and muckraking, the stuff that gave Westminster a bad name — he was in a reinforced steel box with his wife and daughter while terrorists tried to kill him. He cupped his hands together like a man about to pray or a father cradling his infant son's head. Or a politician examining the lines of his palm. He didn't believe in any form of mumbo jumbo but someone once told him that according to palmistry the lines on your left palm represent the destiny you were born with and the lines on your right the destiny you make for yourself. It had since pleased him to note the wide divergence of the two. Heart line, head line, fate line, life line. At what point had he made himself into a man who thought of saving his political career while his daughter was in need of a father's reassurance? He patted the floor next to him and took her hand in his when she sat down, her head on his shoulder. Counted her fingers as he'd done when she was born, though until Eamonn he'd always thought that was some myth of parenting that no one actually did.

"Your mother's right," he said. "Those who can, do. Those who can't, go online." That got a small laugh. "To be honest, I'm pretty sure Suarez is pretending this is a bigger deal than it is as a sort of drill. That's the way he is. Likes to be very certain all his men — and women, before you correct me — know how to act under pressure."

"Are you saying this to make me feel better?"

"I'm the Lone Wolf. I don't say things to make people feel better." He bared his teeth at her, and she smiled at him, trustingly.

Still children into their twenties, this generation. By Emily's age he'd already faced down so much of the ugliness of the world. Had fun doing it too, in places. And for all the political wrongheadedness of the Anti-Nazi League, they'd won. Wasn't he proof of that? Who would have thought in the days he walked around with his RAC-ISTS ARE BAD IN BED badge, spoiling for a fistfight or a fuck, whichever came along, that someone like him could end up where he was now? And if he had thought it, if someone had said he'd be the home secretary in a safe room while men prowled outside trying to kill him, he'd have known without asking that the men were neo-Nazi skinheads. But how dare they — how dare it be *his people.* After everything his generation did to make this country better for them, how dare they. Personal animus — hell, yes!

"Dad?" Emily said, and he loosened the pressure on her hand.

How were they planning to do it? A truck packed with dynamite on a parallel street, a detonation that would destroy the whole neighborhood? Were they in the sewer system? Had they infiltrated his security detail? He looked at Terry.

"Breathe," she mouthed, and came to sit on the other side of their daughter.

So he concentrated on that. On breathing; on holding his daughter's hand. On remembering that there was no correlation between evil and competence. On thinking how he could emerge from this a hero, the party leadership in his grasp. Then back to breathing, back to holding his daughter's hand.

After what seemed an endless time of silence Emily said, "If Eamonn were here he'd be telling us jokes."

Karamat glanced at his watch. His son was there now, in Karachi.

He cleared his throat. "Terry, there's something . . ."

There was a hammering on the door, Suarez's all-clear code, and then his voice saying it was safe to come out. Karamat stood up so fast he felt a moment of light-headedness. He turned the lock, heard all the bolts slide out from their positions of protection. Heard his daughter burst into tears of relief, and turned to help her up, Terry doing the same, the three of them clinging together for a moment. When they pulled apart there was Suarez, smiling in relief.

"Just some kind of a hoax, sir. Useful drill for all of us."

"How do you know?"

"Because they claim they've got you, sir, and clearly they haven't."

The crackle of a walkie-talkie. A voice on the other end — urgent, horrified.

Every television channel replayed it endlessly:

A man in a navy blue shirt walks into the park. He is recognized, the journalists race forward, he holds up his hand to them, calls out the name of the woman he's come for. The cameras turn to her. She is the only person unaware, her cheek resting on the lid of ice that has melted to near-transparency. The journalists move back, allow a path from him to her. Into this path step two men in beige shalwar kameezes. "At last you're here," says one, and opens his arms wide. The man in the navy blue shirt looks over to the woman, but he's in a new place, he doesn't want to offend, he allows himself to be embraced. While one man pulls him against his chest, pinning his arms in place, the other encircles his waist. The two men step away, turn, run. They are climbing the railings out of the park before the man in the navy blue shirt understands the belt they've locked around him.

He tugs at it, he yells for a knife, something, anything to cut it off. But everyone is running, toward this exit or that, screams and voices raised to God, who else can save them now? One cameraman, a veteran of carnage, stops at the edge of the park, beyond the blast radius as well as he can judge, turns his lens onto the new emptiness of the field. The woman has stood up now. The man with the explosives around his waist holds up both his hands to stop her from coming to him. "Run!" he shouts. "Get away from me, run!" And run she does, crashing right into him, a judder of the camera as the man holding it on his shoulder flinches in expectation of a blast. At first the man in the navy shirt struggles, but her arms are around him, she whispers something, and he stops. She rests her cheek against his, he drops his head to kiss her shoulder. For a moment they are two lovers in a park, under an ancient tree, sundappled, beautiful, and at peace.

ACKNOWLEDGMENTS

Jatinder Verma at Tara Arts gave me the idea of adapting *Antigone* in a contemporary context. Jatinder, many thanks, and apologies for doing so in the form of a novel rather than a play.

I'm fortunate to continue to have the Santa Maddalena Foundation in my life; thank you to Beatrice Monti for the space to work, and for her friendship and her dogs.

Thanks also to Dermot O'Flynn for the desk overlooking the sea.

Thank you, Victoria Hobbs, Alexandra Pringle, Becky Saletan, Angelique Tran Van Sang, Jennifer Custer, Faiza S. Khan, and everyone else at Bloomsbury, Riverhead, and A. M. Heath who has played a part in the life of *Home Fire*.

Thank you to my other publishers, and to my translators.

Thank you also to the translators of Sophocles: Anne Carson's *Antigone*

367

(Oberon Books, 2015) and Seamus Heaney's *The Burial at Thebes: Sophocles' Antigone* (Faber & Faber, 2005) were my constant companions as I wrote this novel. I'm also grateful for Ali Smith's *The Story of Antigone* (Pushkin Children's Books, 2013), and for Ali Smith herself.

Thank you to Shami Chakrabarti for permission to use her words, spoken when she was director of Liberty (liberty-human-rights.org.uk), regarding plans to strip British nationals of their citizenship.

Elizabeth Porto remains as trusted an early reader as ever.

The Preston Road sections owe a great deal to Geraldine Cooke — friend, guide, fact-checker — who gave of her time unstintingly without demanding to know what I was up to. My thanks also to her many friends and acquaintances who spoke to me about their neighborhood.

Gillian Slovo's excellent verbatim play *Another World: Lossing Our Children to Islamic State* (Oberon Books, 2016) was commissioned shortly before I started to write *Home Fire*. Gillian showed extraordinary generosity and friendship in sharing her knowledge and resources, as well as in her reading of the first draft of this novel.

ABOUT THE AUTHOR

Kamila Shamsie is the author of several previous novels, including *Broke Verses* and *Burnt Shadows*. She has been a finalist for the Man Booker Prize, the Orange Prize (twice) and the DSC Prize for South Asian Literature, among other honors, and has been named one of *Granta*'s Best of Young British Novelists and a Fellow of the Royal Society of Literature. She was raised in Karachi and lives in London.

The employees of Thorndike Press hope you have enjoyed this Large Print book. All our Thorndike, Wheeler, and Kennebec Large Print titles are designed for easy reading, and all our books are made to last. Other Thorndike Press Large Print books are available at your library, through selected bookstores, or directly from us.

For information about titles, please call:
(800) 223-1244

or visit our website at:
gale.com/thorndike

To share your comments, please write:

Publisher
Thorndike Press
10 Water St., Suite 310
Waterville, ME 04901